D1391865

THE STEPMOTHER'S DIARY

Also by Fay Weldon

FICTION

The Fat Woman's Joke
Down Among the Women
Female Friends
Little Sisters
Remember Me
Praxis
Puffball
The President's Child
The Life and Loves of a She-Devil
The Shrapnel Academy
The Heart of the Country
The Hearts and Lives of Men
Leader of the Band
The Cloning of Joanna May
Darcy's Utopia
Growing Rich
Affliction
Life Force
Question of Timing
Splitting
Worst Fears
Big Women
Rhode Island Blues
The Bulgari Connection
Mantrapped
She May Not Leave
The Spa Decameron

COLLECTIONS

Watching Me, Watching You
Polaris: And Other Stories
Moon Over Minneapolis or Why She Couldn't Stay
Angel, All Innocence: And Other Stories
Wicked Women
A Hard Time to be a Father
Nothing to Wear and Nowhere to Hide: A Collection of Short Stories

NON-FICTION

Letters to Alice: On First Reading Jane Austen
Rebecca West
Sacred Cows
Godless in Eden
Auto Da Fay: A Memoir
What Makes Women Happy

THE STEPMOTHER'S DIARY

Fay Weldon

Quercus

First published in Great Britain in 2008 by

Quercus
21 Bloomsbury Square
London
WC1A 2NS

A CIP catalogue record for this book is available
from the British Library

ISBN (HB) 978 1 84724 204 4
ISBN (TPB) 978 1 84724 205 1

This book is a work of fiction. Names, characters,
businesses, organizations, places and events are
either the product of the author's imagination
or are used fictitiously. Any resemblance to
actual persons, living or dead, events or
locales is entirely coincidental.

10 9 8 7 6 5 4 3 2 1

Printed and bound in Great Britain by Clays Ltd, St Ives Plc.

FSC
Mixed Sources
Product group from well-managed
forests and other controlled sources

Cert no. SGS - COC - 2061
www.fsc.org
© 1996 Forest Stewardship Council

THE STEPMOTHER'S DIARY

March 2008

Emily's Account

I read my daughter's diaries the other day. Let me share with you. You may think you know pretty much what's going on in your own family. Believe me, you do not. You think truly dreadful things only happen in other countries, other cultures, far away: but they also happen in your own back yard, to the nicest people, and at the hands of others who believe that they too are perfectly sane and nice, the kind who sort the household waste and try to save Africa.

Gwen, grandmother of my daughter Sappho's stepchild, turns out to be nothing but a two-faced, greedy bitch. And she had recently been awarded an OBE for services to charity. Mind you, the money had been as good as stolen, and from Sappho.

And to Isobel, my pretty granddaughter, currently doing her A-levels, who spends her Saturdays clearing old people's gardens, and in whose sweet mouth butter would not melt, I was on the verge of saying, 'I think you are evil. Not just ordinary evil, but actually satanic.' I did not say it because I did not want to be cursed. Isobel does not projectile-vomit nor does her head turn right around on its neck, as with the child in *The Exorcist*, but she might as well. You can see that I am pretty angry with her at the moment.

Isobel is not actually my granddaughter; she is my daughter Sappho's stepdaughter. There is a difference. There is no blood connection. I would not want you to think evil ran in the genes. These modern, all-inclusive families of ours, created by the passing sexual interest of a couple in each other, be they hetero or homo, can give birth to chaos. Splits happen: children pack their bags and have no choice but to follow the possessor of half their genes, leaving the other half behind. A week with this parent, a weekend with the other – if they love us so much, think the young, why don't they get the fuck back together? Save us all this?

And as a result of modern times here is my daughter Sappho, Isobel's stepmother, on my doorstep at ten in the morning, pregnant, *distraite*, and suffering.

Usually once I open the door to Sappho she goes on in ahead of me bringing with her a gust of good cheer, energy, and red-cheeked dark prettiness, which has been hers since she burst from the womb. On that occasion she didn't even leave me time to get to the delivery room. It is not in her nature to hang about. But today she just stood hesitantly on the step and thrust a heavy Waitrose bag towards me. She was five months pregnant, and she should not have been lugging heavy stuff about.

'I'm not going to stay,' she said. 'These are my diaries. I want you to hide them. Please don't read them.'

'Good heavens,' I said. 'Surely there are enough places at home to hide things?'

Home for Sappho and her husband Gavin, and his children Isobel and Arthur, was our beloved Apple Lee, a rambling, six bedroomed farmhouse of considerable age and uncertain value, located as it was just off the carbon-soaked Archway roundabout where 'no one' wanted to buy. Only its Grade II listing had kept developers at bay. All around was squalor and random urban development, waiting for decades for a chop which never came. Although the house had been recently and rashly renovated to the glossiest of standards (Sappho had become unexpectedly and wonderfully rich) it was already cluttered, since none of the family put anything away if they could help it. Only Laura the perfect secretary did, and these days she was kept to her quarters.

I had lived in Apple Lee for thirty years and here Sappho had been born, and her father before her, and here I had been widowed young, and assiduously pursued lovers and career. I am a psychoanalyst and work from home. I still thought of Apple Lee as mine, and myself as temporarily absent, and half regretted and half not, that I had put the property in her name so that she, not I would have to cope with garden, stairs, draughts, rumoured ghosts, Heritage building regs, the ancient apple tree which needed treatment for blight and canker, the protected soprano pipistrelle bats in the garage which was once the stable block, the neighbours with their man-eating dogs and feral children, the street litter of fast food cartons and used syringes.

I prefer to live in a comfortable, centrally-heated, ground-floor retirement flat in Hampstead, and my few clients (Freud has fallen out of favour in recent years) certainly prefer to see me here rather than at Apple Lee.

I had not reckoned on Gavin and the children moving in with Sappho. Of course, it was on the cards that she would marry: though she always said she had no intention of doing so. That she would abandon the world and sanity for love had simply not occurred to me.

'Not Apple Lee; it isn't safe any more,' said Sappho. 'Isobel might find them and use them against me. Fucking little tart.' That was quite shocking.

In the four years since her marriage Sappho's loyalty to her new family – though none of them was her flesh and blood – was extreme. But perhaps now she was finally pregnant, and Stubb-Palmer blood (Sappho's) was to mingle with Garner blood (Gavin's) in the new child, her reactions would become less civilised and more Darwinian. She might even try to nudge the rival's children out of the nest. The selfish gene would assert itself: she would begin to act more like a wicked stepmother and less like an angel trying to outdo her predecessor in care and concern for the young she had inherited. We would see. This morning she certainly looked a little wild-eyed and paranoiac. I hoped she was okay – it is nice when one's theories are vindicated but one does not want one's flesh and blood to suffer for them. Better to be proved wrong. 'Fucking little tart' from Sappho was out of order, and distressing; she swore occasionally but mostly at inanimate objects. 'Fucking computer', 'fucking printer!' perhaps, but not this.

'I have to be on my own for a while,' she said now. 'I have things to work out.'

'You and Greta Garbo,' I began, but stopped. There was indeed something really the matter. She was not wearing her usual too-high heels or the silks and suedes she tended to favour: she was wearing a woolly hat with red and blue stripes and was wrapped in an old nylon navy parka, and her shoes might as well as be Gavin's as hers. So much pregnancy can do for you when it comes to fashion, I know, but she was not at all her normal self. She had the stunned look you see on faces on TV when people watch their homes being burned, or stand among the bodies of the dead, unsure whether they're in a dream or it's real. She was wearing a backpack. I recognised it as Arthur's, the one he took to go pot-holing, as was the hat.

'You shouldn't be wearing a backpack,' I said. 'They're bad for the spine. What are you trying to do? Lose the baby?'

'You would say something like that,' she said, forlornly. 'It's projection. You mean you want me to lose the baby.'

I was taken aback.

'Why would you think I wanted you to do that? Of course I don't.'

'Because you hate Gavin,' she said, bleakly. 'And it's Gavin's baby.'

Well, who else's would it be? Infidelity, between them, was just not on the cards.

'You're so full of hormones,' I said, 'you're not going to know who you hate or what you want.'

I wished she hadn't married Gavin but I didn't hate him. Nor, did I imagine for one moment, did she. I had seen and heard too many patients vent their rage about their spouses, how they despised them, loathed them, wished them dead – only to observe them perfectly calm and affectionate again at the next session, good sex having intervened as like as not. Gavin and Sappho had had some almighty row, which they did anyway every month or so. It was always when she was pre-menstrual, a fact she hated me to point out, and so I did try not to. Now that she was pregnant, I felt allowed to mention it. But I clearly shouldn't have.

She glared at me, as if she were seven once again, and turned to go, in such apparent dudgeon I tried to grab hold of her, which is not in my nature – I tend to reserve physical contact with anyone for actual sexual activity. I am too often construed as a rather reserved and remote mother, but I love Sappho very much.

The trouble is that too much awareness of the fragility of the child's erotic development can make one err on the side of caution. So many case histories offer tales of phobias and neuroses – a shoe fetish, say, or a savage Electra complex – triggered in childhood by some random action by the mother, some misinterpretation by the child of what is going on. The knowledge itself can mean one tiptoes through their lives when one should be clumping noisily about. Now, seeing she was unhappy, mother love overcame reserve and took me by surprise, and I reached out for her. And Sappho just pushed me away and said,

'I'm going away for a bit. Just don't try and run me to ground, okay?'

And she was gone and I was dreadfully hurt.

And I went inside and tried to make sense of it. Why did she think I hated Gavin? I was always perfectly polite to him. I daresay I tended to disparage him in the 'Oh, men!' kind of way women of my generation do disparage men, but he was Sappho's choice – inasmuch as women do have a choice when their hormones are running and their expectations are sailing – and I had gritted my teeth and tried not to let her see I was appalled.

And in fact these days I get on rather well with Gavin. He was fascinated by birds and small wildlife, having been brought up on the Yorkshire moors, not far from where Ted Hughes the poet spent his childhood. My deceased husband Rob had been a friend of Hughes, and shared the love of small furry creatures, and some of it had rubbed off on me, so at least I had something to talk to Gavin about, if only rodents, crows and eagles. I am not so hot on the classical stage, which is his other enthusiasm, tending to go to the theatre only if Sappho has written the play. And that, since she married Gavin, come to think of it, and he moved into Apple Lee with the children, simply hadn't happened. Once she had a writing career, now she does not. She has a family, and a job, and obligations. Is this what marriage does? Yes. Partnership is worse. Always peering over the shoulder to see if another is fancied more? Never!

Barnaby declares he wants to live under the same roof as me. Let him come down for a toasted sandwich and a snuggling session in bed – he has problems – but anything more? Heaven forfend.

And 'fucking little tart'? Isobel was usually as good as gold. Girls can suddenly 'turn' when they reach the menarche, I know, and change from little darlings into Winehouse monsters almost overnight, embracing squalor and rough sex in a fit of enanti-adromia, that Jekyll–Hyde, Saul-on-the-road-to-Damascus process so loved by Jung, but surely not our Isobel. Mind you, she was a stepchild. Stepchildren tend to have 'issues' in adolescence.

'Any woman who takes on a man with a daughter takes on trouble,' I'd said to Sappho, when she first broke it to me that she was going to marry Gavin. 'I hope you're aware of that.'

'That's not necessarily true,' she said. 'You just want it to be.' She could not bear for me to be proved right, I knew, any more than I could bear it when my mother was proved right when I married Rob. But that had been a long time ago.

'These days fathers have profound and lasting relationships with their daughters,' I warned her. 'Often it stops only just short of actual sexual involvement. The face on the pillow is liable to change, but a daughter is for ever.'

The daughter remains to share memories, places, laughter and keep past and youth alive, I said. 'Wives may come and go, but daughters stay, to love and be loved and try and drive out any new woman in the marital bed.'

'It will be different for me,' was all she said. 'Their mother is dead, poor things. Why should they not love me, if I make myself lovable? I will do everything I can to make up for their loss. It's not in my nature to be a wicked stepmother.'

She simply did not, would not, get it. She resists me: I don't blame her. It is not much fun being the child of a widowed, sexually active psychoanalyst. But the archetype has changed, whether Sappho cares to admit it or not. Wicked stepdaughters are more common now than wicked stepmothers ever were. Poor ousted Hansel and Gretel no longer roam the forest hand in hand: rather it is awash with lonely, weeping, second wives shivering in the cold and rain, tripping over tree roots, grabbed at by thistles and thorns which can pierce the heart. Hansel and Gretel stay home in the warm.

The doorbell rings again. Perhaps it is Sappho back to make her peace? In theory I can open my door by pressing a series of keys but it never happens. I thank God this is a ground-floor flat and there are no stairs and that I no longer live at Apple Lee, where the stair carpet in my time was worn and dangerous. I am in my sixties; I have a mildly arthritic knee. I open the front door to Gavin.

Behind him pass the citizens of Hampstead, to and fro as they do all day outside my window, with their smart clothes and cotton bags from the organic stores, and nowadays not a plastic bag in sight. I am up near the underground station, opposite the coffee shop. The customers have clear civic consciences, and God knows what they get up to in their hypoallergenic beds at night. Gavin is looking just fine, handsome and only moderately distraught, which is not unusual. He doesn't come in.

'Is Sappho here, Emily?' he asks. I shake my head.

'No,' I say. Well, it is the truth. I don't want to get involved.

'You haven't seen her?'

'No,' I say, crossing my fingers. Freud saw this as an unconscious gesture of seduction, but I do it consciously, to acknowledge and excuse a lie.

Gavin runs his hand through his hair, which I see has suddenly begun to thin. And he had such a fine head of hair once. It was part of his charm, with his intelligent eagle looks and saintly manner: all that brown curly hair, all that vigour! Gavin is nineteen years older than Sappho, and only ten years younger than me. When he is seventy and she is fifty-one, she will feel it. When she gets to my age, he will be eighty-five. I wouldn't want a man of eighty-five. (Barnaby is sixty-seven and that is quite old enough. Barnaby lives upstairs and will be down for a toasted cheese sandwich any minute now.) And now Sappho is pregnant, and not easily able to get out of this relationship. A lot of the young these days have a kind of first disposable marriage before moving on to what they describe as the real one. This has not happened, alas, to Sappho. I want a grandchild, true, and a bird in the hand is worth two in the bush, but the girl has managed to complicate her life no end, and wilfully, not just by shacking up with but actually marrying the man.

'Any idea where she might be?' he asks, as if casually, but it isn't. Something's up.

'No,' I say. 'Didn't she tell anyone where she was going? She usually does, in case she's needed.'

'You know what she's like,' he says. 'She writes an email and then presses delete instead of send.'

'Doesn't Laura know?' Laura is their secretary and in the interests of efficiency tracks everyone's movements, even plays back their phone calls in order to make sure dates and times are put into the Garner Times Diary, and everyone is where they are supposed to be in the right clothes and on time. It is not embossed – one of Gavin's few economies. Once it was the Sappho Stubb-Palmer Economist Diary, her name embossed in gold.

'Laura is temporarily out of the office,' says Gavin. I wait, but he declines to elaborate.

'Have you tried Sappho's mobile?' I ask. Gavin all but shudders. He manages email, but despises mobiles and all things digital. He is a dinosaur, and I am afraid one day he will simply topple over into hot primeval sand and crush my poor Sappho, who is a rosy, delicate flamingo.

'It's switched off, naturally.' He is hostile towards her. What has she done?

'There's an open day at Isobel's school tomorrow,' he continues. 'I just need to remind her.' But it doesn't ring true to me.

Now Sappho is pregnant things will have hotted up. Competition for the father will become overt. From 'fucking little tart' I imagine the row is most likely over Isobel.

I tell Gavin I'll get in touch as soon as I know anything. I suggest he checks out the college where she teaches once a week, but he says there's no reply from her office. And then he asks if by any chance she left a carrier bag with some papers, and I think: oh, that's it. For some reason he's after Sappho's diaries.

'No,' I say. 'Why?'

'There are just some papers there I need.' He is on his way to a weekend conference in the Faroe Islands.

'Ah,' I say, 'the red-necked phalarope!' He is pleased at my ornithological knowledge, and darts me one of his charming smiles, and I hope that whatever has happened between Gavin and Sappho is not too bad, and all will yet be well.

Gavin goes. I offer him a drink but I'm glad he doesn't take up the offer. I do not want to keep up the deceit, and besides, he might catch a glimpse of the Waitrose bag.

These diaries, which Sappho doesn't want the 'fucking little tart' to get hold of, and which now Gavin is searching for, are safely with me. Of course I meant to read them. I am a mother, and have my daughter's best interests at heart. In a Waitrose bag, too, and therefore homely yet aspirational. A Tesco's bag would somehow have diminished the contents.

Was it my duty as a mother to read them, or not to read them? I had read her diaries when she was a child until she found out I was doing it. She said nothing but began to write them as letters to me, and then we both got bored and stopped. Or perhaps she just had too much homework, being at an academic all-girls school. Did she mean me to read them while saying she didn't? Yes, I decided. Of course. Otherwise she would have handed them to one of her friends. I made myself a cup of coffee.

I take my mildly painful joints back to my desk, where I somehow fit. The Waitrose bag sits there and defies me to open it. I am putting it off. Do I really want to open it? Isn't it bad enough remembering what you choose to remember, let alone facing your daughter's memories of a mutual life?

I go back to considering the plight of the modern child in the current climate of multiple serial partnerships. The one-life, one-spouse model is outmoded. The child of the much-married or serial-partnered must live with a mere half of the provider of their genes, and as like as not the wrong half. The bed where they were conceived vibrates to the *cris de jouissance* of new partners, and it a rare house built to modern building specifications where the walls are thick enough to muffle animal cries of human congress. The primal scene, which Freud felt to be so important to the unconscious sexual development of the child – the first awareness of the parents' sexual entwining – is not necessarily between the joint creators of the personality, the self, as nature intended, but is tainted by the intrusion of a stranger. In Isobel's case, by my daughter, Sappho. The more the father loves the newcomer, the more the child hates.

Isobel's real mother is Isolde Garner, ten years deceased, invalid and martyr of perfect memory but still very much alive, I fear, in the Garner household. Sappho and Gavin sleep with a painting of Isolde above their bed. It's a rather gloomy composition by a fashionable but not very good artist, in patterns of greys, as if all the life had been drained out of the subject, as indeed when it was painted it was soon to be. The only light allowed is around the head, in the form of what amounts to a halo. A depressing piece.

I said once, when Sappho was having trouble conceiving the grandchild I so wanted, that perhaps the painting of an ex-wife above the bed was not a particularly good fertility omen.

'I tried to get rid of it,' she said shortly. 'But Isobel had hysterics. Gavin would be more than happy to see it go, but Isobel sees it as a disloyalty.'

'Why can't she have it in her room?' I asked.

'It would upset her colour scheme,' said Sappho. 'The greys are too blue. She's very artistic.'

'Or Arthur's room?'

'Even I wouldn't wish that on Isolde,' said Sappho. 'Arthur's room is all dirty socks and plates of old baked beans.' For all her money she is hopeless at running a house.

The doorbell goes again. I open it to Barnaby, my lover. I like to describe him like this, of course, and he technically is, but Viagra would help. He is more of a cuddler than a lover. Barnaby has the flat above mine: he is a Jungian who specialises in dream analysis and dream therapy. We are in and out of each other's homes all the time, and quarrel all the time. I think, bluntly, that Jungian therapy sucks: he thinks the same of Freud. Sometimes I suggest we get married, knowing that this is the best way to keep him at a distance. Sometimes marriage seems tempting: most of the time, no. I mean, *why*? Company is good but I might meet someone else, not in so much need of Viagra. The problem remains decade after decade. Settle for one and you have to go without the other, unless you're prepared to put up with an almighty fuss. But then he might meet some nice, kind, soppy Jungian, younger and sweeter than me, who would be only too happy to snap him up – and I wouldn't want that at all. So it goes. Whatever changes?

I tell him Gavin has been round, looking for Sappho. I tell him Sappho came earlier and left her diaries.

'I hope you're not reading them,' he says.

'Of course I'm reading them,' I say. 'That's why she left them.'

'Bloody Freudian,' he says. 'Sometimes people mean what they say.'

'Very seldom,' I say.

He asks me how worried I am about Sappho, and I think and say six out of ten. Not too much at all. My normal level is about five. A contrite Gavin is coming after her: she's pregnant and extra-hormonal at the moment: they have rows as a normal part of life and quickly recover: she has enough money to do as she pleases; she is one of fate's favourites.

'It's the children I'm sorry for,' I say, 'and since they're no blood relations of mine even that's fairly theoretical.'

He accuses me of a Freudian impartiality which adds up to coldness. I accuse him of a Jungian moral-high-ground nicey-nicey soppiness. We split a bottle of wine, and I make cheese on toast, using cheese slices, which offends him. He would prefer some kind of double-distilled Cheddar but I can't be bothered. Processed slices are perfectly good. I ask him for his views on the primal scene as it must affect stepchildren in our modern society. He chatters on about the archetypal mother Gaia and how she conspires against the consort to free the son from the father's control. I say I am talking about the too-early eroticisation of the growing child.

'Picture it,' I say. 'Gavin, discontented with his empty bed after seven years, joins Sappho in hers, and drags his children with him to witness this new connubial bliss, and obliges them to overhear their cries of joy. Apple Lee may be old, but only its outer walls are made of solid stone and inside the partition walls are thin.'

'Perhaps it's her idea,' says Barnaby. 'Perhaps she's the one who's done the dragging. Perhaps she is in a conspiracy with the son against the father. How many times has she been married?'

'Only once,' I say. 'It's his second.'

'And they all live under her roof. That goes against the natural grain, in which the man provides the home and introduces the wife and eventually their children into it, and all breathe the

same air, smell the same body smells, from the beginning.'
Barnaby can be quite astute. So intense is the experience, so
strong is that initial birthing, that siblings, if separated when
small and reared apart, will meet as strangers and fall in love. We
can agree on that.

'So which of them did the dragging?' he persists.

'It was only sensible for them to live in Apple Lee,' I say. 'It's a
big house with a garden, near the children's schools, and it's been
Sappho's family home for generations. I moved into it when I
married her father. He died, I took it over, and so far as I was
concerned the house was cursed. It practically killed me with its
dry-rot. So I put it in Sappho's name. She doesn't seem to mind,
and anyway she's rich so curses don't affect her. She just employs
builders.'

'I would have thought,' he says, enigmatically, 'that the primal
scene is the least of anyone's problems. Why does it obsess you?
Is there something you are hiding from yourself?'

I get fed up with Barnaby, and shoo him out when he has
finished his toasted cheese and chutney. Now I am ready to face
the diaries.

They are stuffed into the heavy plastic bag – six rather shabby
cardboard folders with rubber bands holding them together,
miscellaneous typescripts, a number of lined, handwritten A4
pads, and many extra loose sheets of paper. Sappho has clearly
packed them in a hurry and not under the eyes of Laura, who
would have had them properly labelled, in date order, and copies
made and on disc. These are my daughter's diaries; they are her
self, her life, her being. They are my own creation, up to a point,
since I brought her to life. How sensible are children who, in
search of their own selves, normally hide all such material from

their mothers. Sappho must indeed be desperate. As it happens the first page I take out is an account of her wedding to Gavin Garner, four years back. Disaster day, if I'm to face facts.

Sappho's Diary: *June 26th 2004*

Dear Diary,

Last week I married Gavin. It was a good wedding. It was on the longest day of the year, and the sun shone, and the guests were on the whole happy, except for my mother, my secretary, my agent, some of my closest friends, several colleagues, and the mother of my new husband's deceased wife.

'*I, Sappho, take you, Gavin, to be my lawful, wedded husband.*'

But they will all come round to it, I am sure. Love conquers all. Those most against it are those who have most to lose by it.

My mother's complaint is that Gavin is so much older than me, and comes with two children, and his income is uncertain; why do I bother with marriage, which is an outmoded institution; why doesn't he just move in with me? What she really means is she worries that if I am legally married to Gavin his children may end up inheriting Apple Lee. She says she only wants me to be happy. All mothers say this, but I think she means it. Just trust me, Mother. I will watch all legal contracts, make wills, this kind of thing.

'*I, Sappho, take you, Gavin, to be my lawful, wedded husband.*' *Love him, comfort him...*

My agent says married women don't meet deadlines. What he really means is that a husband may feel competitive, start checking the statements, reading the contracts, try to bring down his percentage and generally interfering. He might even get fired.

'*I, Sappho, take you, Gavin, to be my lawful, wedded husband.*' *Honour and keep him...*

Laura my secretary says a husband will distract me from my work, but what she means is that until now she has full control over my life, and she is frightened that things will change if I marry. She is not against sex, nor, so far as I can see, passing lovers, but she is against men in general and certainly against marriage. She may be a lesbian. I don't know. She comes to my house to work every day and knows every detail of my life, but I know remarkably little about hers.

All my life I have been observed. My mother sees me as a case history and I'm sure takes notes. When I was at drama school my every step and vowel was scrutinised. Now I am famous (moderately), journalists consult Google before coming to talk to me and know every stupid thing I have said or written, and I know nothing about them. They see me as a media object, not a human being. Gavin will save me from all this. There will just be him and me, and every now and then his children, too.

'*I, Sappho, take you, Gavin, to be my lawful, wedded husband.*' *Not to be entered into unadvisedly or lightly, but reverently, deliberately, and in accordance with the purposes for which it was instituted by God...*

My friends don't want their own social lives disrupted: they're afraid our all-girl evenings will stop. Weddings within the group unsettle everyone. Many have stepmothers of their own and prophesy disaster so far as Isobel is concerned. But I know all that will be all right. Her real mother died: there was no divorce. There is no animosity in the background, on the contrary. I was there on the day of her birth and her mother trusted me with her care. That is to say I was the au pair. And though Isobel was too small to remember, I don't forget. She was the sweetest, prettiest thing. My friend Belinda says my stepson Arthur will try and seduce me, because all stepsons vie with their fathers to possess the new wife, but that is nuts.

'I, Sappho, take you, Gavin, to be my lawful, wedded husband.' As long as we both shall live...

Gwen, Gavin's ex-mother-in-law, stands to lose her grandchildren. She doesn't want them coming under my influence. Well, they will and too bad. I don't want them coming under hers. She doesn't like me, and never did. I am too real for her, all over the place, and she is so perfect and clear from the beautiful arch of her eyebrows to her cute Prada shoes, and she suspected me from the beginning, even when there was nothing to suspect, when poor Isolde was on her deathbed, and I was holding everything together. The children love me; they put up with Gwen, with whom they have been living for the past seven years, poor things, since Isolde's death, other than holidays and weekends with Gavin.

Snap, snap went the paparazzi outside the registry office: flash, flash. I don't know who told them. 'This way, Gavin! This way, Sappho.' But most of the flashes were for me. I hope Gavin doesn't mind. I hope he manages to finish his novel and his star outshines mine. I hope he doesn't get bitter and twisted because he is a serious person and I am a trivial one and the world is too stubborn and dumbed-down to notice. 'Give us a smile, Sappho, give us a smile.'

I could feel my mother raising her eyebrows when Isobel went up to the front during the marriage ceremony and held Gavin's hand and just stood there, and didn't let go even when he kissed the bride, that is to say me, but I thought it was brave of Isobel. She was only eleven and didn't want to be left out. She had no mother of her own, only now, me. I want her to understand she is gaining a mother, not losing a father. So I included her in the embrace and we stood in a close, contented little ring and I could hear the breath of the sentimental, approving sigh from the audience, and I thought: I will make all this come right for everyone, I will.

Poor Isobel! That morning she had woken us up. It was five-thirty in the morning. I hate early-morning telephone calls. They are usually bad news. Someone in prison, in hospital, something awful. But it was Isobel. She was at her grandmother Gwen's. She had been woken up by a nightmare. She was sobbing and gasping in terror. 'Daddy, I'm so frightened. In my dream you were getting married, and it looked like Sappho, but she was really a shape-shifter like in the film and started to eat you alive. And I tried to scream but my voice came out all tinny and squeaky, and I woke up.' He calmed her down and reassured her, and reminded her that since she was going to live with us she was quite safe, it was only a dream. She shouldn't watch films after the watershed. What was Gwen thinking of?

But it was ages before the sobbing stopped and long after the erection I had felt pressing against my side dwindled, that the phone went down. Gavin went back to sleep at once, but I couldn't settle because it was midsummer and the birds knew it, and soon it was time to get up and prepare ourselves for the cere-mony. And I wasn't going to look my best. I was all puffy-eyed from lack of sleep.

'*I, Sappho, take you, Gavin to be my lawful, wedded husband.*'
Life gets so boring if nothing happens, nothing changes. Hold
your nose and jump!

Emily's View Of The Matter

I closed the diary, but only temporarily. Of course I meant to
carry on reading. I just needed a little rest. I could see it was going
to be disturbing: Sappho was evidently preparing for publication
as much as self-expression. It was in my daughter's nature to be
published and be damned – it was after all how she made her
living. 'Hold your nose and jump', forsooth, into a diary as into
marriage and the devil takes the hindmost, which in this case
would be me, the one who sees her as a case history. Other
mothers measure their children's height on the door post: I tended
to write down landmarks in her psychosexual development in a
notebook – though goodness knows where I had put it. But I was
confident enough in my affection for her, and hers for me, that I
trusted her not to write anything too terrible. What I got I would
deserve; I would read on.

I wondered if I should call up and ask Barnaby about Isobel's
dream but desisted. He would probably say the child had
invented it for the benefit of her stepmother, in order to disturb
and upset. I did not think Isobel at eleven was capable of quite
such sophistication, though you never knew. Four years of
marriage since, and Sappho had made few complaints about
Isobel, and none at all about Arthur, but then she wouldn't,

would she? She wasn't going to give any of us grounds for being right about the wrong-headedness of the marriage. Until now, when she had arrived quivering and quavering upon my doorstep, she had turned its good face resolutely to the world.

But she was quite right. It was a good wedding, as I remember it. Everyone said so, and most meant it. When we'd all given vent to our doubts in the weeks leading up to the ceremony and Sappho still insisted on going ahead, there was nothing for it but to wish the couple well. We all knew how well Gavin had behaved when Isolde was dying – and she took two years about it. For eighteen months of those Gavin had written a newspaper column on the subject, tenderly and tastefully enough, and how could one not hope for his happiness? Thirty guests came to the ceremony in the Camden register office and another fifty turned up at the Groucho's upstairs bar, closed for the occasion. It was an all-generational affair: Gavin's father was eighty-eight and like some old and dignified eagle, an older version of his son and still vigorous, smart and *compos mentis*, which was reassuring to those of us on the bride's side and was a matter of congratulation to those on the groom's.

'Like Michael Douglas and Catherine Zeta Jones,' someone said, 'and that's lasted, hasn't it?'

Sappho did show some resemblance to the film star, bright-eyed, long-legged and looked good in anything. Gavin had wise eyes and a firm chin and enough hair left to look good at the altar, or the desk or whatever, it being a register office. One would like one's daughter to be married in a church but since I had not had her christened I could scarcely expect it.

Luke, Sappho's agent, came up to me at the party and said he'd been counting wedding rings.

'Only fourteen, darling, amongst eighty guests. One wonders what the world is coming to! And four of those embedded into now mottling heterosexual flesh, as was the custom of yesteryear.'

Luke's partner Hugo said he's counted ten rings between five gay couples after civil contracts. Hugo's ex-partner Lionel claimed stable relationships were more a feature of the gay community than the heterosexual.

I had done something very unusual for me and written to Hilary Alexander on the *Telegraph* and asked her what the mother of the bride should wear. I was very conscious that Gwen Lance, mother of Gavin's first wife Isolde, and none of our favourite person, was going to be present. With the aid of nannies and helps she had looked after her grandchildren Arthur and Isobel since Isolde's death from lung cancer. She had modelled in her day for David Bailey and although now well into her sixties was ineffably well-dressed and still occasionally appeared in *Vogue*. I did not exactly want to outdo her, but I did want to be her equal.

Hilary Alexander suggested I simply contact Gwen, and I did, on the phone, introducing myself. Gwen was cool, and distant.

'It isn't exactly a wedding, my dear, is it, being in an office. And a second marriage at that. Has Sappho been married before? No? Extraordinary! But not too much of a fuss, I would think. I found a nice vintage Chanel knee-length suit in yellow and white on my rail the other day; probably something like that. No hats or anything. But I have to go now; I have a taxi at the door.'

I bought a very restrained Dior dress at great expense, which when on looked as if it could have come from Marks & Spencer, and Gwen turned up in an Yves St Laurent cream dress with a kind of safari jacket over it and a jaunty hat, and looked about thirty-five and totally outshone me. Barnaby wasn't properly in my life at the time so I had to go on my own. Thank God Laura was there to do the organising so it went like clockwork. Isobel was wearing white, more like a wedding dress than the one Sappho wore, which was grey chiffon and did nothing for her but which had probably been chosen by Laura at Fenwick's. Sappho was usually too busy working to bother much with clothes, even for her own wedding.

The groom's father engaged Gwen in so lively a conversation some wondered whether, if the bride's mother was free to marry the groom's father, how the younger couple would take it. The age gap would be about the same. The youngest guest was five, daughter of Sappho's friend Polly, and widely rumoured to be the child of a sperm bank. Arthur stayed away – ostensibly because he was in the middle of his biology exams. It was understandable, all agreed, that if a lad didn't want to come to his widowed father's wedding, he should not be pressured to do so.

But that's enough of all that wedding stuff. That was then and this is now. Back to the diaries.

I am rather pleased there are no entries dating back to her childhood. The ones she has seen fit to leave with me date from when she left home, so I will be spared much. The first pages were written when she had just started drama school.

I'd hoped she'd go to university but no. She was wilful. She was such a pretty girl, graceful, obstinate, straightforward, guileless, with a great generosity of spirit, a lively mind, a certain naivety and an ambition to write for the theatre, which I discouraged, interpreting the desire as an evasion of the central role of the self. I was so proud of her, and so worried for her. She was forever trying out other selves for size. I dreaded her settling on one that wasn't quite *her*. She'd found boys her own age spotty and dull, preferring to sit in her room and do her homework. She'd gone straight from My Little Pony to *Lord of the Rings* via Georgette Heyer and bodice-rippers, to posters of Arthur Miller, with his big boots and double-tied shoelaces all over her wall. I suppose she thought what was good enough for Marilyn Monroe was good enough for her.

She was all set to go to Cambridge when she was taken by a fit of anti-elitism and wanted to join the real world. I was against it, and from the evidence of the diaries I was right. It was a mistake. She met the Garners.

Sappho's Diary: *January 1st 1992*

Dear Diary,

Here I am, in my new home, in a new year, life beginning. Allowed to live away from Apple Lee at last, live unobserved, everyone too busy and involved with themselves to care what I do. No one nagging or reading my mind or making notes on my psychosexual development. I shall be a famous actress. I have talent, I know I do, though if I try and do a Geordie accent everyone laughs. At least here they are able to laugh, even though they are a bit thespy and affected. I spent one term at Cambridge and everyone was so superior it cracked their faces if they so much as smiled. So I came to the Royal Academy of the Dramatic Arts. Mother was furious, but I have my trust fund and can do as I like. The boys are a bit of a disappointment, they're so young, and all the girls say they're gay, but I reckon they're just trying to put me off. They can't all be gay. One day I will open this diary and remember what it was like to be me just starting out.

There's a woman who teaches the playwriting course at the Royal Court called Isolde Garner. She is quite famous, and has plays on in the West End. She has just had a baby boy and called it Arthur. Her mother is called Gwendolyn, so it's all very Knights of the Round Table. I wrote a little sketch about it which the group acted, and she said I had a real writing talent but I don't think I have. I can act, but writing? I don't think so.

I saw her husband the other day. He came to collect her and had the baby in this sling thing in front of him. She had a couple of pages to finish, and tried to breastfeed the baby still at her desk, but the baby muttered and moaned and stayed hungry. So the husband whipped out this bottle of formula, ready prepared, and I warmed it under the tap and we tried that. Arthur was quite hungry, you could tell, but seemed well satisfied afterwards. He is a lovely baby but I can see babies are a great nuisance.

'I'll have to give up breastfeeding altogether,' says Isolde. 'Do you mind? It turns my brain to porridge.'

'Lactating is not a nice word,' agrees the husband. 'So it may not be a very good thing.'

I try to follow the reasoning, and fail, other than that they live in a world in which aesthetics rule, and the mere sound of a word can turn you against its meaning. But it makes you think having a baby mightn't be so bad if it had a father who would look after it. His name is Gavin Garner and he is a famous writer. You see him and her sometimes in the arts pages of the Sundays. He is tall and broad and looks like a lordly eagle, and she rather like a robin with her head on one side while she considers what has been said. A thin robin after a bad winter, mind you. She is very slim and pale and totally beautiful, and he seems to adore her. Anyway, he is too old and powerful and clever for me. I would just be tongue-tied if he asked me for an opinion. I'm just another drama student. He writes reviews, really long ones, on classical theatre, and can be terrible about people.

Emily's Understanding

And Gavin of course was the man she ended up with, a dozen or so years later, Isolde having disappeared from the scene. And Arthur grew up to be not gay, but lacking in what one might call testosteronic qualities of aggression and sexual drive. I blame bottle-feeding. Not because of any necessary superiority of breast milk over formula – breast milk is a minimum require-ment for infant survival not a maximum – but because bottles were no longer made of glass but plastic rich in oestrogen-mimicking chemicals which it liberates fifty-fold when you heat it up.

But that is by the by. I have not told Sappho because she washed and wielded the plastic bottle many times for Arthur during his infancy, and I do not want to increase the feelings of guilt she has towards her stepchildren and which makes coping with them more difficult than it ought to be.

Poor Sappho, she misses her own father, as is clear from the above entry. Her father died when she was three. His name was Rob, he was a GP. She was our only child. It had been such a long hot summer: I remember everything was so parched that year the apple tree could hardly bring itself to bear fruit. I had just been welcomed into the Institute of Psychoanalysts. It is a long training: I had qualified as a GP and then became so interested in the id, the ego and the superego that I moved sideways. I knew so much now about narcissistic and borderline states, character and personality disorders, psychosomatic states, simple and complex trauma, the interaction of neurotic and psychotic forces I scarcely noticed what was going on around me in real life. It had not crossed my mind that Rob would take his own life. He suffered from depression and a degree of paranoia, but so did nearly all the men I knew; angst was part of the male fashion of the day, for feminism was bursting upon the world. Some say depression is repressed anger, but at the time I saw it as repressed guilt. Men were guilty about their patriarchal attitudes, and rightly so. I had just taken my first patient, under supervision. He was, as I remember, a rather good-looking if anorexic business man.

'On top of everything else,' Rob said to me, 'I now have to worry about you having affairs with the patients.'

I promised him I wouldn't. I thought he was joking but perhaps he was not.

'But I know what you're like,' he complained. 'And now I'm told there's this thing called "positive transference".'

I said it was probably balanced by negative transference. The patients were as likely to hate me as love me. Neither emotion, I assured him, necessarily had an erotic element.

And I thought no more about it. Rob had ceased practising as a doctor, the better to fight off the developers who were as determined to demolish Apple Lee as he was to save it. It was a full-time job. Compulsory purchase orders bounced through the letterbox. I was all for selling: the house had been in the family for generations but that did not mean it had to stay there. The roof leaked, the wiring was hazardous, the plumbing noisy.

'It will fall down by itself,' I remember saying, 'if you don't do something. And that will cost thousands we don't have. Sell, for God's sake, sell!'

'Over my dead body,' he said, and he wasn't joking. 'They'll have to drag me out feet first.'

And so they did. That is exactly what happened.

After Rob died I went through a patch of what the supervisor of my self-analysis described as a pre-oedipal, polymorphous sexuality: that is to say I slept around, with anyone or anything, and I don't suppose that did little Sappho any good. I justified it, as one does, by believing I was acting on principle rather than out of despair: pursuing a free sexuality, saving the world as well as myself, making love not war as Marcuse instructed us. Sex good, repression bad. I have worked through it, more or less, through my advancing years, and now content myself with Barnaby, while rather hoping to up-grade some day.

But this is meant to be an account of Sappho's life not mine. It's just that, as Freud explained to us, the psychosexual development of the growing child is interdependent on that of the parent. And Sappho's choice of Gavin for a husband is a source of mystery to both Barnaby and me.

'My dear Emily,' Barnaby says, 'there is a simple and obvious answer – she is replacing the father who died when she was three.'

'But why an older man with a daughter? There are plenty of unencumbered men about. Why Gavin? Unless it's his daughter she's identifying with.'

'Or perhaps,' says Barnaby cunningly, 'you over-exposed her to the primal scene when she was small. Too many lovers, too many cries in the night? I fear it is yourself you are talking about.'

Enough of all this. Sappho at seventeen. What does she mean? 'Mother was furious, but I have my trust fund and can do what I like.'

For fuck's sake, has the girl no idea? What bringing up a child on your own can be like? What I gave up for her? How I didn't marry again for her sake? Because I don't think stepfathers are a good idea for a girl: because the tensions growing up with one, especially such a pretty, dreamy one as her, do no one any good. And all right, because whenever I did meet a man I thought I could marry I started worrying at once in case he preferred her to me – being younger and fresher. And as for her feeling guilty when she moved out when she had a perfectly good home with me, I am really glad she did; so she ought. Seventeen years she had spent with me and then she's just off? I daresay it happens in nature: you bear them and they grow up and are ready to leave the nest, and if you did it properly you're pretty relieved when they do go. Some of my colleagues indeed argue that the bad behaviour of teenagers is designed by a beneficent nature so the parents are happy when they go. But I had never noticed that 'nature' had the slightest concern for anyone's happiness: all she's concerned with, the bitch, is the propagation of the species and the minute the mother is past child-bearing age nature has no further interest in her whatsoever and casts her off like an old glove – but there you are.

And as for the trust fund and she could do as she liked, that is nonsense. I had charge of her trust fund, though if she really needed something I would never, never stand in her way.

What am I avoiding that has made me so angry? What are these diversionary tactics? Primal scream stuff? I fear so. Back to the diaries.

Sappho's Diary: *March 10th 1993*

Dear Diary,

Isolde says to get into the habit of writing one's life in scenes. It fosters a certain detachment. So here's the scene for today. I'm not likely to forget it. (Actually, it happened last week, on my birthday, but I've only now had time to write it up.)

Lights up on Sappho, aged nineteen, cleaning out the tea urn backstage at the Royal Court. She is doing this gladly, though some others on the course think they are just being used as cheap labour. Personally, Sappho thinks she is the luckiest person alive. She gets to see Isolde at least two or three sessions once a week, which means she has occasional individual tuition from one of the greatest playwrights living and goes to all the plays at the Royal Court free, and Gavin now speaks to her as if she were a human being. The phone goes.

SAPPHO: Hello, hi, Gavin. Any news of the baby? No? *Death and the Maiden?* Yes, of course, I filed the re-writes last week. I'll bring them right over. But surely she can't want to work today. Isn't the baby due any minute?

Lights up on Isolde, grabbing her stomach from time to time but still writing at the kitchen table. Gavin puts down the receiver and goes on squeezing oranges for the little boy Arthur, who is three and a poppet. Gavin Garner is the best father and husband in the world.

Enter Sappho with notes.

GAVIN: Thank you for this, Sappho! I don't know what we would do without you.

ISOLDE: Thanks for coming over, Sappho. Oh dear, my waters seem to have broken.

Not a good scene for on-stage. Better if it happens off.

(*N.B: always worry about water on stage. It gets into the electrics. Rock stars keep electrocuting themselves, sometimes fatally, by using water as a part of an act. Never mind. I'll see to it later. On.*)

ISOLDE: How very messy. Gavin, I think you had better phone the hospital.

SAPPHO: Can I help?

ISOLDE: You could wipe up, I suppose, but it seems so very personal. And I promised myself I'd never use you for domestic labour. It's a temptation because you're so willing.

SAPPHO: Yes, but this is rather different. Kind of an emergency?

GAVIN: All I get from these bastards is a recorded message. All our operators are busy. I'll call 999.

ISOLDE: No, honestly, why don't you just drive me in? Sappho, you wouldn't mind looking after Arthur, would you? Give him some tea and put him to bed? I don't want you there at the birth, Gavin, don't worry. These things are not for the squeamish, nothing like that.

Exit Isolde and Gavin, arguing about the merits or otherwise of fathers being present at the birth.

Inset scene of Gwen, Isolde's posh mother, talking to camera if this is to be a film or to the audience if it's stage.

GWEN: What, a man there at the birth? Never let it happen. He'll be put off sex for ever. Women who insist on it are digging their own matrimonial graves. If men go off with younger women it's not because they're younger *per se*, it's because they've never had to witness them in an animal state, grunting and screaming and sweating.

Cut to, or lights up on, Sappho phoning her mother.

SAPPHO: Hi Mum, Isolde's going in to hospital in a hurry to have the baby and they've left me with the little boy. What do little boys of three eat?

Lights up on Emily in Apple Lee, answering the phone. She is distraught.

EMILY: But Sappho you are meant to be round here. It's your birthday. I have made a chocolate cake especially for you. Young Piers has flown all the way back from South Africa especially to see you. And oh my God, now the bath is overflowing. Water is pouring down the stairs. Those Garner people take the most fearful advantage.

SAPPHO: Mother, please don't lay a guilt trip on me.

Emily, Or Freud, On Masochism

' "Lay a guilt trip on me!" Can she have really said anything so lamentable?' I complained to Barnaby, whose washing machine had broken down, and so had dropped by with his weekly bag of socks and shirts. I was pleased enough to abandon the diaries. They were going to make a disturbing read. I had read the entry to him, and now we sat in front of the washing machine in the kitchen and watched while a stray red sock turned everything a pale pink. Short of draining the machine by hand there was little we could about it but accept.

'Why not? How old was she? Nineteen? It's the kind of thing the young do say. Thus they shrug off any fleeting pangs of conscience.'

'But it's so crude,' I said. 'Such an over-simplification. The shopping mall version of the language of the mind. A primal power struggle between mother and daughter and it gets called *laying a guilt trip*?'

'It's understandable,' said Barnaby mildly. 'The mother reproaches: the child projects its own sense of guilt back onto the mother, and leaves her feeling bad. Look at you – you're smarting all over. Calm down.'

'I don't like her wandering round on her own,' I said. I felt helpless. When children are little you can pick them up under one arm and run to a place of safety. But then they grow up and how can you save them from themselves? 'I remember that day well,' I said. 'I got very annoyed with her. I'd made her a chocolate cake for her birthday and asked some friends round to celebrate. Then it all had to be cancelled because of the bloody Garners. Everything had to be cancelled. The water wasn't pouring down the stairs: why is her instinct to exaggerate everything so? It was dripping through the kitchen ceiling.'

'She did turn out to be a dramatist,' said Barnaby. 'I expect that's part of it.'

It was quite companionable sitting here beside him. He was a very calm and reassuring person. It was probably a good thing that his shirts would have to be abandoned. They were fairly grey to begin with and there was no hope of them coming out a clear bright pink – they would just end up a yet murkier grey with a reddish tinge. He needed a woman; just not me.

'I should have gone round to help her out. I would have seen what was happening and headed the Garners off. But I was annoyed with her and everything was going wrong. The chocolate cake had sunk horribly into a gooey dark brown mess. I am not into baking at the best of times, but one does like the material world to echo one's good intentions rather than one's incompetence.'

'You have missed a trick,' said Barnaby. 'I would have thought cakes sinking and not rising was distinctly Freudian. I am sorry to have failed you so often.'

'Forget it,' I said. 'I blame the oven. It was rusty old iron and had not been cleaned since it was installed, I imagine around Nineteen Thirty. It was narrower than modern ovens. My hands are still quite scarred around the edges from that oven. Of course the kitchen is all very smart now. The cooker must have cost Sappho over three thousand pounds.'

'I didn't know cookers could be that much,' says Barnaby.

The leasehold of his flat comes to an end in a couple of years. Is this why he is being so nice to me? Because he wants to move in? Well, he can think again. He can share my washing machine but not my life.

'Laura believes in buying the best,' I say. 'She says anything else is a false economy.'

After Sappho started making money and took over Apple Lee, the house was renovated to the taste of the last decade of the last century, not to mention Laura's, and by the time Gavin moved in the kitchen was all stainless steel and granite surfaces, and everything whirred and blinked with little beeps and red lights. It was not at all cosy, and not particularly to Gavin's taste, which Sappho described once as Northern Moor Brutal.

'Who was Piers from South Africa?' asked Barnaby. 'What happened to him?'

I said I couldn't remember, but he was probably a medical student. I tried to introduce Sappho to young men who were her intellectual equal: the boys at RADA seemed such a flimsy, self-obsessed lot. The last thing I wanted was for her to end up with some actor.

'Emily,' said Barnaby, 'take comfort. Considering how you

liked to control her life, you must have done something right or she'd have taken to drink and drugs by now.'

'She was the only child I had,' I said helplessly. 'Poor Sappho! I can see I must have driven her mad.'

'She seems sane enough to me,' he said. 'Just a little neurotic.'

Neurotic? Allowing herself to be used as a skivvy by the Garners? Marrying Gavin? Practically twenty years older than she, lugging two children behind him, giving up her own career to suit him and getting herself with child when she had her whole future before her?

'Neurotic is putting it mildly,' I say. 'My daughter is almost pathologically masochistic. Masochism exists on the moral plane as well as the erotic. It belongs to the super-ego as much as to the id.'

'Bloody Freudian,' says Barnaby. 'Bloody metapsychologist. You and your landscape of the brain. I suppose you think it is all your fault?'

'Yes,' I say. 'Of course I do. I was too repressive a parent. Her father died when she was three. The worst age. She thinks she is responsible. Masochism is how we convert pain – whether it be physical or moral – into pleasure. It exists to assuage some great unconscious guilt. Masochism and repression are intertwined. To suffer, to be helpless, to be free from choice, is to be free of guilt. Why else do people wander round Anne Summers sex shops, looking at velvet handcuffs and day-dreaming of guilty pleasure?'

'You are preoccupied with sex,' he complains. 'Foucault's dirty little secret, the one that powers all human activity, is at least productive. Be positive. Look how rich your little daughter got after she left the Garner household, look how smart her oven! Scribble, scribble, little Sappho! "Scribble, scribble, Mr

Gibbon!" What guilty secret did Edward Gibbon have that drove him on? A productive age is a guilty age. The proletariat sweats and suffers through the Industrial Age for the sadistic pleasures of its masters. What secret did your daughter have? Guilt is why Sappho's kitchen now gleams and glitters and your stove was never more than rusty iron. Guilt equals wealth: wealth equals guilt.'

'Bloody Marxist,' I say.

The spin cycle comes to an end. Barnaby investigates his ruined wash. He looks at me longingly.

'Am I staying the night?' he asks.

'No, you are not,' I say. 'I need to be alone.'

'You and Greta Garbo,' he says.

I say he is not to drape his wet washing over the backs of my chairs. He can take it back upstairs. He does. He is very biddable. Perhaps he wants me to take out a whip and beat him, but doesn't like to say so.

The diaries disturb me greatly. My worry level stands at seven out of ten, and rising. Doing nothing is irresponsible. Sappho is my daughter. She has wandered off into the metaphorical night, into blankness, demanding that she be left alone, while offering me her past to scrutinise. I can't just leave it at that. She requires me to do something but I am not sure what. I will ring and ask Laura what's going on. But I don't want to give her any hint that I am concerned.

I call Apple Lee but the call goes to answerphone. This in itself is strange. Laura the super-efficient is usually there until late evening, manning the phones – or personning them, as she would say, with her little trilling laugh, half serious, half not. But perhaps she's gone off in search of sustenance? Camden Council has spent millions trying to refurbish the neighbourhood, and a few brave tapas bars have recently opened up. The Garners keep Apple Lee unpainted and dishevelled on the outside, the better to confuse robbers. More to the point, they have surveillance cameras covering the house and security lights that spring into life at every city fox or prowling cat that wanders by.

I will wait a couple of hours and then try Laura again. I could go and meet Isobel out of school and see what she has to say. I remember that it's Friday, and she usually stays with Gwen on Friday nights. Arthur has just started at Warwick University, where he is studying marine biology, otherwise I'd ask him. Arthur and I get on well, and always have. There are various friends and colleagues I could ask of course, but I don't want to start unnecessary hares running. Sappho would be furious if I did.

Back to the diaries. I am sorry now I sent Barnaby away. Company is a good cure for anxiety, a sliver of which, pure and unadulterated, unexpectedly sticks me under the ribs and twists. I look for the reason and find none. Barnaby is right. I too am in denial.

Sappho's Diary: *April 10th 1994*

Dear Diary,

A scene from today I can't let go unrecorded.

Gwen, Isolde's mother, cashmere-clad, supremely elegant with her long model's back, long model's legs (if over-long feet) and her normal, slightly surprised and vaguely condescending air – it

*may of course just be the over-plucked eyebrows – is visiting
Isolde and Gavin. She comes into the kitchen while Sappho is
giving lunch to Arthur and Isobel. Sappho is wearing jeans and
a grubby T-shirt and it is a long time since she has had her hair
cut. She hasn't had time. Fortunately both children are being
sweet and idyllic, so Sappho is spared the usual barbed
comments. God, how she hates this woman. It is mutual. Gwen
puts on the kettle, and speaks to Sappho as if casually, but she is
not casual. She has something to say and has decided to say it.*

GWEN: So how are you, Sappho? Is it Sappho by name or
Sappho by nature? Or both?

SAPPHO: I'm sorry. I don't understand what you mean.

GWEN: I'm talking lesbians, darling.

SAPPHO: Oh. No, I don't think I'm a lesbian. My mother is a
feminist, and a psychoanalyst by profession, but a
normal heterosexual. Indeed, rather more than normal.
She called me after a lyric poet who just happened to
live on the Isle of Lesbos a long time ago. I wasn't the
product of a sperm bank or anything like that. I had a
proper father but he died in an accident. She is a widow.

GWEN: Because we all rather wonder why you don't have a
boyfriend. A pretty girl like you.

*Sappho has wondered the same thing herself for some time, and
has decided she puts men off by being too clever. She gets bored*

and starts being the life and soul of the party and too loud. Stray men certainly like to bump up against her in the street. She is persecuted in the Underground. The boyfriend potential like to have her as a friend but don't fall in love with her. They tend to fall in love with the still, slow, disdainful types with thin arms and long ironed hair. She is planning to work on it and never show that she is clever, let alone that she has a GSOH. But all this is too long to explain to Gwen, who is only looking for trouble anyway. Gwen's talking too fast and eating raspberry jam by the spoonful from the children's tea table. Gwen may be on cocaine, or if it's the munchies perhaps it's spliff? (Must fact-check: or does it apply to both drugs?) But Sappho continues to speak the truth because this is her life policy.

SAPPHO: I don't have time for boyfriends, I expect that's it. All that exchange of bodily fluids seems a bit gross. I don't say that kind of thing at home because it's such a source of discussion and concern. Or perhaps I'm just not attractive to men. I don't have the proper pheromones.

GWEN: Because if you're after my son-in-law, lay off.

This is so startling Sappho drops the teaspoon with which she is feeding Isobel, splattering soft egg yolk all over the place, including Isobel's hair. Isobel's face puckers. She can't bear mess. She begins to whimper.

GWEN: Either you're a very good actress – which, having seen you once on stage, I know you are not – or you are indeed Miss Innocence. Forget it, Miss Lesbos, drop it. I apologise.

Exit madwoman, still spooning jam. Sappho comforts Isobel.

Well, that was a nasty crack about my acting. I know I'm not very good but I'm not that bad. Anyway, I'd rather write the lines than say them. I love the power writers have. 'There is a massive explosion' – just four words, but they mean at least ten people have to use all their skill and training, which I don't have, to create something more real than reality. Better to be a writer than an actor. The puzzle is why does Gwen manage to make me feel so inferior? All she can do is swan around in nice clothes. And she has a nasty, vulgar, stupid mind. Gavin is old enough, just, to be my father and naturally I'd never do anything to upset Isolde. Though I sometimes think Isolde does rather neglect Gavin: she is so wrapped up in her work. And she doesn't seem even to hear the children when they get rackety. Mind you, it must be hard for Isolde to have Gwen for a mother. Gwen was really famous back in the fifties and did a lot of work for *Vogue*. She looked forty when she was seventeen, which seems to have been the fashion then, and she still looks forty today. I suppose it's the face creams. Gwen is really rather disgusting and quite daft. Gavin is a God anyway, not a man. Gods and mortals simply do not mate. My mother gets weird ideas in her head sometimes, but at least she's not totally daft. And she doesn't spoon jam straight from the jar into her mouth.

If I ever did marry, if ever anyone wanted to marry me and I don't see why they should except for my money, and I don't have any of that, just a miserable trust fund which has to be signed by my mother as if I were a child until I am twenty-five when it runs out anyway, I would like it to be to someone like Gavin. (I must remember to keep my sentences shorter and avoid the breathy style, Isolde says.) He is very gentle and a good father, and has this great shock of hair. If he's on TV and lit from behind he looks like a saint with a halo. Little Isobel adores him. When she was tiny he'd carry her round in a kind of sling thing on his chest. Next to his heartbeat, he said. And she would stare up at him, so solemnly with her big round greeny eyes: I wanted to get between the gaze and interrupt it. It seemed indecent – such trust and faith. How could two people have such confidence in one another? Don't they know how things go wrong in the world? I wish I had had a father like Gavin and not be fated to be an orphan. I might have more self-confidence. And Arthur just puts one foot in front of the other and gets on with life. He was born untroubled, and lucky.

Emily's Apology

What does she mean, an orphan? She had me, didn't she? And her father until she was three? And he adored her, and he also carried her round in one of those sling things. She too was the apple of a father's eye. So much so that I got jealous, fleetingly, just every now and then, but still decidedly jealous, the way Sappho puts it – wanting to get between the pair of them. To interrupt the gaze. Me, me, me, what about me? Don't I exist, too? Pity the poor mother, whose fate it is to give birth to a monster that takes what you have, sucks you dry and spits you out. The child exists at the mother's expense, steals the father's love, the emotional nourishment that was once the mother's, and runs off laughing.

The horrible truth is that when Rob died there was one thing less for me to cope with. Sappho's existence was no longer a constant reminder of my own depravity – me, Emily Stubb-Palmer, psychoanalyst, jealous of her own daughter! Pathetic. It wasn't just every now and then, either. It was pretty much all of the time. Poor mothers, poor daughters. Two's company, three's none.

Consider. Just consider. No such thing as an accident, said Freud, always right, the bugger. Sappho's birthday. (Barnaby's interpretation is solipsistic, naturally; forget it.) Mum makes a terrible, uneatable cake, lets the bath run over, and brings down the kitchen ceiling. Invites a young man the daughter is bound to dislike on sight in order to embarrass her. What kind of birthday was I wishing on my daughter? I was wishing her ill, because this was her nineteenth birthday, and she was blooming into womanhood and I was fading. When things go wrong, consider yourself and your real motives. Let the free association rip. Thanatos, the death wish. Masochism. Repression. False memories. Fantasies. Guilty secrets. No need to go on. What am I hiding from myself?

I call Laura again. Still no reply. I remember Sappho's mobile, better late than never. It's switched off. My God, what's going on? Forget *her* life; what about mine?

I suppose I'm not jealous because Gavin married her, not me? Old enough to be her father? No. That is going too far, even for Freud.

I am glad she says my ideas aren't as weird as Gwen's. Thank you, Sappho. She has written exclamation marks along the bottom of the page, and then ha-ha-ha-ha down the sides. She's still a child.

What I objected to most about the Garners in the beginning was that they used Sappho not just as a domestic skivvy, but as an intellectual slave. I knew for a fact that whole scenes in some of Isolde's celebrated TV dramas were written by Sappho. But she never appeared in the credits. 'Additional scenes by' or some such. No.

'It's too bad, Sappho,' I'd say. 'They're exploiting you.'

'Oh Mum,' she'd say. 'They're not. I'm an apprentice. I'm learning. I'm so lucky.'

'My left foot!' I'd say, but she'd get upset and I'd drop it.

When the plays were screened the Garners liked to give a party to their followers and admirers, not to mention a few critics. Sappho would work late preparing food after the children were in bed. No caterers were hired though they could well afford it. They were both earning good money. God, they were mean.

And then Gavin or Isolde would say, 'Wouldn't you prefer to watch at home with your mother?' Which was their way of saying a) you're just the skivvy and b) we don't want it leaking out that this line or that is yours, not Isolde's. And she'd come over to Apple Lee and we would watch together. Why did she never fight back? In retrospect, of course, it is obvious. It was the massive guilt – she fancied Gavin from the beginning, and could hardly admit it to herself. Just obliquely – Isolde didn't 'look after' him well enough. Women who take skivvies into their homes really do need to be careful. The Chinese have their concubines; the Muslim world has its four wives. That's half the world taken care of. It is a natural enough situation. The woman likes a particular man in the bed. The man falls naturally into whatever's available.

And it wasn't just Isolde taking advantage, and credit where none was due, it was Gavin as well. I'd seen a photo Sappho had taken of a stone curlew circling over Kenwood in the *Ornithologist* and it was attributed to Gavin – no mention of Sappho. Mind you, it was Gavin who had taught her how to take and develop photographs. (He scorned all things digital.) And I knew that Sappho would sit in the Gods and watch plays while Gavin sat sleeping in the front row of the stalls with his little pencil light drooping from his hand. The fathers of young children never get enough sleep. One way or another it was Sappho's judgements, Sappho's opinions that found their way into Gavin's review columns. I knew because I read them. Hand Sappho a stick and she would run with it. It was her great talent, or had been. Now, after four years married to Gavin, she huddled under some old navy parka and handed me her diaries to hide. Why?

And in the meanwhile, while she toiled for the Garners, her degree had been postponed for a year and then another year: at least they did pull strings for her, and she became one of the troops of extras at the National Theatre, and was even allowed, when her skivvying duties permitted, to speak the odd line in public from time to time.

'I never get any further than serving wenches, brothel girls and one-line messengers,' she complained. 'I don't know why, others do. Perhaps I have no natural talent. Perhaps I'm just an embarrassment and no one likes to say so.'

'You're good enough,' I'd say. 'But perhaps you're needed elsewhere.' She'd have none of that. The Garners would never be so devious.

'I like being on stage,' she said. 'But I'm not a natural. Isolde is right, my forte is writing.'

She may well have been right, though I never liked to admit it. She was too definite a personality herself to be able to slip easily into other people's skins. And still she didn't have a boyfriend. What was the matter with her? Me? Perhaps, in my concern for the poor girl's psychosexual development, I had somehow halted it? Was she perhaps stuck in the homosexual phase? Or imprinted, following the Garners round as a baby goose follows the first thing it sees when it hatches? If she was in love with either of them it seemed at the time to be with Isolde, not Gavin.

I went up to Barnaby's flat to offer him the use of my clothes dryer. I also asked him what he thought about Freud's theory that Oedipal wishes in the female were initially homosexual desires for the mother, which then shifted to a more overt sexual desire for the father.

'You're seeing Isolde and Gavin as substitute parents? I suppose that figures,' said Barnaby. He had the heating turned right up the better to dry his washing, and was going round his cluttered flat naked to the waist. 'Only do we have to think about Sappho all the time? Can't we think about me? All this to-ing and fro-ing from your place to mine is a waste of time.' He was quite a fine figure of a man, for sixty-seven. Flat-stomached and well-muscled. A pity about the sexual dysfunction. If that was what it was. He seemed to like me well enough, though once in a dream, he complained, I had appeared in the form of a shark – and I could see perhaps he feared me as some kind of sexually voracious predator. If only he would consent to take Viagra or Cialis I could feature as a gambolling lamb and he would have confidence to rise to the occasion. Perhaps I could grind some tablets up and put them in his tea? I didn't mind his propensity to snuggle in bed rather than actually fuck, but it could get frustrating.

Sappho like a baby, re-winding and starting her psychic life over again? Driven to it by me, in order to develop unobserved? It made sense.

'You mean Sappho might have arrested in the mother phase?' I pressed him. 'And then moved on to Gavin, Isolde having no penis to envy. Gavin has a very long penis; so I have heard. And used it quite actively, I believe, when he was on his own, and before Sappho came on the scene. It is also not beyond the bounds of possibility that he seduced my daughter after Isolde became ill. She was little better than a slave girl.'

'It is really a matter of indifference to me,' said Barnaby. Well, he was a Jungian. Jungians tend to be afraid of sex – they prefer religious and spiritual metaphor. We Freudians stick with the sex. He and I would never get on. There would be no spiral staircase.

'For heaven's sake, Emily,' he said (I seemed to have really annoyed him), 'I find that unlikely. They were of different generations and Gavin is, by and large, a worthy person who apparently was very much in love with his dying Isolde. I too read his newspaper columns and very moving and illuminating they were. How the person is loved and not the body.'

'Sanctimonious poppycock,' I said.

'You could think many things of Gavin Garner,' he said stiffly, 'but not that he was into trivialising his own emotions. Married, literary, theatrical, bird-watching academics take themselves seriously. They do not fall into bed with naive twenty-year-old girls.'

'Dry your own washing,' I said, and went downstairs again.

I pulled out another sheet of paper. I could tell from the Waitrose bag that Laura has not been allowed near the diaries. Frankly, they are a mess. One must learn that if a folder says 1993 it is likely to contain papers from another year. I have the feeling

Sappho left the house in a hurry. Got all the folders together at leisure, marked up the years, and then had to just shove papers in any old how and get out of there. But why?

It is no use worrying about her, which of course does not stop one. I wish I had said something less self-indulgent than, 'What are you trying to do? Lose the baby?' This was no time to have a dig about unconscious motivation. She had worked hard enough trying to get pregnant. As so often happens when women put off having babies it can be difficult. And Gavin wasn't exactly a young man. I daresay his sperm had got rather tired. But she was clearly in trouble and I should not have said it. More to the point, why had Sappho thrown it back at me? A great deal of projection goes on between mother and child, I know well enough. The child blames the parents for its own misdeeds. The parent blames the child when its own inadequacies make their appearance in their offspring, and judges them more harshly.

I read on. The next sheet I extracted went right back to the beginning, before Isobel was born, when she had just appointed Isolde and Gavin her new parents.

Sappho's Diary: *January 16th 1995*

Dear Diary,

Come to think of it, I have only you to confide in. I have no one else to talk to. You might as well be dear. Other girls talk to their mothers, I believe, but it's impossible for me. All she does is peer at me from a distance and wonder if I have yet reached the genital stage of my psychosexual development. In other words, if I am a virgin. Which I am, Dear Diary, and hope to remain so as long as possible, but I don't mean her to know that. I want her to know nothing at all about me. She is not really very interested anyway. To her I am just another case history. She talks to patients in our front room. They come at ten to the hour every hour, a constant stream. She listens to what they say all right; I can listen to them talk from my bedroom. The floor is so thin that if I droop my head down towards the floor and move the rug I hear what is being said. It makes a break from homework. The voices can get blurred sometimes, which is good, because some-times they tell her the most disgusting things. There was one man who liked doing it with dogs, and paid girls to join in. I think it's bad of her not to take better care that I can't overhear.

'Stop listening, then,' is all she'd say. But I have to spend years trying hard not to fantasise about being one of the girls. I bet Mother knew I listened, too. Do not think, Dear Diary, that I am going to tell even you all the things that go on in my head. It is dangerous to write things down, let alone speak them: vague memories become certainties once you do.

They talk all the time; she only says a word or two. It is a pecu-liar thing to do for a living. Listening. A paid listener. You'd think people could talk to their friends. But then most of the patients look too unhappy to have friends. I don't have many, mind you, but not because I'm unhappy. I'm not a loner or anything like that. I just tend not to go round in a group. The patients probably put on that expression when she opens the door to them. They pay her to be sorry for them. I read the books from her shelves to try and make sense of it, but she found out and began to censor my reading. I got really upset about that.

A constant flow of men to the door. Mostly men; she likes men. There's one girl who comes to her at three o'clock on Saturdays. She's an anorexic. She's been coming for years. At least she's not dead yet. I suppose that's worth it. But it meant we could never do anything normal like go to the mall on Saturday afternoons.

Anyone could be excused for thinking Apple Lee was a knocking shop. They come in the evening, too, of course, but then they were 'Mum's friends' not 'Mum's clients'. Sometimes they spend the night. She doesn't necessarily take them up to the bedroom, and I try not to listen but I can't help it. Once I swear there were three of them at it. You'd think someone like her would have more self-control. They're all politicos. I am simply not interested. I told her once I was sick of all the Marxist talk I was exposed to and she said, 'Darling, they're Trotskyites,' so that put me in my place. I go round to the Garners a lot now. I have supper there once or twice a week, and can actually have quite a conversation with Gavin; Isolde feels more like a real mother to me than Emily.

Emily Is Distraught

It is all fantasy! It is simply not true. There is no way Sappho could have heard what was going on in my consulting room. She heard what she wanted to hear. No patient of mine ever said anything about a threesome with dogs. I would have remembered. Why would I be in denial? Where did she get this nonsense from?

I once found her reading a volume of Krafft-Ebing she'd nicked from my shelves and I took it away from her. She must have been about twelve, just moving out of the latent stage, when children can get acutely sexually suggestible and I didn't think Kafft-Ebing on zoophilia was particularly sensible for a girl of that age. That is why I took the book away. And yes, she did make a dreadful scene when I did, out of all proportion to what was going on, a kind of six-year-old's tantrum. At the time I took it to be some kind of regressive behaviour, triggered by my thwarting of her spirit of enquiry, instead of fostering it, which I normally tried to do – certainly not triggered by the contents of the bloody book. So she internalises the trauma and out it comes as something actually remembered and I get blamed for it. I'd write it up as a case history only it's my own daughter, and anyway I have this talk on gender to write.

I am calming down now. I suppose I must be grateful she remembers the incident as reported by one of my disliked patients. How did she think she lived, other than by my earnings? The money from Rob's insurance policy had been spent long since and I had a small private income and a trust that was coming to an end, but I had to work for a living and I was good at what I did. I'm glad she remembered Alison, who was suffering from an ascetic neurosis, and it's true she took up our Saturday afternoons, but it was worth it: she sent me an invitation to her wedding and she was finally pregnant.

But at least Rob died when Sappho was so small – such was her masochistic nature I could see her growing up into a father abuser: a girl who projects her own sexual desire onto the father and then mistakes fantasy for reality and years later claims actual sexual abuse, sadistically destroying the family in the process. I was spared that particular anxiety. It is an ill wind, etc. At the same time I could never judge from my own experience with Sappho which was the more likely to be the case – Freud's early conclusion that all girls fantasise about sexual abuse from the father, and that it seldom happens in actuality, or his later conviction that if a girl denies it has happened it certainly has, and more, they need to be compelled to remember it in the interests of their psychic health. I solved the dilemma – which has clouded the recovered memory landscape for so long – by sitting on the wall, and thinking about other things, such as primal scenes. I am all too good at sitting on walls. I only hope Sappho didn't osmote through her placenta my then preoccupation with the fantasy/reality debate, and use Gavin to replace the missing father. Who is to say what goes on between mother and child in the womb?

The memory that I brought lovers into the consulting room is hopelessly false. That I indulged in threesomes down there is nuts. I went through a wild stage at one time, I remember, in middle years, trying to keep age at bay, no doubt, but never when Sappho was around. That is just for the record. I hope it is obvious in case Sappho ever does decide to publish these diaries. (Judging from his appearance on my doorstep Gavin worries too. So far he appears as a hero, but what next?) The trouble with three-or-more-somes is that there are bound to be witnesses. Nothing, nothing stays private for ever. The dirty little secret is too interesting, powers too much of our lives. My difficulty with Jung is that he is just too spiritual, too nice, for words; doesn't see the vulgar energy of sex as powering the universe. Give me Freud and a bit of miserable, tedious, hard-working super-ego any day.

I forgive Sappho. What girl doesn't go through a stage of rejecting her mother in order to be herself? Mothers ditto, to lessen the pain of parting.

I call Apple Lee again, but all I get is the answerphone. Then I remember that Gavin said Laura was 'temporarily' out of the office. Does this mean she's ill, or on holiday? I usually look after her cats when she's away – she brings them round to stay with me, and they bring chaos, fleas and yowling into my life and their hair makes Barnaby sneeze. But I do it because I am Laura's fan, and I know without her Sappho's life would be a mess. So she's probably just poorly.

I call Laura on her landline at home, in case she's there, but the bell just rings on and on into silence. I can't believe she's forgotten to turn on the answerphone but she must have. Laura's life is altogether orderly, too: she is a no-nonsense person; she doesn't approve of love, on the grounds that it leads to instability and lack of purpose, though she is quite keen on sex. I know because I once found her watching the porn channels on her computer. I imagine she is a sadist to Sappho's masochist: she is the whip-wielder, the time-keeper, the obsessive compulsive who must have everything categorised and under control. A left-brainer, as opposed to Sappho's right brain, with its scatty, fuzzy, muddled tendency. Between them they made a good money-making team, or had done till Gavin came back and distorted the clarity of the scene.

The phone goes. It's Laura, calling back.

'Was it you who rang just now?' she asks. Her voice is cold. Her normal professional courtesy, its contrived ebullience, is lacking.

'Yes,' I say. 'I'm looking for Sappho.'

'Yes,' she says, bleakly. I wait for her to say more but she doesn't.

'Do you know where she is?'

'No,' she says.

I stay silent. If I say nothing the next response will have to come from her. It does.

'I don't care where the fuck she is,' says Laura. 'Or her wanker of a husband. I've handed in my notice, and the cunt accepted it.'

This time I am shocked into silence. Not at the language – I had heard Laura sound off before, though only prudently once the phone was safely down – but at the very idea that the Garner household could function without Laura. When I'd put Apple Lee in Sappho's name and moved out, I'd done it mostly because I knew Laura would be there to notice when the house was falling down, pay the builders, get the right email to the right person and the deadlines met. All the things that Sappho tended not to be able to organise, or come to that, Gavin later.

'I don't understand,' I say.

'I am not staying under the same roof as Gwen.'

'The other granny can be difficult,' I say cautiously. 'I know Sappho had trouble with her at one time.'

I like to refer to Gwen as the 'other granny' if I can. 'Grandmère' Gwen could have endured, or 'Nona', after the Italian, but 'granny' is downmarket. It annoys her, which she demonstrates by licking her perfect lips with her little pink tongue, and then dabbing them with a tissue for fear of their chapping. I don't know why this annoys me so. Perhaps because my own mother would do it. Lick the lips, then dab. In her determination to have a 'proper family' when she first got married

Sappho urged Gwen to accept the title of 'grandmamma', but Gwen declined.

'Why on earth would one want a title,' she said to Sappho, 'when one has a perfectly good name? Being called Gwen is bad enough: it is short for Gwendolyn. Don't you think it's a little diminishing to be referred to as the mere adjunct of others? Do you want to be addressed as stepmother all the time?'

'No thanks,' said Sappho.

'And why should anything change just because you and my ex-son-in-law have gone through a marriage ceremony? It still doesn't make you one of the family, a blood relation. You know I was Guinevere of the Round Table in a past life?'

'How do you know?' Sappho asked, curious.

'I was regressed by a very reliable hypno-therapist,' Gwen replied.

'Poor woman,' I'd said to Sappho at the time. 'Cut her some slack. She lost her only daughter to cancer. Suffering doesn't ennoble people: it makes them worse.'

'You don't like her, either,' said Sappho. 'Don't be such a hypocrite.'

It was true. Gwen was a difficult woman to like. Isobel had inherited the cool, clear-cut beauty, lucky her, but with it the knack of speaking painful truths, designed to hurt. After this particular brush with Sappho the relationship between the two women had been the more distant.

Laura and I have been silent for a while, she inwardly pursuing her grievance and me mine. Now suddenly she begins to talk.

'The old bitch called me a liar. She said I was not one of the family and wasn't needed any more. The only reason that fucking house keeps standing is because of me. Well, let it fall down.'

And she goes on to tell me that Gwen had turned up in the office wanting money from the petty cash to pay off her taxi, and Laura looked but found the key was missing. Gwen had delivered the not-blood-relative barb and Laura had suggested that Gwen should look for the key in Isobel's top drawer, where it would probably be under the knickers Isobel had shoplifted from Victoria's Secret. Gwen called Laura a liar, and Laura had gone to Gavin and said she was handing in her notice. She was not going to be called a liar by anyone. And Gavin had said, 'I think it's for the best if you do go, Laura.'

'But it's not up to him,' I say. 'Sappho employs you, not Gavin.'

'Not really,' says Laura. 'Gavin re-negotiated my contract way back. I was to type up his novel as he wrote it. Not that he ever did.'

'But where was Sappho?'

'She'd just walked out,' says Laura. 'I reckon they'd had a row about the credit cards. I was sorting it out; Isobel had been screaming up and down the stairs as usual, they were all up there in the attic, then Sappho goes down to the basement, and packs a bag and she's off, saying we all have to look after ourselves. Quite the drama queen. I daresay she just wanted a bit of peace and quiet to get on with her novel.'

'Her novel?' I ask. 'I didn't know she was writing a novel.'

'I told her there's no money in it,' said Laura, 'but she won't listen to me any more. She should stick to what she's good at, TV soaps, but she never delivers in time so they've stopped asking. And then Granny Cow turns up. It's impossible to work under such conditions.'

'I'm sorry about all this, Laura,' I say. 'I'm sure everything will get back to normal soon. Whatever happens, I'm sure they'll see you right financially.' Laura just laughs. 'The bank sent back my last salary cheque "refer to drawer". Can you imagine anyone paying by cheque in this day and age? He's a dinosaur. And now she's pregnant and has to put up with him for ever.'

The cheque I could believe. 'Return to drawer' I could not. Money had been so plentiful in the early days: Laura was being lavishly paid.

'You're mad to be so generous,' I'd told Sappho at the time she first took Laura on, but as it turned out, when *Ms Alien* went on at the National and Sappho grew rich and famous practically overnight, it was Laura who held everyone and everything steady. Any financial difficulty would surely be temporary. Sappho was, to the best of my knowledge, working on another play, which presumably would be an equal success. It was called *I Liked It Here*. Mind you, she was taking her time writing it. The delivery date had been put back once or twice. I had wondered about that at the time.

'Mother, they can wait. I am an artist not a hack. Sometimes I just don't *feel* like writing. Sometimes there is nothing to be said. We weren't put on this earth to labour ceaselessly, we can afford to stand still and stare, just sometimes. Why do you have to come on like the Spanish Inquisition? You're a psychoanalyst, you should understand if anyone can. It's in the word. Delivery dates. If I deliver a play I won't be able to deliver a baby. They're alternatives. Isobel pointed that out to me. The gynaecologist said I would be more likely to get pregnant if I just sat around and did nothing for a bit. So I am. It's not exactly nothing, anyway. Running this house, coping with the children, I've applied for a teaching job—'

'What on earth for?'

'Just one day a week – I want to put something back, the way Isolde did. Then perhaps destiny will reward me.'

When a girl is determined to get pregnant nothing stands in her way, not even the work which has been her passion for a decade. What would she care if her income stream was drying up? I could see her expenses were enormous. She'd spent an unconscionable amount on Apple Lee – to a mixture of Sappho and Laura's tastes, which, when combined, were indeed lavish. And the money spent could not necessarily be recouped in the market. But what did I know any more? Other than that *Ms Alien* must surely still be bringing something in.

'They're up to their ears in debt, the fat cunts,' Laura now confides in me. 'At least I have my savings.'

She was certainly, I thought, what is known as a disgruntled employee. She might even have an undiagnosed Tourettes, triggered by shock.

'But that's not possible,' I said. Laura laughed, really quite cheerfully.

'Isobel's quite the big spender,' she said. 'When she and Gwen go shopping together it's a hoot.'

'Hang on a minute, Isobel's a child.'

'And Sappho's a fool. And Gwen hates her. You've no idea.'

Laura laughed some more and put down the phone.

The telephone call reminded me of the French nursery rhyme about the monsieur who comes home after a long absence and asks his servant how things have been. *Très bien, très bien*, very good, very good, comes the answer, except the stables are burned and the horses are dead, and the house is burned, and the family is dead, *mais très bien, très bien*.

Much as I disliked Gwen, I had been worried for some time

about Sappho's attempts to win the children's affections away from the 'other granny'. I told Barnaby so when I crept upstairs in an attempt to lessen the impact of my conversation with Laura.

'Your Sappho seems to be asking for trouble,' Barnaby observed. 'Most girls would want the burden of stepchildren to be spread as wide as possible. She goes on regarding them as spoils of war. Actually, they are always a danger. Nicostratus, stepson of Helen of Troy, drove her from her kingdom and we all know the fate of Snow White's stepmama. And Cinderella, from her ashy grate, won riches. "Shiver and quiver, my little tree, silver and gold throw down over me," Cinderella begged her dead mother, in the form of the hazel tree. And the dead mother obliged. Or there was Phineus, son-in-law of the north wind Boreas, patron saint of anorexics everywhere. Anorexia flourishes in the reconstituted family – how is Isobel doing body-wise?'

'Thin and fashionable,' I say, and shut him up. Too much information.

It was Sappho and Gavin's noble aspiration to move the children gradually from Gwen's place – where they had lived since their mother died – to Apple Lee. They had remained at the same school since their early childhood, and great efforts had been made to keep them there and undisturbed. At first they spent weekends and holidays with Gavin and Sappho and went to school from Gwen's place. Little by little, moved by her conviction that Gwen was too odd for comfort, and Isobel too influenced by her, Sappho poached them away from their grandmother. The school bus came up through Archway and along the road past Apple Lee. After her last unfortunate brush with Gwen, Sappho would urge the children to drop off for tea – white toast and Marmite – which would soon drift off into TV-watching or cinema-going and so on, until it seemed only reasonable for them to stay over at Sappho's, until they were more often with her than they were with Gwen.

'You'll regret this luring act, Sappho,' I warned her. 'Let sleeping children lie.'

'How do you mean, "luring"?' She was quite indignant. 'I am not "luring". I am offering Marmite on toast. We're weaning them away from Gwen. They'll be much better off with us. We're just trying to do it gracefully and tactfully, so the decision seems to come from them – no one's forcing us down their throats.'

Well, so be it. I do have a sense of duty towards my step-grandchildren: I did not hold their Garner blood against them. It is impossible not to keep at least some affection for young people in one's care. If asked who I'd push out of the lifeboat first, it would be in this order: Gwen, Gavin, Laura, then Barnaby, then Isobel, then Arthur, and last of course Sappho. Though I'd probably jump out myself to make sure Sappho lived. She is *my* daughter, a blood relative. The children take precedence over Barnaby simply because they are children; Isobel goes before Arthur because, frankly, the boy is just nicer to have around. Sometimes he even forgets and calls Sappho 'Mum', which always pleases her no end.

Isobel never does: she refers to her stepmother variously as Sappho as Sap, or 'your wife', or 'my stepmother', and Gavin had caught the habit and called her Sap too: it could sound affectionate but sometimes, from Isobel's rosebud lips, it was simply dismissive – but since Gavin did it too, there was little that could be said by way of objection.

After my disconcerting phone call with Laura I rang round a friend or two who said as far as they knew everything was fine in the Garner household. Someone involved with the League for the Protection of Birds of Prey said how pleased they'd been to get a donation of £25,000 from Sappho. Everything was fine. Laura was spreading rumours, trying to cause trouble. Sappho was pregnant: Laura had flipped. When women get pregnant all kind of hostilities come to the surface. Vengeance is mine, says the obstetrician with womb-envy, the midwife who's barren, the friend who's infertile, the single parent too poor to have the next one, the employee with the vasectomied husband – so many people to say *why her and not me?* And also of course the P.A. who's been in a symbiotic relationship with her beloved female employer, has managed to come to terms, just about, with the eruption of a husband, but finds a pregnancy the last straw. Laura felt abandoned and deserted by Sappho. But why had Sappho told me so little of this?

And there was another interpretation. Laura was a woman scorned. She was in love with Gavin, had made an advance, had had it rejected, and now her anger against him knew no bounds. This would also account for the allegations she made against Isobel, who was next in line, I fear, for her father's affections.

The difficulty with the human condition is that two is company and three is none, and this loving company of two keeps producing a third. The Laura/Sappho union is disturbed and distressed and angered when Gavin enters: the Gavin/Isolde union is disturbed by the arrival of Sappho, Gwen has decided only family counts and her status depends upon a bloodline dating back to King Arthur – and all are driven a little, temporarily I hope, mad.

A blessed few, like Arthur, seem to escape trouble, by virtue of sheer placidity of temperament. He did not, thank God, inherit his parents' brains. If he had he might have been autistic. Parents with very high IQs between them – especially when linked with mathematical ability – seem to produce children on the autistic scale. And there is of course another union which I ought not to deny; it's the Emily/Sappho one. I have managed so far not to resent Gavin too much, and am positively magnanimous when it comes to his children.

If I took a taxi now I could go and meet Isobel out of school and see what she had to add to my knowledge of the situation. But that would be interpreted as stirring, and rightly so. Or I could go straight to Gwen. On the other hand, if I left my flat Sappho might phone me and I'd miss her. I was between mobile phones. I'd had my bag snatched coming out of Hampstead tube, and my phone and its SIM card with all my numbers had gone. And besides, I dread confrontation. And more, when you have children surely there is a cut-off point at which you just let them get on with their lives?

There was an hour to spare. I would read more Diary.

The contents are handwritten, and dated from 1995. The writing is all over the place.

Sappho's Diary: *October 17th 1995*

Dear Diary,

This is the worst day of my life. I went with Isolde to the hospital. She'd been complaining of a little cough and wouldn't go to the doctor, and wouldn't go, and finally she did, and he sent her round at once to the chest clinic, who did tests and now they wanted her to go in and see them at the hospital. She didn't want Gavin to go with her, because he's so neurotic about hospitals, unless it's for her giving birth which he quite enjoys, so I went with her. I'm trembling so much I can hardly write. I can't believe this. They've made a mistake. I said so when we were on the way home in a taxi – and she just shook her head and said, 'No, they're right. I feel it. These are my last days.'

'How do you mean, you feel it?'

'I know it,' she said. 'Did you notice a black crow sitting on the fence when we got into the taxi? That was a sign.'

I can't be sure whether she's joking or not. Perhaps she's in shock. The way the doctor told her was enough to unhinge anyone.

'You can't think like that,' I say. 'Even if they've got it right, which I bet they haven't, you have to fight it.'

'Bloody rubbish,' she says. 'Think about it. What does "fighting" mean? Why waste strength? It always wins in the end. And the quicker the better.'

'Not any more,' I say. 'Cancer isn't a death sentence any more.'

'Not if it's lung cancer,' she said. 'Not if it's metastasised to the spine.'

'How do you know?'

'Because I've looked it up, idiot.' I noticed she was really wheezing quite badly. She smoked a lot. She and Gavin both did. They rolled their own. 'The prognosis is eight months at most if it goes untreated.'

'But you're not going to let it go untreated?'

'Yes,' she said, coolly and flatly.

She's only just forty.

When we got there this man in a white coat looked at his notes but not her and said she had advanced lung cancer and she was going to die, it was terminal, death could be expected within the year, but she could be made more comfortable with radio- and chemotherapy. She might lose her hair.

I said foolishly, 'But she's Isolde Garner, she's famous.'

The man in the white coat shook his head. He hadn't even heard of her. His glasses were smeary and old-fashioned, and his face was puffy and his eyes were small. He wasn't at all impressive.

And Isolde said, 'Don't be silly, Sappho, everyone dies,' and for some reason started quoting the Shelley poem *Ozymandias King of Kings*. The doctor shrugged and she got up and left the room, slamming the door. I followed her, with what is called an apologetic shrug – the kind my mother would give to other people when I was small and misbehaving. I hated it when she did that, and I hated myself now for finding myself doing the same. It's spooky the way mannerisms get inherited.

'He loves his work,' Isolde observed. 'He gets his rocks off telling people they're going to die. That's the only reason he got a job in oncology.' She lit up a cigarette. A strong smell of dope wafted down the corridor. I supposed she'd taken quite a lot before we'd set off.

I thought she was being uncharitable. He might just be embarrassed and hadn't yet taken the bad-news training, but I didn't say anything. I suppose I was in shock, too, and without the benefit of the marijuana. She at least had had her suspicions. She should have made her husband or her mother go with her, not me. It wasn't fair.

It was such a mean thought. But I wasn't family. And I thought of what my mother said, that they were exploiting me.

Not just looking after the children but me writing her TV scenes without acknowledgement. She did the shaping, at which I was hopeless, true, but if the dialogue wasn't 'working' she'd hand the pages over to me and I'd see to it. A lot of what I said to Gavin after the theatre ended up in his column, and he didn't even buy me a drink in the interval. And then there was the matter of the stone curlew photo which went in under his name not mine and got a prize. It was only £25 but even so, he could have acknowledged it, or even split it. They only paid me minimum rates. On the other hand she taught me dramatic construction and he taught me photography, for nothing, and I got to know the right people.

In other words I was thinking of anything other than Isolde's death sentence. It was clearly absurd, they had made it up, got the plates mixed, were covering their own ineptitude, and she was right, the loon with the smeary glasses was just in it for kicks, and probably said it to everyone who came through his door. 'Bang bang, you're dead.' Isolde would get home and tell Gavin and he would put everything right.

I am writing this at my mother's. She looks okay, thank God. She isn't wheezing or coughing. She's a bit miserable because a) she's just shown the latest boyfriend the door and b) because she's just had the gas bill in, and is threatening to sell Apple Lee yet again. But she'd better not, it's my home, even if I don't live here any more, and c) one of her patients who had been sent to her as a suicide risk actually went and did it, in a closed garage with the car engine running, and she feels a failure. But I'm not surprised it's got to her, because this was what happened to my father, when I was three, only his was an accident. He was cleaning the mud off the headlights while we were out shopping and he'd left the engine running and the garage door slammed and he didn't notice.

I don't remember much about it. I have a kind of memory of being in the garage and someone opening the door and a man falling out of it, but I said this once to her and she went mad and said I'd been nowhere near the garage that day and we never mentioned it again. All the talk, talk, talk that goes on in this house and the important things still don't get talked about. In case it reminds people of what they'd rather forget or want to put off thinking about until another time.

Like Isolde's sentence of death.

Emily Feels Better

At least she was glad I showed no signs of illness. Daughters often wish their mothers would just die. Another of the dirty little secrets held in common with the rest of the human race, the ones that power endeavour and capitalism. I remember going to see *The Wizard of Oz* with my best friend Teresa when I was about eight, and singing along with the Munchkins, 'Ding-Dong the Witch is Dead' – and seeing my mother as the witch. I felt guilty and confessed to Teresa.

'No,' she said. 'Why do you think the wicked witch is your mother? She's mine. Now she's dead I can look after my dada properly.'

'It was only a film,' I said. 'It wasn't real.'

'Oh,' she said, and went bright red.

Then she said, 'Anyway I liked the song.' Which exchange I daresay put me on the road to my present profession. So at least if Sappho had ever harboured such secret desires she had grown out of them.

As to the suicidal patient I have no memory of him at all, which is very odd. Perhaps in my distress I said something to Sappho when she came round to me in tears, Isolde having just been diagnosed with lung cancer, and I was breaking my rule and talking to her about Rob. And Sappho interpreted what I was saying as being about a patient, because she could not take it on board that I was talking about her father. I am in denial, forgetting, or she is in denial, remembering. Good Lord, so many skins to the onions, layer after layer. Peel away and peel away the memories, weeping the while.

Or perhaps I was drunk. It's possible. I was certainly in distress. My boyfriend had indeed walked out on me, and I was indeed sorry. You only know what you want when it's gone.

His name was Harry. He had wanted to marry me and it would have been suitable, but I had dithered for so long he gave up, and met someone else and married them. Lost to me for ever, a senior research psychologist with a steady income, supplemented by international lectures – good-looking, early forties, drank a little, not too much. In those days I drank rather a lot.

But I mean, who wants suitable? All the suitably conjoined people I know have long since split up.

Come to think of it, Barnaby is a re-run of Harry. I shouldn't have walked out on him like that just now. Perhaps I will call him up and apologise. I wouldn't want someone else to offer Barnaby the backs of their chairs for drying his washing. Ursula the aromatherapist on the fourth floor of this block of flats has her eye on him, but she's not very bright. He can't be bothered with women who aren't bright. Or so he says. She's forty.

It's much easier to be the one doing the casting out, not the one cast out.

Also, I had lost a very good DIY man in Harry. In those days at Apple Lee the need for DIY loomed large. He came back to bed in the middle of the night and said, 'I can smell dry rot in the bathroom,' and went downstairs and came back with some of Rob's old tools and said, 'I'll see to it.'

'Please,' I said, 'not now. I've a patient at nine.'

But Harry, being a real single-tasker with Asperger's undertones, took the side of the bath down there and then – and found the crumbling wood and fungus beneath, and turned on the radio and sang and worked – forget my night's sleep, and for many a night thereafter.

'I can't afford builders,' I said.

'I know,' he said, and up came the floorboards, and down came the kitchen ceiling where it met the outside wall of Apple Lee, and he saw that the rot had got into the brickwork, and back and back and down and down he traced the tendrils, with hammer and chisel and metal bars – what a terrible mess he left – until he found the tuber. It was monstrous, like a kind of sprouting potato from outer space with searching strands: but also something here in the heart, lurking in the unconscious, an infection, which you can only tell when you get a whiff of something wrong, terribly wrong, sometimes by accident. It's the dry rot of the soul. Then back and back into the past you go, uncovering the infection, rooting it out, everything rubbishy and rotted away. That's why I'm glad to be out of Apple Lee. Let Sappho deal with the place, throw money at it, try and heal it, and us.

Perhaps now finally she has had enough of it; the rot has spread too far, too deep.

So I borrowed money to pay for the builders to clear up the mess, and they found more fungus, and had to take out the whole staircase and so it went on, one side of the house exposed to the fresh air and the heating bills enormous all that winter, and with every penny I spent on the house I loved Harry less, blaming him. The way my patients blame the breast cancer on the mammogram. They are mad but you see the point. And I put off marrying him and put off marrying him, until the day the builders finally marched out of Apple Lee when he said, 'I hope you don't mind, but I've met someone.'

The 'someone', a lady architect who had built her own house to the highest specifications, lasted ten years and Harry is now on visiting terms with me again, and how we laugh about old times. Barnaby hates him, I say with some satisfaction. Barnaby hasn't a DIY bone in his body, thank God.

I still don't love Barnaby, though I like him well enough. I wait for the flood of oxytocin which wipes away doubt but it doesn't happen. Perhaps I have outgrown it. I explained the same to Barnaby one day when he was discussing the building of the spiral staircase that would link our lives permanently.

'Oh no,' Barnaby assures me. 'It's always available at any age, though of course at its peak during late adolescence. I have known a woman in her nineties fall in love with a man of seventy-odd. It seemed to be just as painful and shaming to her to understand she wasn't fancied as it would have been to a woman a third of her age.'

'Then I'll wait,' I say to Barnaby, which wasn't the answer he expected, poor man.

I explain to such of my patients as are victims of unrequited love that it is only a neurotic dependency, but I cannot cure myself. If I am in love with anyone, it is a dead man, Rob, Sappho's father. That sounds really soppy, but it is true.

'You must reach closure sooner or later,' Barnaby insists, but he would, wouldn't he, being a Jungian. Me, I'm very bad at 'reaching closure'. It just doesn't happen. It's like 'fighting cancer', a comforting illusion that effort and hard work will achieve something. It won't.

I prefer what Freud said, but then I would, wouldn't I: '*We find a place for what we lose. Although we know that after such a loss the acute stage of mourning will subside, we also know that a part of us shall remain inconsolable and never find a substitute. No matter what may fill the gap, even if it is completely filled, it will nevertheless remain something changed for ever.*' There was no way that Barnaby could metamorphise into Rob.

So I remember that evening well, when Sappho came home crying, because she'd taken Isolde to the hospital and come home in a taxi with a corpse-in-waiting, and I was too preoccupied with my own troubles to be much use to her. That's motherhood.

A loose page from the diary. It comes from before Isolde's visit to the hospital. I shan't call Barnaby and apologise. It's pathetic. Let fate push him into the arms of the aromatherapist upstairs. So be it.

Sappho's Diary: *February 11th 1994*

Isolde says try a description, the kind you find in novels.

'But I don't want to write novels,' I say. 'I mean to be a play-wright like you.'

'You may be driven to many inferior forms of fiction during your lifetime,' Isolde says, 'in the attempt to make a living. And it is different from set description. Longer, for one thing. You have to build up a picture in the reader's mind, not just in the mind of the designer, who is trained to pick up clues from the writer.'

'So when you're writing TV you'd say of this place, avoiding indefinite articles to save space, "cluttered middle-income home of intellectual married couple, evidence of small children, theatrical posters on the wall" and she does the rest. Stage would be "cluttered home of literary theatrical couple with intellectual leanings, not over clean", and a team of gay artistes would descend upon the set.'

'Exactly. And talking about clean, the kitchen floor does need a good scrubbing. Really down on your hands and knees, Sappho, not a casual smearing over with the Squeegee. And don't think because it's a novel that means a lot of adjectives and adverbs. It doesn't.'

Isolde's in the kitchen eating toast and honey without due attention. Some honey drips onto the floor. She ignores it. Soon some of her cigarette ash will fall down and join it. She is not good at ashtrays. Gavin is meticulous. When she stands she will tread both into the carpet and not even notice. Compared to the office floor, which is carpeted, the kitchen floor is a doddle. At least it's tiled. You only see the smears when the winter sun shines in low, but she sees everything, notices everything. She's like my mother, but she doesn't try to interfere with what goes in my head, just gets me to do more housework. It's preferable.

'What shall I describe?'

'Use your own initiative, Sappho, for God's sake. Anywhere, anything; this place.'

Okay. Here goes.

The Garners lived in one of those redbrick mansion flats in Bloomsbury, as befits a literary couple; handy for everything cultural, theatres and the Royal Academy of Dramatic Arts, where Isolde teaches and Sappho is a pupil. It's on the ground floor so people walk up and down the street outside all day and the windows are barred. It isn't frankly very cheerful. But people drop by because it's so central which is nice, and Isolde and Gavin give lots of parties for which I bake the canapés. I'm hot on cheese straws. Stars of stage and TV screen turn up, and critics and directors and famous journalists, and if they're serious they are Gavin's friends, and if they are hippy-ish they are hers. Everyone smokes a lot. Photographers and film crews call and set out their tripods and cameras because Gavin is so famous, though it's a long time since he has finished a book, and Isolde is even more famous, and I love the atmosphere, and make good contacts, even though it means I have to lug the children to the florist at Russell Square station to buy flowers for the set.

Yes, sorry, the flat. Physical appearance of. There is a long central corridor with rooms leading off it, so the rooms to your right when you come in the front door are rather dark, and in the winter the rooms to the left are always cold and not all that bright even on a sunny day, because of the bars. There is a wonky boiler which was put in around 1910, and the central heating is noisy and doesn't get to the kitchen. The children race up and down the corridor on their tricycles. My mother comes round from time to time to help out and says it reminds her of *The Shining*, but she would, wouldn't she?

'What, you mean tides of blood following them down the corridor?' I say. 'Hardly.'

'A very menstrual image,' she says. Sometimes I can do without her helping out. She doesn't much like the Garners and thinks they exploit me. She's jealous, I think. On the one hand she wants to be rid of me and live her life in peace and have her lovers and make the bedsprings ping without worrying whether I can hear. But for another I'm her only real companion and we do things together and I stop her from being lonely.

I can tell I'm a drama writer not a novelist from the way I leave places and things and go at once into feelings and undercurrents. Stop it.

There isn't a garden. It is a hopeless place for children, but frankly children are not high on the list of the household priorities. It is assumed they will grow up into the next generation of geniuses simply by the passage of time, and by the cleaning, feeding and nurturing talents of a succession of girls like me, though I doubt any of them get asked to do the re-writes or lie in the grass on the heath waiting for the blue-titted warbler or whatever to come along and then take a photo. Sometimes I take the children back home with me to play in the garden at Apple Lee, fifteen minutes up the hill on the Highgate bus, to get some fresh air. They love the garden there and the apple tree in the front makes them excited. 'I spy with my little eye,' shrieks Arthur as the bus turns the corner, and they can see it.

'Apple, apple,' says little Isobel and holds out her tiny arms to be lifted up.

Emily's Comment

No comment. Except Sappho must have really held her ear to the wall to hear a single thing.

Sappho's Diary: *December 18th 1995*

I'll do this part of what happened as in a TV scene. It's less painful.

INT. THE LIVING ROOM. DAY
Isolde and Gavin stand in the kitchen in each other's arms. No children.

GAVIN: We must get a second opinion, of course.

ISOLDE: What is the point? The answer will be the same. I feel it. When I got into the taxi a crow sat on the fence and stared at me. I knew then. It's okay. I regret nothing. Not even the cigarettes.

She goes to the shelf and takes down a clutch of photographs. They are portraits of herself, typical poses of Isolde as she has appeared on TV programmes and in the press for the last ten years. Her pale, beautiful face wreathed in a halo of smoke, her languid, elegant fingers hold a drooping cigarette. She is a kind of Virginia Woolf figure if Virginia had been born beautiful. Gavin is in some of them, leaning over her, inspiration and savant in his own right: tall, strong-featured, like Ted Hughes, infinitely masculine.

ISOLDE: But you won't leave me, will you.

GAVIN: I will never leave you.

ISOLDE: And you will look after the children.

GAVIN: Isolde—

ISOLDE: And you must marry again.

GAVIN: Isolde, stop telling me what to do. You know I hate it.

ISOLDE: Good. You have accepted. We will go on as before, then. We will pretend it hasn't happened. That I never went to the hospital. When I feel ill I will take an aspirin or perhaps two. If I can no longer receive guests standing I will receive them sitting or in bed. It will be quite glamorous. We will play Verdi – *La Dame Aux Camellias*.

GAVIN: But that will make you a courtesan. How about *Traviata*?

ISOLDE: She was a courtesan, too.

GAVIN: You see, it is impossible for a good wife to die.

ISOLDE: Anyway, we will have Verdi as a background.

Cutaways to Gwen.

GWEN: It is unthinkable. No one in our family gets cancer. Heart, yes, but cancer, no. If anything does happen, I'll take the children. You know that. What do you mean, Isolde, better if he re-marries? Who's going to take on a man with two children? Someone like

Sappho? That silly, neurotic young girl? With the psychoanalyst mother with the disgusting ideas? You're joking. Not that I'd put it past her, she's a devious little thing. What happened to the father anyway? There's a rumour the mother drove him to suicide with her promiscuous ways. The children are far too much in that girl's company as it is. God knows what ideas she's putting into their precious little heads. You should think more of your children and less of your silly career. What does it amount to? A lot of empty chatter. All this is just another silly, worrying fancy of yours, Isolde, and not fair to the children, let alone me. If you really think you're ill go and see someone privately. These hospital doctors will say anything just to be able to fill in boxes. Can someone turn off that dreadful racket? I hate Verdi.

Yes, Dear Diary, that was a direct quote about my father's death, which stuck in my mind and put a lot of other things out of it, even on that dreadful day – Gwen saying that rumour had it my mother drove my father to suicide because of her promiscuous ways. Well, that was definitely not the case. My father died by accident. He was cleaning his car in the garage and the door swung closed. If there's a rumour to the contrary then Gwen is the one who put it about. What a bitch! My mother would not lie to me about something as important as that. It could be acute depression in which case it might be in the genes and would have to be guarded against. I wish Gwen liked me more. It is horrible being hated and suspected by someone. I want to be universally loved.

Back to Gwen's cutaways. On and on.

GWEN: And what's going to happen to me? How am I going to live? My rent has gone up again. And no, I am not going to find anywhere cheaper. This is my home. I was born a Kensington person and I shall die one. Not my fault my protected rent has suddenly gone up to market rent, which is four hundred per cent: they have no right doing it. I shall go to law, of course. And no, I won't sell any of my 'treasures' as you call them. Now is a really bad time to sell. You wouldn't get half what they're really worth. They represent me and everything I am and ever have been: you don't sell yourself off in chunks. I hope you have good insurance. [*Pause*] I told you, you smoked too much.

ISOLDE: Poor Gwen, she flickers into denial and out again.

GAVIN: While we stay firmly in it?

ISOLDE: I reckon that's about it. Why not? I want you to bring up the children, not Gwen. I don't want them growing up as idiots. But how can you look after them and earn a living? What do you think about marrying Sappho when this is over? She's good with the children, and I know you fancy her.

Isolde looks at her feet as she says it, and licks her lips. Not as her mother licks hers, which is with a little flicker of pleasure and self-congratulation, as if she had really enjoyed hurting someone, but like a child, gearing herself up to some great effort. His arms go round her again.

GAVIN: Isolde, Sappho is a bright, pretty, very young girl but I don't fancy her one bit. Young girls bore me to bits, you know that. They have nothing in their heads.

ISOLDE: This one has. And I don't want to spend the rest of my life feeling jealous. So if I appoint her as my successor it will be just fine. So please.

Enter Sappho with Arthur and Isobel, one in each hand. Sappho overhears this last part of the conversation though the rest she has inferred. The others fall silent.

Cut to little Isobel, rising three, who runs to Gavin and clutches his knees with her little thin, translucent arms and tries to pull him away from her mother. She does this a lot.

ISOBEL: Daddy, stop talking to Mummy.

End of scene.

I remember Isobel saying that, but the rest I infer. I have put all the bits and pieces together and made a scene of it. For a lot of it I won't have been in the room, but that is the art of the playwright. You make connections. Bits I will have overheard. The Garners weren't the 'hush, not in front of the servants' type. They were too proud to have secrets: it would have meant they were ashamed of something and in their cosmology there was nothing to be ashamed of. There is certainly planning for after

Isolde dies. The idea that Gavin could marry me and everything just carry on with me in Isolde's place surfaces from time to time, and sinks again. It is just speculation. Gavin did once describe me to Isolde as bright and pretty, though not to my face. I was really pleased by that – you never quite knew what either of them really thought of you. And as for her being jealous of me – if it's true and not just her annoying Gavin, it's only because I have my life before me and she doesn't. At least I think so. I don't like to think of Gavin having sexual desires. If I ever do my thoughts veer off very quickly. I suppose that's what 'taboo' means. I shall ask my mother for further definitions. But I certainly don't want to be appointed as Isolde's successor, in some kind of arranged marriage. I have my own life to live, thank you very much. What, move into her bed just as her side of it grows cold? Yuk.

I shock myself. It's as if her dying puts me off her. Actually, I love her. If I put my arms around her she would stop this dying business. I have enough spirit for both of us. I guess I'm just stunned. My mind circles round and round and won't settle between resentment and gratitude, hate and love.

But most of the time it is really difficult to remember that Isolde is dying at all. She potters and chatters around the place as usual, just sometimes she goes into spasms of coughing, and in the locked bathroom cupboard as from yesterday are stacks of painkillers and pills of different persuasions, some which look legal and some don't. I think she really means to carry on as if it wasn't happening. She's not going to try to get cured or even have the death sentence delayed. She hasn't stopped smoking.

'She's embracing Thanatos,' my mother says. She's not. She's fucking dying. Stopping. Blotting out.

Today while the children were at nursery I spent a couple of hours ringing round and asking friends and acquaintances to a supper party on Sunday night. They want me to stay and help, and I said I would, though this guy called Martin is meant to be taking me to a party. I expect if I don't go he'll just find someone there who'll go to bed with him which I won't. But what can you do? I don't really mind losing Martin and Isolde is dying so I reckon I'm here for the duration. She is a wonderful, original, brave, courageous, talented woman and I can't leave her.

I am a bit disappointed in Gavin, because he hasn't somehow made everything come right, but then he isn't God.

Emily's Lament

Well, I'm sorry, too.

And 'didn't really mind losing Martin!' Good God. Was the girl mad? (No, don't answer that.) I remember Martin. He had a title, though precisely what I can't remember, a lot of money and was hopelessly enamoured of Sappho. He was extremely pleasant, studying to be an architect, and went everywhere with his dog, a black and white border collie. If she had gone to the party she might have married him and ended up with a wholly other set of diaries which she could leave with me at a time of crisis. The way chance affects the lives of the young is terrifying. Which is a silly thing to say, I know. Chance affects us all. Lamentations are pointless. If I had gone another way home when Sappho was three and I hadn't taken her shopping and we had not chanced to see a red and blue striped woolly hat and stayed to try it on, we might have got home minutes sooner in time to save Rob. If, if, if. If this, if that. Forget it.

Where had the rumour come from, that Rob's death was no accident? Gwen? What would she know about it? I had never spoken of it – except that once when I did try to tell Sappho and she misheard me, by accident or on purpose. Though I daresay in the past something might have slipped out, because the secret lay so heavily upon me, and I may have whispered the truth in the ear of some lover or other, hoping for pity, or an excuse for my own drunken behaviour.

'I am a widow, you know. My husband killed himself.'

And whoever it was would pretend to be interested but of course he wouldn't be. Harry was mildly interested but then he was interested in everything. If there was dry rot he wouldn't rest until he had traced it to its source and rooted it out, like a therapist worrying away at a neurosis. Indeed, you could see him as a veritable DIY therapist. You have to admire that.

'My last girlfriend's husband was a suicide,' Harry might well have said to my successor, the lady architect. 'He put the hosing from the exhaust through the car window, turned on the engine, and just sat there.'

'Why did he do that?'

'I expect she drove him to it. She slept around, even when she was married.'

'How do you know?' the lady architect will have asked.

And Harry would have said, 'Because she told me,' and given her my name, because at that time one of my more famous clients was a leading film actress who got her name in the papers and kept going into rehab. And I had suddenly become fashionable and people boasted of the acquaintance. Yes, and then Gwen was modelling for the older woman at a charity fashion show for the Architectural Association and got into conversation with a woman who just happened to be sitting in the front row who turned out to be the architect and who said when my name came up in the conversation, 'Her husband killed himself, you know, and she managed to keep it secret from her daughter.'

Yes, it was possible, just unlikely.

Gwen probably just made it up. She did not like me any more than she liked Sappho, and perhaps she identified with me over-much. She too had lost her daughter's father when her child was small, though through divorce, not death. Perhaps she wished him dead and better still by his own hand. Perhaps she was projecting forbidden desires on to me?

All the same, it was unsettling, and thank God Sappho had not taken much note of what had been said, at least at the time, and just assumed that Gwen got it wrong. It was, as a political party adviser said on 9/11, a good day to bury bad news.

Now Gwen lives with her grievances in her Kensington apartment, where you couldn't move for fear of breaking a piece of ancient Assyrian glass worth £3,000 or brushing a scarab worth £8,000 onto the floor. Though, mind you, that was what she said they were worth. How would one ever know? She lives in fear of moths getting at her cashmere. How the children put up with her at all I don't know, but they even seemed to like her.

I reckon Gwen's conviction that Sappho was up to no good was straightforward projection. She had so seldom been up to any good herself when young. She had taken gifts, though I daresay never money, from the many wealthy and distinguished men that cluster around leading models. She specialised in antiquarians and art collectors. Isolde's father had been a Lebanese jeweller. The mother affected gentility but did not, honestly, know how to behave.

A terrible thought occurs to me. I call up Barnaby. He has gone to bed. At least he has not nipped upstairs to the aromatherapist. Another telling fantasy. He asks me up. I go.

'Barnaby,' I say, 'this thing about protected rents. Could they really put up someone's rent by four hundred per cent overnight, back in Nineteen Ninety-Five?'

'Landlords can do just about anything. Probably.'

'And Sappho could have ended up paying it?'

'Can we talk about anything but Sappho? For example, us?'

'No. Not for the time being. What would be the market rent be for a four-bedroomed flat in Kensington?'

'Astronomical. Any sensible person would have moved out long ago. But not Gwen. So yes, it's perfectly possible she's paying Gwen's rent: Gwen looks after the children. But Sappho can afford to pay, can't she? Why?'

'Another thing. Have you ever heard anything about Rob committing suicide?'

'Rob? Your first husband? Do we have to talk about him now?'

'My only husband. Yes. There isn't going to be any sex, I can tell, so we might as well talk.'

'But he died more than thirty years ago. Why should there be rumours?'

'Because I used to go to parties. One talks too much. One forgets things. Never too badly. I have a healthy super-ego; what use would I be to my patients if I didn't? It never affected them.'

'Of course not.' Is he being ironic? 'You're a social creature, that's all. You would just go to parties, drink too much, pick up men as a diversionary tactic, to distract you from widow's grief, tell all and forget about it by the morning. I knew he died, I didn't know he killed himself. How did he do it?'

I told him.

'There were no witnesses. There was only the policeman who broke down the garage door for us and found him.'

'Us? You and Sappho?'

'Good God no, me and Mary who did the cleaning. Little Sappho was in the hall trying on her new woolly hat in the mirror. She can't possibly have seen unless what got imprinted on my mind so shockingly got imprinted on hers as well.'

'A kind of ghost thing. I see.'

'It isn't funny,' I said. 'None of it's funny. Children can be very telepathic.'

'Anyway, it isn't your fault, if that's what you want to establish. I accept it. What was the vision?'

'The policeman opening the door of the car and a body falling out. It was Rob. Every now and then when she was small Sappho would ask me about "the man falling out of the car" and I'd explain no, it came from something on the TV, or a film, or some description she has heard.'

'The simplest explanation is usually the best. Sappho saw. Like all that regression to past lives stuff; how does the hypnotised person know the street plan of some mediaeval city? Answer, because she saw it in a book stuck away on the father's shelves.'

'Or the brilliant pianist washed up by the sea, an amnesiac, who turns out to be an ordinary Albanian asylum-seeker and a very poor pianist, and the crop circles are done by pranksters not aliens, and the UFOs are – well, whatever they always are. How disappointing life can be.'

'How nice it is to be talking about something other than your family, Emily. Can I stroke your leg?'

'No, stroking leads to expectation and expectation leads to disappointment.'

I felt like my patients do when they talk about anything that isn't important rather than face the matter in hand. But I told him how I'd got home from shopping with Sappho and called out to Rob, and got no reply, and asked Mary if she had seen him, and she said no, she thought he was in the garage. He was. But he was dead.

'The same garage Harry found the tools in to investigate the dry rot?'

So Barnaby did listen to some things.

'Yes,' I said. 'Though Sappho had it pulled down and the conservatory extended. When she was small you went through the kitchen to get to the garage. Usually Rob left the door open if he was working in there but today it was closed. I could hear the engine running and I tried the handle but the door was locked from the inside.'

'So it didn't slam shut.'

'I got frightened and ran outside to try and look through the window but could only see shelves with old tins of paint and spare clutches and yellowed newspaper and so on, and a policeman was walking by – those were the days – so I called him and he came inside and gave the garage door a good shove and it gave way easily – the wood was rotten – and I saw him go to the car and open the driver's door, and before it happened I knew what I would see. Rob's body tumbling out.'

'Did you pass Sappho as you ran out?'

'Why are you so interested suddenly?'

'I thought you wanted me to be.'

'The police officer was quite old. He had a nice face. He was a kind man. He told us to go back inside and we did. Sappho was in the kitchen by then dancing about with her little woolly hat. When he came back in he referred to the "terrible accident". Somehow he had managed to overlook the length of hose that might have connected the exhaust to the car window. So I've never really been sure. In his report he wrote that he had found Rob slumped on the ground at the front of the car: he must have been scraping mud off the headlights and the garage door had slammed shut and Rob hadn't noticed. There was an inquest and a verdict of accidental death, and a rider about how you must never leave the engine running in an enclosed space.'

'That was good of them,' said Barnaby.

'How do you mean "good of them"?'

'*Felo de se* is as catching as measles. One does it, the rest does it. They were kind to you.'

'But I might have seen wrong.'

'You said the door was locked from the inside. So you've been going round getting drunk and confessing to strangers that your husband committed suicide because that relieves the guilt. When really you've no idea.'

I got out of bed and got dressed.

'Emily,' said Barnaby, 'I wish you'd stay in one place and just settle down. How am I ever going to get to sleep?'

Drop, splash, drop, splash. I was actually crying over my daughter's diary, not for her, but for me. There was no getting out of it, no matter how Barnaby tried to help. Rob had killed himself, no matter how I wriggled and squirmed. Sappho had witnessed the circumstances of his death, and if she ever linked up memory with reason could work out what had happened, and not be fooled by kindly coroner's reports. She would not be too fond of me if she did. Or indeed of Rob, who had wilfully taken back the gift of life God gave him. Suicide is indeed catching. And she is running off into the night – well, mid-morning – looking dreadful. What has the new generation got against forgetfulness? They feel it is their right to be told the truth, the whole truth and nothing but the truth, to know about family insanities, genetic tendencies, circumstances of birth and so on, all of which an older generation felt wiser to keep hidden. Me, at any rate simulacrum me, the talking interactive puppet, which was all that was left when Rob died, has always felt it much kinder to tell untruths, half-truths, and downright lies than 'the truth'. Especially to myself. My anxiety rate is running so high I have to take a sleeping pill.

Why Rob did what he did I have no idea. Or has simulacrum me simply forgotten this, too, being the wrong side of the with-Rob/without-Rob divide? He had seemed cheerful enough the last time I saw him. The car headlights were muddy, he said. It had been raining: he could scarcely see the way ahead. Rob was not by nature a cleaner of cars: not for him the vacuumed interior, the polished bodywork of the proud suburbanite. His last words to me were that he needed to see clearly. Is that the statement of someone bent on suicide? Or someone who had somehow found out that his wife, albeit casually, was frequently unfaithful? Or just of someone who feels safer if the car's headlights show the way ahead? Look, it was a long time ago, in the age of infidelity. Everyone now is old and grey and many have died. I am strictly a one-man-at-a-time person now. One learns.

He left me well insured: the coroner's verdict of accidental death gave the insurance company no choice but to pay out. Apple Lee had been crumbling round our ears, to his distress. I had been able out of the proceeds of his death at least to re-roof the place, re-wire, see to the garden and so on. (I didn't find the dry rot, at the time.) Perhaps Rob died to save the house, and trusted me to do it? I don't know. It had been his family's home for generations. Could Rob have thought his life was worth less than the well-being and re-wiring of Apple Lee? Men are mad fucks, if you'll excuse me, and it is possible. Dr Shipman the serial killer hanged himself in prison so his wife could cash in his life assurance policy. But then Rob was an honourable man and not a mass murderer.

I had always consoled myself that Sappho's intrinsic good cheer would save her from any catching suicidal intent – but of course I worried. The children of suicides often end the same way. Does not any parent worry at sometime or other that their child will take it into their head to cease to be alive? Rob's mother's child did that, and died in the very house where he was born. Rob's mother died in a road accident: she stepped in front of a lorry while on holiday in Spain. An easy thing to do for a tourist looking for traffic in the wrong direction. But who is to say the wrong way was the way she looked? Rob's mother, Sappho's grandmother, Sappho now pregnant. Lord, one could worry oneself to death.

I slept, but woke early and as dawn broke took the Waitrose bag into my lonely bed.

Sappho's Diary: *February 23rd 1996*

It was a good party here at the Mansions. I had rather a lot to drink. I made the champagne cocktail for everyone the way I like it, with two lumps of sugar, not one, and quite a lot of brandy. Peter Hall came briefly, and Kenneth Branagh, a clutch of people over here for *Natural Born Killers*, the editor of the *TLS*, a playwright over from New York, the usual wives and friends, and a handful of girls with long legs and short skirts whom all the men looked at. I was just the one serving the drinks and taking the coats and opening the door. If I had time and money I daresay I could turn myself into one of the looked-at girls, but thinking seems to take up too much of my time. Also of course writing the diary takes up real hours. I am too preoccupied to have my nails done or my hair put in rags or sniff a little cocaine in order to be the life and soul of the party. No one went home until one o'clock in the morning or so.

Isolde wore a new grey Ghost dress – she's so thin now it looks great: she had rather wide hips before she got ill – and had borrowed some real pearls from Gwen (though how would one know?), and Gavin and she laughed and chatted most of the way through the party as if nothing at all was wrong. I thought then perhaps the scene in the hospital was just some kind of *Candid Camera* joke for my benefit. Some hope!

At around eleven Isolde left the room and I went after her to find her, and there she was on the stairs in paroxysms of coughing and her beautiful long hand on her chest, and she asked for water. When I got back the fit was over and Gavin was sitting next to her and had his hand on her forehead and they were both crying.

'I'm going to put an end to it before it gets really bad,' she said. 'You understand that?'

'Don't be silly,' he said. 'I want you with me to the last minute.'

In five minutes they were both back at the party as if nothing had happened. I guess it is going to go on like this.

I'd write up the party scene as a play, but there are too many characters to handle. Truth comes more easily when turned into drama: you can tell what is going on. Everything invented is pointed and means something: everything 'real' is random and you have to sieve through it for the truth.

The children stayed the night at Gwen's. They love it over there though I can't think why. Gwen makes them keep to strict mealtimes and finish everything on their plate. They'll be going to church this morning, though I don't suppose they'll be praying for their mother because they're not going to be told a thing. Over at Gwen's they can't run up and down the corridors screaming as they do here; they have to steer their way carefully between *objets d'art* and things that break if they're touched. They seem to rather enjoy being told off, I expect because it's a novelty. Isobel is naturally precise and careful in her movements, and takes after Gwen, but Arthur tends to be really noisy and boisterous. He manages to fall on and off the furniture, and break it. The store room here is full of three-legged chairs and split side tables waiting for a carpenter who never comes. Isolde and Gavin don't believe in discipline and I'm not allowed to slap them though I am sometimes tempted. Isobel can read already, Arthur doesn't even know his letters yet. But Arthur's a delight, and Isobel... well, I dunno, I expect she'll get better.

Isobel is the snuggling-up and sucking-her-thumb kind, and if she can curl up on her father's lap so much the better. She wiggles around and that sometimes seems to annoy Isolde.

'Just stop that, Isobel!'

'Not doing nothing,' Isobel will say, and goes on doing it, staring at her mother with those smiley eyes which aren't smiling. It is her favourite response, these days.

'She's only little, Isolde,' Gavin will say, 'for heaven's sake!' But he will get up, I notice, when pride allows, and fetch his lighter and move the child off his lap.

And then all of a sudden Isobel will be all over her mother and tossing her head if ever her father approaches and saying, 'Go away, Daddy.'

'But that's what children do,' my mother says. 'It's normal behaviour in small children: they're trying out gender for size. They switch affection from parent to parent at whim: it's an important part of their psychosexual development. You need to be aware of this. One or the other of the parents is always going to be annoyed.'

'You mean two's company and three's none.'

'In a nutshell, Sappho. You're very good at nutshells.'

I can never tell whether she's approving or mocking.

'Then single mothers get it easier?'

'Yes, but their children get it harder. No way can they do the trying out for size.'

I can see why people have gone right off Freud. And thank you, Mum, you lost me my dad, so I'm shafted anyway. Nor is my mum one for stepparents: it's too confusing for the child. She once said to me this is why she didn't ever re-marry. Thanks for the guilt trip, Mum. All my fault, not hers. Personally, I think it's because marriage would curtail her sexual activities.

Emily Reacts

Okay, okay, I can take it, you're right, Sappho. Sorry. Okay?

Sappho's Diary: *February 24th 1996*

Dear Diary,

This morning they made love. I tried not to listen but the walls are thin and I couldn't be bothered to get up and go and make breakfast I was so tired. It takes them for ever. I guess that's meant to be good. Movements and rustlings and little gasps and shushes because they know I'm next door. I wonder what it is like to be her, and I wonder what it is like to be him. Or perhaps I don't really want to know; I want to listen but I don't want to do it, supposing I hated it? No wonder I put men off. I don't know anyone my age who is still a virgin, so I expect Mother is right to worry about my psychosexual development – it's all to hell. What the fuck. Perhaps they want her to have a baby before she goes? The doctor said a year, but I don't suppose they can be that precise. They might have to snatch it from the womb like Caesar, or was it Macbeth? I could go and count her contraceptive pills to see if she's stopped taking them but I'm not that kind of person, even for research purposes.

Once it was over I got up and squeezed them some orange juice and we all had breakfast and Gavin wanted to know my opinion of Eugène Ionesco's *Here Comes a Chopper*, which we'd both seen last week. Me in the Gods, he in the second row of the stalls. It confused him: it was easy class warfare, he said, and really he was a Chekhov man and a soupçon of Ibsen possibly. I said the underprivileged everywhere would love it – as I had – and an anagram of Ionesco is 'Ice Soon', and of Sheridan, 'Dasher In' and of Arthur Miller, 'Hurt, I'll Rearm'! They both stared at me and Gavin said, 'Give that girl a rise.' But they won't, of course. They can always find reasons for not spending money. Then they set to doing their own anagrams.

P.S. This afternoon the black bird was back sitting on the wall. Gavin went and took his .22 rifle from the locked cupboard in his study and went outside and actually shot it. A few lace curtains twitched but that was about all. People in these mansion flats tend to be elderly. The man above us is in his nineties and stone deaf, which is just as well because of Arthur. Gavin, the bird man, killing a bird! I was shocked. He just picked it up by its leg all bloody and limp and dropped it in the bin. But he says crows are different. They have to be culled or they take over. But I'm pretty sure it was a raven. Ravens are tricksters and creators in mythology – writers, in other words – not harbingers of death, so I hope he hasn't done any damage.

Emily's Analysis

Actually, to dream of a raven is to dream of a man's sexual organ, according to Freud. I don't know why Sappho's so resistant to all things Freudian. She's perfectly intelligent. As to Isobel wriggling around in her father's lap, that's just to defy mother and claim possession. Obviously there is phallic intent. Why be surprised?

It's dreadful to read how events unfolded, how the re-run of the primal scene with her new parents was presented to my poor daughter: of course she was bound to end up in bed with the father figure, and acting the mother to his children.

And what a cow Isolde was, and how little any of us recognised it. If only she had done what she promised, and done herself in earlier, everyone from her family to her friends to her colleagues would have been saved from her courage, from her 'fight'. Length of life is not what any of us should be after, just quality of life.

'Personally,' I said to Barnaby the other day, 'I mean to do away with myself before I become incompetent.'

'Everyone says this,' he said. 'But when it comes to it they don't. We all cling to life.'

'Except suicides,' I said.

'They're exceptions,' he said. 'The wiring in the brain has gone wrong. An inheritable flaw.'

Thanks, Barnaby, as Sappho would say. But Freud saw suicide as internalised aggression, and I could see how it could apply to Rob, so amiable and cheerful was his outward appearance. Rage built up inside him and the volcano imploded. I would have worried even more about Sappho had she turned up on my doorstep looking bright and cheerful, colourfully clothed and high-heeled, rather than navy parka-ed and flat-heeled. Whatever her problems were, they were not internalised. They were all around her, in the open, ready to be dealt with.

Barnaby knocked on the door and told me I should stop brooding and come out to the deli and have a cup of coffee and a chocolate croissant. I said I couldn't go out, I was waiting for Sappho to call. He said to take my mobile with me, for heaven's sake, and I explained she normally called me on the landline because she had mislaid her mobile and Laura was usually our point of contact.

'And Laura has been fired.' I said. That made an impression. So he bought the coffee and croissants round to me and we sat in the sun in my kitchen, and he dunked his croissants in the coffee, having buttered them first. Patches of melting butter and chocolate floated on the top of his latte but he didn't seem to mind. I did. I would hate to be married to him.

He told me he had to leave the house in twenty minutes for a meeting at the Tavistock Clinic but I could spend the time telling him about Sappho's life at the Garners in her sick-nurse capacity, and he would not charge me.

Oh, thanks. So this is what it's come to. He thinks I'm mad.

As I spoke I grew angrier and angrier but whether at him or at the Garners, or even Sappho, I cannot say. I told him how Isolde's little cough had turned into a lung cancer so far advanced as to be inoperable. How she would not stop smoking, or Gavin either, but they had no thought for the lungs of their own children, let alone Sappho's.

'The evidence that secondary smoking is damaging is flimsy,' Barnaby observed.

'You would say that, wouldn't you, you're a smoker,' I said.

'What makes you say that? Have I ever smoked in your presence?'

'No,' I agreed. 'But your flat stinks of old cigarettes.'

'You are angry,' he said.

'How do you know that?'

'Because you say stinks instead of smells.'

He was right. I gave up and carried on. I described how a sense of tragedy had overwhelmed everyone – someone so young, so fair, so talented et cetera – to be thus snatched away. I too fell under her spell. I would go up and help Sappho, take the children off her hands so she could see to Isolde, and as time went on to help lift her in and out of bed if Gavin was away. I never queried that this was the best thing to do, that she might be better off in a hospital, having the treatment she refused, or in a hospice, dying gracefully, out of full sight of the children, and setting Sappho free to get on with her life. Gavin rose to the occasion, I must say. He too became almost saintly, stroking brows and bringing gruel, and reading stories to the children, working round the clock to get the articles out and the money in. And Isolde's talent for improvisation remained, no matter that the crow had been killed. She wrote two plays in a year, or she and Sappho did between them.

'What has the crow to do with anything?' Barnaby demanded.

'Crow equals raven, equals the male sexual organs,' I explained. 'He shoots the crow, which equals his sex life, when he hears she has terminal cancer. Sex and creativity are inseparable. Eros overcomes Thanatos.'

'I thought he was killing the bearer of bad news,' said Barnaby. 'But have it your own way. Sex, sex, sex, Freud, Freud, Freud.'

I refrained from comment. It would be so easy on an occasion like this to crumble Viagra into his latte. As it was, dead crows lay strewn round his feet, and he didn't seem to realise their importance.

'She turned into a deathbed heroine,' I said. 'She became Violetta in *Traviata*, Marguerite in *Camille*, Mimi in *La Bohème* all at once. Verdi and Puccini and the odd drop of Purcell was piped to every room. It was mad. She held court at her bedside: friends, family, children, lovers and the media clustered round, summonsed or dismissed should the illness grip and the hour become ugly. She was beautiful and brave, she took a wonderful photograph: everyone adored her.'

'But you resented her, and her influence over Sappho.'

'How could I, in the face of her dying? Everything was

subsumed to it. Isolde had turned into a wise woman, a guru, an icon, an oracle. A Sunday newspaper paid Gavin well to write a column every week about the course of her demise: *Only The Brave – A Genius Battles Cancer*. It went on for eighteen months before coming to its hideous end.'

'I remember that. It was rather well written and quite moving.'

'Gavin got to be quite the Sunday expert on death and dying. A lot of talk about finding closure. It didn't take him long to find it. Seven years on and he was married to my Sappho.'

'Seven days would be worth commenting on, I suppose. Seven years comes over as rather bathetic, Emily. Though seven is a good Jungian number, I suppose.'

Yes, I said, I gathered that Jung had studied alchemy for seven years, but he didn't take my point. Which is that whatever way you look at it, Jung sucks. But Barnaby looked at his watch so I continued.

'The editors had taken medical advice and planned for a six-or seven-month stint for Gavin's column but Isolde kept going for three times as long. So, fortunately, did the readership. It was one long Victorian melodrama: overlong.'

I hastened through the rest. How through it all my Sappho washed and cooked and cleaned and measured medicines and arranged flowers and opened the door to visitors and kept the worst of the illness away from the children and took on the business of dealing with the press. Gavin had his column to write and his novel to finish. But I will not be mean about this: he did his best, considering he is a man, and came through it very well. Sappho's acting career at the National fell by the wayside. Not that I minded that very much either. Frankly, it was not her forte.

I saw Barnaby was looking out of the window and not

concentrating. I noticed that Ursula the aromatherapist in her high wedgies, cropped jeans and bare midriff was coming down our steps. She was far too old to dress that way, but I had to admit she had style. Barnaby was watching her as men do watch bouncy, attractive women, with a kind of suspended disbelief. I didn't think there was much more to it than that; the woman had to leave the house sometimes. She got into her little car, parked badly in the Residents' bays. The car was pasted all over with Save the Whale, Spare the Planet and Watch my Carbon Footprint posters. I didn't think she was his type.

'Time's up,' he said. 'I hope you feel better now. But there wasn't much catharsis.'

'Moan, moan,' I said. 'Typical man. See you this evening perhaps?'

He looked at me suspiciously and then said,

'Extraordinary what a little competition can do for a woman.'

He reads my mind. Is this a good thing or a bad thing between man and wife?

I went back to the diaries. Forget that she had specifically asked me not to read them. She had handed them to me. I was her mother. The daughter conceals – the mother investigates. This is the normal order of things.

Sappho's Diary: *September 12th 1997*

Dear Diary,

On Thursday afternoon last week I lost my virginity. Not before time, you might think, but I wish it had happened in different circumstances. I suppose the phrase 'losing one's virginity' dates from the time women first had sex on their marriage night so what you lost was innocence, unknowing. Now we all know everything and there is nothing to lose other than ignorance. What you have to gain is an awareness of a whole set of physical experiences which words are hard put to define. I reckon I'm in shock, because I can hardly remember, or only vaguely, what happened. And only then can I be really sure because there was blood on the cover of the bed in the spare room, and I had to take it off and put it in the washing machine and it shrunk. I had put it on at 60 degrees and the cold wash would have been safer.

I am staying at Apple Lee with my mother as I write this. I cannot go back into the Garners' apartment: they will have to get on without me.

After the event, the deflowering, Gavin fled straight to his study mumbling something about his column and I took Isolde a cup of tea and her pain-killers and she asked for more as usual and I said no as usual.

'Not even now?' she said. 'Not even now will you help me, Sappho?' I pretended not to know what she was talking about. 'It would be so much better for everyone if I was off the planet.'

The point is that she is quite able to save her tablets up herself and take an overdose any time she chooses, she just doesn't choose. She would rather involve me and I won't be involved. I am not family. There is very little time left for her anyway, according to the doctor.

Gavin looked in and said goodbye to both of us and kissed Isolde on the forehead, ignoring me, so I gathered this was the way he meant to play it. We were not going to talk about it. But

I had been elected to the succession in some way, by unanimous vote, by tacit agreement. If I waited until after Isolde's death I would find myself stepping into Isolde's shoes, live in, and go on looking after the flat and the family. How would I find the moral strength and energy not to? I couldn't just leave the family in the lurch.

'Give them my love, darling,' whispered Isolde. 'Tell them Isolde would be there if she could be.' And Gavin went off to chair some meeting of the Royal Society of Literature while I counted Isolde's uneven breaths, knowing that the long pause between them would quite soon be permanent. 'Taking a last breath' has some of the connotations of 'losing virginity'. The cliché overcomes the meaning. It's not that you don't take a last breath; it's that you don't take the next one. I was babysitting so I spent the night in the other spare room, the one I had not collapsed upon with Gavin. I got breakfast for the children and Gavin came in and behaved as if the incident upon the bloodied coverlet had not happened. If I'd had any sense I could have spoken up there and then and said,

'Gavin, it is not possible for me to stay under your roof a moment longer, in the circumstances,' and packed my bag and left, but I didn't.

What I did do was to begin to doubt whether anything had happened at all. If everyone behaves as if nothing has happened then you begin to wonder whether it did. I looked for external clues. I was a bit sore 'down there' as Gwen describes it when telling the children off for playing with themselves – 'down there' seems to be non-gender-specific, so far as Gwen is concerned. The coverlet was back on the bed and I could have imagined the wash – except the satin binding had shrunk and was puckered in places. But the evidence was a bit thin, other than that. Soreness can happen anyway: a puckered satin binding isn't much to go on.

The problem was solved when Gwen turned up with her suitcase on the Friday morning telling me she was moving into the spare room and I would have to go. I was taken aback. One thing to want to leave, another thing to be asked to leave.

'There are two spare rooms,' I said. 'There's lots of room. Why? Who will look after the children?'

'I am perfectly able to look after my own grandchildren, and family will be coming to stay. There simply isn't room, Sappho. We're very grateful to you for your help, but you're not family. How much does my daughter owe you?'

'It's not a question of money.'

'I am well aware of that, young lady.' What did she mean? And why the 'young lady', as if I was a child given to misbehaving? How could she possibly know what had happened? She was either telepathic, the flat was bugged, or it was coincidence. Or, most likely, she was in touch with the doctor, and she knew the end was coming, and wanted to be by her daughter's side at the end and didn't want me, as she put it, littering up the place.

So I declined a week's money in lieu of notice and just walked out into the fresh air, away from the smell of death, and the shuffling of the deaf old man up above, and the noise of bicycle wheels on parquet floors, and the shadow patterns made by the bars on the windows, and memories of dead crows, and heavy carrier bags in pouring rain with the handles digging in and little hands tugging at you, and Isolde's soft plaintive voice and Gavin's deep commanding one, and Isobel's demands and Arthur's mess, and now Gwen, and oh, it was a blessed relief.

I take refuge with my friend Belinda who is too interested in her own life to take much interest in mine and I sleep and sleep and sleep. I don't go to my mother's for a day or two. She'll take one look at me and know what has happened, and will be pleased because my psychosexual development has taken a turn for the better, and furious that it was Gavin. And guilt comes sweeping in like a tide. I have crept out from under. I am a worm. I did not see it through. The Queen Mother banished me, sent me into exile, just as Isolde and Gavin claimed me as their heir. I should go back, face up to Gwen, have it out with Gavin, and speak the unspeakable. If I were a proper person that's what I would do. But I'm not going to do it. I am both glad and appalled. The Garners are my life. Without them I am nothing. Any day now Isolde will fail to take the next breath and I will not be there at her bedside. How can I look her in the eye? For all I know she may have already closed those large eyes for the last time. Gavin cannot look me in mine. Does anyone care that I am gone? Is it a relief to Gavin, or a sorrow? There is no message from them. Well, they have other things to think about. I will never know and don't want to know. Will they tell me? It may be a long time before anyone gets round to it. Gwen is right. I am not family, only help.

I should have written 'how I lost my virginity' the day it happened, and then I might be able to remember more clearly. Perhaps I really am a writer, because for me reality begins on the page; what others see as 'real life' shifts ands blurs and changes all the time. No wonder I can't find anyone to marry me. But then I haven't tried very hard.

Imagine some future boyfriend. People do have them. I can't be that odd. A passing plumber, perhaps.

'So tell me about your first *experience*, Sappho? Know what I mean?'

'Well, see, I was working with this couple, and she were dying, weren't she, just down the corridor, and I was looking after her two kids – yer, it were a real tragedy, all over the *Sunday Times* it was, every fucking week, but they called me Saffron not Sappho – read it, did you? Yer, that was me – and me and the father were sort of pushed up against each other, and before you knew it—'

'Dirty old bugger! Did you like it?'

'Can't remember.'

Pause, pause, scuffle, scuffle.

'I'll give you something to remember.'

I see that in my expectations of the future I have already de-classed myself, given myself a plumber and joined him in incoherence. Punishment, I suppose, will now follow me all the days of my life. But at least I allow myself a sex life. There is something to look forward to.

I know the theory of this kind of thing: it's like getting back on a horse straight after it has thrown you. You mustn't skirt the memory, but face it head on. The trouble is the 'spare room' becomes like the cave in E. M. Forster's *A Passage to India*. Less than a week and I don't go in there in my mind any more. I read the book while I was at the convent, and re-read it, in case I had missed some sexual detail. Allegations are made but no one ever really knows, not even the protagonists, not even, I sometimes suspect, Forster himself. Perhaps it doesn't matter anyway who does what to whom, or where, or how?

'The fantasy of experience is just as real to the psyche as the fact,' Mother says. And Jesus, I seem to remember from my days in the convent, said to lust in your heart was the same as to lust in the act, but who these days is going to believe that? We are far too literal. I can clearly remember a wrong decision made at the washing machine, if only because it left the satin binding of the bedspread puckered, but where do we see evidence of any lasting effect on the psyche?

What I remember, rightly or wrongly, is that Gavin my employer and I lay on the bed together in the spare room and both of us wept, while Isolde slept or pretended to sleep and the children ate their tea unsupervised in the kitchen, and every tear of Gavin's was worth ten of mine because his came so rarely, and mine so plentifully. I could not bear his grief.

The doctor had just been and had said Isolde's death was imminent. This was why we were crying. Or perhaps it was just relief. She had taken so much of our lives and strength to keep herself going as the promised one year now moved almost to two. The parties and bedside soirées had stopped months back: we had become boring and tragedy had turned into tedium. People stayed away and talked in hushed whispers. Verdi and Puccini fell quiet. This was the reality sandwich and it was awful. Gavin's theatre column had come to an end; he had stopped work on his novel, and wrote his eleven hundred words a week for the benefit of morbid readers who wanted to follow every detail of 'my wife's struggle against cancer'. *Only The Brave – A Genius Battles Cancer* paid the rent but exposed his life in a way which offended his dignity – and there was no hiding from the truth because his mother Gwen read every word, and I had to read it to Isolde, censoring it as I read. Gavin's life was on hold, as was mine. But I was young: I could spare a couple of years: he could not.

We were both of us torn by conflicting hopes, one) that she would just for God's sake get it over with and die, and we would not have to hear the wracking coughs, the gasping for air, the little cries of pain so bravely borne, and two) that she would live for ever and not put us through the pain of her death.

I let the doctor out: the long corridor to the front door. We had gone to the kitchen so he could wash his hands. The children were sitting at the table eating tea. They were subdued, poor little things. *Timor mortis conturbat me*, even though everybody pretends for the children's sake everything's just fine. I close the door after the doctor. On my way back to the kitchen I lay down upon the spare bed. Isolde has the room across the way, next to the front door. I had to take some time out of life. Gavin, coming out of Isolde's room, saw me lying there and came in and lay down beside me and put his arms around me and I cried into his shoulder. He cried, too. It was like brother or sister, if only I had had a brother: the thought came into my head that it was more like niece and uncle, and the thought made me want to laugh; I suppose it was hysterical. He began to laugh, too, kind of. Isolde called out from the next room. The walls were thin.

'I can hear you crying,' she said. 'Do stop it. Get on with it. Do it for me.'

It was not so much permission, as an instruction. We were to create another drama for her, to make her passing easier, more entertaining, and more dramatic. She was me: she would go out in a cloud of sexual ecstasy. And I looked at the scene from afar as if it were on a stage. I left my body and now I floated in the top right-hand corner of the room, and watched the girl's body and the man's, but it was nothing to do with me, and I'll swear Isobel never came into the room. That's all I can say, Dear Diary; post traumatic stress can do all kinds of things to the memory, I looked down upon the act as if it were nothing to do with me, and if little Isobel came into the room I have no idea. Why do I even entertain the idea that she did? Why should she have, just because she could have?

I never want to see Gavin, or Isolde or Isobel, or Gwen or any of them. I wouldn't mind seeing Arthur because he's sweet and not all complicated, but I can see I will have to forgo that pleasure. They're out of my life.

I don't know how I can live with myself.

Emily's Told-You-So

Fantasy? Well, perhaps. I doubt it. It explains so much. Why Sappho butted out of her job at the Garners a couple of weeks before Isolde died, and came home to me.

She wept. Me, I was pleased enough to get my daughter safely out of the madhouse and home. But as mothers do, I felt obliged to suggest she did not behave intemperately.

'Gwen despises me,' she said. 'She told me to go. She said I was not family.'

Well, you're not, I thought, but did not say. Her voice was thick with tears. 'But everyone must be under dreadful strain,' was all I said. 'Death doesn't make people behave well, it makes them behave worse. Just ignore it.'

'She needn't think I'm going to go on being the skivvy if she talks to me like that. Let her empty the bedpans herself for a change. No, I'm out of there.'

'But darling,' I said, 'there is something to be said for seeing things through to the end.'

'The end smells,' she said violently, and I was taken aback by the savagery of her response.

I did wonder at the time whether it was Gavin, not Gwen, who had disturbed her psyche so. The son-in-law, not the mother. If 'something' had happened between her and Gavin I was not surprised. He was an attractive man and had a degree of fame: she was a pretty girl with an eye for drama. Circumstances pushed them together, and in the face of a lingering death, those obliged to witness it are all too likely to take refuge in sex. Thanatos and Eros are forever linked. If her return to me, her escape from the Garners, was at the cost of her virginity so be it. She wasn't pressured, she was willing, it just happened. And who am I to say it shouldn't have happened? Far, far better than that she should have stayed on as skivvy and slave to the widowed Gavin Garner. Then indeed there would have been psychic damage. I shuddered at the possibility.

'You just want to make me forgive everyone,' she said. 'Don't you see any virtue in righteous anger?'

'Not much,' I said, truthfully. And then someone offered her a part as Anne Boleyn in a play at the local theatre, the lead having fallen ill, and I encouraged her to take it. She could act out self-pity to her heart's content.

But then when Sappho wouldn't go to the funeral, I argued with her about that with more energy. Those poor children!

'If they've just lost their mother,' I said, 'and they lost you just before – don't think your sudden departure won't have been a psychic blow. Your not being there won't be at all helpful.'

'Gwen should have thought of that before,' Sappho said. 'And it will be helpful to me.'

'But surely, for the children's sakes – and Gavin will be hurt. You've been part of their lives.'

'Gavin will be just fine,' she said. 'Nature abhors a vacuum. Someone else will turn up at the funeral and catch his eye across a crowded cemetery, and make it their business to look after him. Someone suitable.'

Usually so tender-hearted, she wouldn't go. She was stubborn.

'What you're really afraid of,' I remember saying, 'is that Gavin will ask you to stay on as the skivvy and nurse, and you won't be able to say no.'

'I never want to see or speak of any of them again,' was all she had to say to that, other than, 'You care more about other people's children than you do about me', and she spent the afternoon of the funeral shut in her room crying, and missed a rehearsal and nearly lost the Anne Boleyn gig. Which would have been no bad thing: it was an awful show.

The funeral made headlines in the papers and was on the news, with shots of notables from stage, screen and literature, and some good dresses and hats. Gwen was magnificent and tragic in white. The children looked enchanting and piteous both. Sappho's absence was not noted. Thank God, I thought, that's that. Now she can get on with her life.

The children went to Gwen. She employed a nanny. Gavin downsized to a smaller flat near Russell Square station, and found jobs on various literary magazines, appearing on TV arts programmes from time to time, and the odd up-market quiz show. Without Isolde he became a minor rather than a major celebrity. As far as I knew, or Sappho told me, no one suitable turned up to fill the vacuum, at any rate visibly or permanently. No doubt he had affairs – he was a vigorous and intelligent man.

Nor do I know what happened to his novel – perhaps he never finished it, or perhaps I missed the reviews.

I talked the matter over with Barnaby when he popped by after his Tavistock meeting. I had quite recovered my equilibrium, and he his. These cuddling encounters of ours have to stop. They upset us both.

'I don't suppose the Gavin encounter, shall we call it – and on balance it probably did happen –' he said, 'will have done her much permanent harm. Losing a virginity in the wrong time and place with the wrong person is no longer the big deal it once was. All the other things going on at the time will have left her no space or energy to brood.'

'It will have worked away in her unconscious,' I said, 'but events you don't talk about or put into words have a habit of dissipating like smoke in air. But then I'm a neo-Freudian, not a Freudian—'

'You could have fooled me,' he said. I ignored him.

'And I don't see remembrance as essential to cure: rather, I am a believer in forgetfulness.

'And Sappho had her own defence mechanisms in good working order. She disassociated her ego very effectively from her id.'

'You can say that again,' said Barnaby. 'She went up into the ceiling and observed.'

I do have the benefit of hindsight, of course, which Sappho in her diaries does not. Away from the Garners she flourished. The Anne Boleyn reviews were so bad she gave up acting, thank God, concentrated on writing, and worked part-time for the Royal Court's office of dramaturgy. She moved out of Apple Lee altogether and got a small flat. She slept around – she was right to anticipate rather a liking for rough trade – but there was no one special. I muttered and murmured about her lack of sexual dedication.

'Mother,' she said, by way of explanation, 'come off it!' She seldom called me 'Mum', or 'Mummy', though occasionally 'Ma'. I rather envied my friends the touchy-feely relationship they had with their daughters – Mummy, Mumsy, Mommy and so forth – but Sappho preferred to keep our relationship marginally formal. 'The price of a long-term relationship, let alone a marriage, is so high. Men sap life and energy out of you – they either want to be part of your world and take everything you have, emotionally and financially, or you have to be part of theirs and tailor yourself to their specifications. There's no middle ground that I can see.'

I said that my experience was otherwise.

'Oh yes, you and Daddy,' she said, 'the perfect relationship. But how did that end? Death? You're not exactly one to talk, anyway. How many boyfriends in the past year? Perhaps I just take after you.'

I did not deign to reply.

She conceded that if you 'fell in love' it might be different, but she had never found herself in that predicament.

And then there was the sudden rise to fame and fortune, as I explained to Barnaby. She'd made friends and acquaintances during the Garner years and they were a help to her now. And then she wrote her own full-length play. It was called *The Long, Long History of Ms Alien*. She was as surprised as anyone when the work was taken up and produced. She had written an early draft during the Isolde years; a brief comedy in one act about a young girl turning to drugs for recreation and discovering that she was a lesbian. Someone at the Court found it discarded in a drawer, liked it, and persuaded Sappho to work on it until it was a 'gritty' full-length play without a single funny line in it. She was more taken aback still when it hit the zeitgeist, became a fashionable success, moved as *Ms Alien* to the National and had a vast stage all to itself. Too vast, she told me, for its substance. She began to make money: the play sold abroad. For a time Sappho became the voice of the Cool New Brit culture. I explained all this to Barnaby.

'Youth finds its voice, and so on,' said Barnaby. 'Good for her. We can take it that the loss of her virginity under less than perfect circumstances did not affect her too badly.'

'I used to think that,' I said. 'Now I am not so sure. It was on that assumption that I moved out of Apple Lee and handed it over to her, and now I wish I hadn't.'

'You're just a control freak,' said Barnaby and went upstairs. Sometimes I get the feeling he is me in another body speaking my thoughts aloud. An alter ego. Does this mean we should be together or apart? And still I haven't heard from Sappho. Apple Lee is still on answerphone. There will be nothing for it but to beard Isobel as she comes out of school.

I looked through the diaries for excerpts from those years, but after the last Gavin 'how can I live with myself?' entry they are remarkably sparse.

The answer to 'how can I live with myself?' for most people is 'very well indeed, thank you'. The thing about guilt is that, like pain, it is short-lived. You get better or die.

But here's a sheet. Thank God, typewritten. Her writing gets worse with the years, in inverse proportion to her maturity. I suppose this is true of most people's handwriting. At first we long to be understood: as life goes on we get more protective, more defensive, defying interpretation.

Sappho's Diary: *August 21st 2000*

Dear Diary,

This is awful. Supposing someone finds out the truth about *Ms Alien*? I am going to be exposed, unmasked. I remember what Isolde once said to me: 'All female writers expect that any moment now people are going to turn and say you've no right to call yourself a writer. We've found you out. You're an impostor. You're not a proper writer at all.'

She was right. I'm convinced I'm going to be found out. On my old passport it says as occupation 'childminder' and that's about right. That's what I was: I'd got it to go on holiday with the children to Majorca one year while Isolde and Gavin went on tour in Canada. The question arises because the old passport has run out and I need a new one to go to New York. How am I meant to describe myself? 'Writer' sounds so presumptuous, and is.

The fact is *Ms Alien* isn't a proper play: at heart it's just a one-off, one-act exercise done off the top of my head for one of Isolde's classes. It might even be one of Isolde's own. It had become difficult to tell the difference between her work and mine. She'd often say so. It started out as a comedy. I'd done a bit of work on it and put it in a drawer and forgot about it and then someone came across it and showed it to the dramaturge here and I took out all the funny lines and lengthened it and before I knew it I was a genius. That is not the way a real writer works. It is all a dreadful mistake. There are proper writers out there trying to make a living. Sometimes I try to confess this in interviews but they think I'm joking or on drugs. I hardly ever take drugs: if I do have this peculiar ability to write plot and dialogue and make a convincing whole, I don't want my brain cells interfered with, thank you very much.

The assumption also is that I'm a lesbian, because of my name. I've given up denying it, and I really do like Lucy Florence, and have spent a night or so with her but really I am not into it: it's just embarrassing. A kind of medical interference, an internal examination by a doctor whose intentions you are not quite clear about, and then you spasm and are meant to feel happy and grateful. Perhaps I am low on hormones, all round. I know my mother thinks there's something 'wrong' with me. She doesn't exactly say so but I can tell. If only I had the time I would get to a doctor and find out. I hate dildos, I really do. What am I to make of myself? But then I hate caviare too, and other people love it. Is there some sensual element lacking in me which is normal in other people? Perhaps the 'intelligence' which they attribute to me all the time is counter-sensuality.

Last night I dreamt of Gavin Garner. I haven't thought of him for years, but he was on some comedy quiz show on TV which I happened to see. I was sitting in the audience of a play I had written – second row of the stalls over to the left – and I realised I had no clothes on. Which was bad enough but I was called back stage and told I was going on in five minutes for the last scene and it seemed I was expected to know the lines. The play was *A Winter's Tale*, and they're rather feeble lines anyway, but I couldn't remember how they went. I had to wait for the prompt and the audience hissed. I still had no clothes on but no one took any notice. When the curtain fell Gavin Garner was standing on the plinth not Hermione. I think Lucy Florence was playing Leontes for some mad reason – perhaps it was one of those shows when the director chooses to reverse the genders – and spoke the line, 'But yet, Paulina, Hermione was not so much wrinkled, nothing so aged as this seems.'

There was the sound of a shot and Lucy fell dead. When I looked at the plinth again Gavin had turned into a crow. There was a second shot, and the crow fell dead and rotted away until it was just feathers and blood, and it suddenly stood up and re-formed and flew off with a flapping of wings, blotting out the sun. The shadow passed, and everything was bright again. Dazzling. And then I woke up, because sunlight was showing under the blind and was in my eyes. I must have worked backward from that shaft of light. The dream took seconds but in my mind it covered hours. It started as a nightmare but ended okay. I shall not report this dream to my mother, she will only analyse it.

Too Right, Emily Will

Sappho's dream begins as an exhibition dream; the nakedness of the young child is experienced as thrilling, exciting and erotic, and is repressed by its elders, who are made uneasy by the sight of the naked child dancing round and shrieking its delight.

'Stop that, Sappho, and get some clothes on,' I daresay I would have said, even though the mother in question is me and a trained psychoanalyst. Maternal irritation can get the better of maternal training. After that rebuke repression would have cut in and the nakedness be seen as something to be ashamed of. What have I done? Sappho in the diary has already written about her fear of exposure as a writer: same thing.

I talked the dream over with Barnaby. Dreams are, after all, his speciality. He had lunch upstairs and I daresay smoked a cigarette with the window open and then came down again. He went across to the station and came back with a dozen red roses. What is going on? I find out: he says he's changed his mind and wants to marry me, not just live with me. He claims my preoccupation with the diaries is a diversionary tactic so I don't have to give the matter my full attention.

'I will think about it,' I say. When he wants to marry me I quite go off him. When I want to marry him he quite goes off me. We both want what we can't have.

'But I thought that was what you wanted.'

'I am not sure now I can face the upheaval,' I say. 'I am really so nicely settled here. And it's what Sappho says. Men either want you to own them or them to own you. There's no middle way.'

'Sappho this and Sappho that,' he says. 'What about me?'

'Jealous of my daughter already,' I say and he denies it but I'm right.

Nevertheless he consents to talk about Sappho's dream.

'It's a kind experienced a lot by people who are involved with the stage,' he says. 'The not knowing the lines fear repeats the bewilderment and panic of the child who does not know the rules of the life-game. Acting keeps bringing the fears to the surface – as you delve into the lives of others, the better to construct them, you have to delve into your own.'

'And Florence is playing a man – that's an obvious one,' I say, 'though in the dream thank God Sappho kills her off.'

'Why thank God?' Barnaby asks, narkily. 'Do you have anything against lesbians? Your arrested development theory is crap.' I have made him quite cross. He wanted this evening to be given over to rejoicing at our coupledom, and instead he must talk about Sappho.

'Only that I only ever wanted to be a grandmother in the normal way,' I reply. Thus, now Sappho is pregnant, I can dismiss years of worry.

'And behind the curtain,' I go on, 'lurks the wronged and longed-for object; in the play, Perdita. The lost one. In the dream, Gavin. Oh God! She was bound to end up with him. I should have seen it. The wrinkles are the passage of time, her awareness that it can't be done, he's so much older than she is. The father. Taboo. But he's never really been out of her head since the encounter in the cave. I see it now.'

'If you know so much why ask me?' asks Barnaby. He is really pissed off.

'Gavin turns into the crow, which is Isolde's death. Gavin dies, is reborn, and flies away. Death blots out the sun. But only for a time. The sun must rise.'

'Just as well she didn't tell you the dream then,' Barnaby says. 'She'd have known years earlier it was Gavin she loved and sought him out, and brought on her fate even earlier.'

'I'm not daft. I'd probably have lied and said she was telling herself about the death of love, rather than of its continued existence,' I say.

'Never trust the fortune-teller to be impartial,' says Barnaby. 'Not if it's your own mother. She will tailor the truth to suit her fancy.'

I say he's the fortune-teller not me. He says he has to go. He looks at the red roses speculatively. He has an impulse to take them back, which he controls. I ask him if he doesn't want to stay to supper and he says no. He has some notes to look over, and I am in a bad mood. I say I'm not in a bad mood. It is just that thinking about the past is always disturbing.

'You mean you have other things to think about than me,' says Barnaby, and stomps off upstairs. Indeed I do.

I think about Lucy Florence. She made her name playing Gertrude in a rather good production of Hamlet. A tall, dark, vigorous girl with hairy arms and a strong jaw, too young to play the part. I remember saying at the time she must have been at least ten when she gave birth to Hamlet. But it was an all-woman show and I daresay the director had her favourites.

Freud suggests we dream of the deaths of those we love the most. As odd a reaction as that of schizophrenics who want to hurt – or in extreme cases even kill – the ones who most love them. But I don't think Sappho loved Lucy Florence, though I worried for a time. She had a series of liaisons with men as well, after all, men uninvolved with the theatre: a journalist, an electrician, a film lighting director, a builder, a TV historian, all of them noticeably older than she was. She may of course have been trying to throw off the lesbian tinge with which the media had invested her, but I doubt it. I should have thought and not called her Sappho – it just seemed such a nice name to Rob and me. Though actually a lesbian image – or certainly being known as a bisexual – was an advantage in the theatre at the time. Perhaps it was only that, and she was shrewder than I imagined.

I thought about that, and how she managed to make a name for herself. She tried to keep out of the gossip columns, or assured me she did, but she didn't wholly succeed. Perhaps the media profile was contrived, after all. Intellectual but sexy. She was snapped getting out of a cab with a cabinet minister, drunk, her knickers showing. She apologised publicly to his wife. The wife, a real bitch, said she graciously accepted the apology, since it was well known that Sappho was 'otherwise inclined'. That may have paid off. Lesbianism was 'in'. The play went to America, Germany and Sweden. Money poured in. She was too busy to spend it. She had fan mail. She needed somewhere bigger to live: she needed an equipped and staffed office. Laura had joined her, a tall, plain, efficient girl from the North, with qualifications in office management.

I think more about the wisdom or otherwise of my putting Apple Lee in Sappho's name. I have thought about it quite a lot since she married Gavin. She might do something stupid and put the property jointly in her and Gavin's name. But surely she would have told me? The worry has come creeping to the surface since my conversation with Laura. Did I really know so little about what was going on? I thought I knew so much.

It was my idea, not Sappho's, that we made the move.

'It's yours by right,' I said. 'More yours than mine. Yours by genes. I'm not really one of the family, just married into it.'

'But you've lived here for more than thirty years,' she said. 'It's your home. You've polished the furniture and wiped the floors. Of course it's yours. Like in *Mother Courage*: the land, like the child, belongs to those who look after it. It's yours legally, anyway.'

Apple Lee had been 'in the family' since 1903 or so. Stubb-Palmer males had looked out at a changing London for ten decades and watched the house crumble as their incomes fell.

Rob took it, more fool he, as the humiliation of something loved, and I suspect died to save it, though I couldn't tell Sappho that.

'I've had enough of property,' I said. 'I've had enough of dry rot and the bats and the heating bills and the faulty boiler and the ghost upstairs – probably just creaking doors and groaning pipes. I can't sell it, it would be far too emotional, but I could hand it over to you. Please?'

I don't think I had ever said please to her before, other than in the 'please don't make that racket' sense. This was serious.

'You have the money to keep it up; you need the space; it's central enough for taxis to risk the area, although I admit it's increasingly downmarket. We'll split the value and I'll buy a smaller place. Laura will help organise. You could entertain.' Sappho shuddered, perhaps at the memory of Isolde's smart if grisly parties. 'You should take on the burdens as well as the pleasures of life. A cockroach ran across my surgery floor the other day and frightened a patient and when it rains I listen for the drip, drip, drip as it comes through the ceiling.' And I told her about one of my patients, an obsessive compulsive, who had billed me for the price of a personal alarm, he was so nervous of being mugged when he came to the door. She said she supposed I didn't worry that if she lived there we might be mugged?

Laura and she were by now so bound together by the common cause of running Sappho Stubb-Palmer to advantage that Sappho had taken to referring to the Sappho–Laura unit in the plural 'we', as did Queen Victoria of herself. 'We'll see if we can make that date.' 'Yes, I think we'll take on the commission.' And Sappho wrote and Laura wrote up what Sappho wrote and read her mind so that she could edit as she went, so Sappho could never even be bothered to read what Laura wrote in her name. She knew it would make sense even though it might not be quite what Sappho originally had in mind. It made others giggle, I fear, but I always thought it was out of respect for and acknowledgement of Laura's input rather than the conceit of being a royal 'we'. She stopped doing it after Gavin moved in.

Sappho said she'd think about it, just as I said I'd think about it when Barnaby said he wanted to marry me. Presented by what you want you suddenly don't want it any more. I had grown out of Apple Lee, grown out of its bourgeois, property-owning, concrete boots. If the house came to her early I could be free of the past and what I had taken on when I married Rob and had a child by him. If I waited until I died the house would have fallen down and tides of property developers would have rushed in and taken over, and twelve luxury flats built instead of one family house, and though that might have set the whole area on the path to genteel living I wouldn't be there to see it.

I'd told Sappho half the truth: that I was paying out for personal alarms for my patients. Actually I had been mugged myself last summer, on my way up the path, under the apple tree. My handbag had been stolen. And me, I was beginning to feel my age. It had been brought home to me when I wanted to run after the robber and found I could hardly run. My knee was troubling me and I needed a replacement hip. I couldn't go private even if I'd wanted to: I was scraping money together to re-paint the outhouses. Sappho would have helped me out, but I did not like being indebted to my own daughter. All the insurance money had long been spent and a new wave of expenditure was now required to keep the place standing. I hated it when it rained because of the roof. I wanted to live somewhere quiet and respectable and with no stairs.

'On no account,' my lawyer warned me, 'hand the property over to your daughter. You are too young; so is she. You're relinquishing all control over what goes on. You can put in a clause that gives you the right to live in the house until your death – or to be notified about any changes to the title, but that's all.'

'Sappho has her head screwed on the right way,' I said, and told him I didn't see her easily falling under the sinister influence of a husband. We would soon be in the new century and the days were gone when women had to be protected against themselves. 'Anyway, she's a Cordelia not a Goneril.'

The lawyer, Mr Clive Maidment, shook his head and pursed his lips but went ahead with the documentation. Sappho bought me the Hampstead flat and became owner of Apple Lee. She had Laura to help her deal with it, Laura the dungeon mistress, keeping builders busy and heritage at bay. Laura loved every minute of it, ordering and re-ordering, checking colour charts and prices, choosing tiles, bossing workmen, as much as I had loved not doing it. And then of course Sappho re-met Gavin.

I went back to the diaries: Barnaby called me from upstairs.

'I'm sorry to have been so grumpy,' he said.

'I'm sorry for needling you,' I said.

'You need to crush the end of the roses,' he said. 'To make sure the water gets through to the buds. They were very expensive.'

'Okay,' I said, and decided I would be mad to marry him. That was quite enough emotion for one day, thank you very much.

Sappho's Diary: *July 18th 2004*

Dear Diary,

I have been having another go at writing a novel. It is very different from a stage or screen play, and more difficult. You don't have actors to help you. The bits between the dialogue are a problem because I am not accustomed to writing these to be read by anyone other than those involved in a production. Novel writers have to do all the work themselves – design, casting, lighting, costume – everything. It's a nightmare. By the time I was a few pages in I gave up pretending it was fictional and turned my heroine's name – Sophie – back into my own, Geordie back into Gavin, Isobel remains as Isobel, and Rosalind became Laura. If ever anyone wants to publish it, a click or so of the mouse and all the names can become other once more. In the meanwhile it's just easier to describe and not invent, and useful to look at oneself, one's life and times, in the third person…

Sappho's Novel

Part 1
Sappho And Gavin Find Each Other

It seemed to Sappho that life was good, at least so far as her small corner of the world was concerned. She was young, healthy, bright, successful, so far single, had the good opinion of her peers, owed nothing to the bank and owned her own house mortgage-free. She had no father but she did have a mother. So far as she knew she had no enemies: although critics could be unkind about what she was writing, their barbs were usually softened by, 'Well, she is young and will learn.'

Like all the other women in her age group so far unpartnered, she had been vaguely waiting for the Mr Right of the kitchen maid's prayer to come along, the mythical knight in shiny armour fate had in store for her, to sweep her off her feet and explain to her everything that had been left unexplained – from who shot Kennedy to why we were fighting in Afghanistan. He had to be a well good-looking knight, of course, and tall, and with a tight butt and well-working parts, and with money off-shore, etc. She had been having a few moments of despair, God knows – if such a man existed Nicole Kidman would have nicked him or Sandra Bullock nabbed him – and she had even been having unsettling visions of a childless and lonely old age. But suddenly here he was, actually in her bed upstairs and showing no inclination to leave it, and better still, back from her past, and she from his, so there was no need for too many explanations.

And if when the knight came bursting out of the forest (my mother would certainly find a phallic interpretation of that: she looks over my shoulder all the time while I write) he was a little older than expected, and a little wrinkled around the eyes, at least his hair was still luxuriant (he was lucky in his genes). She had always liked older men (okay, okay, my father, Mother, just fuck off!). And if he was far from being a money-off-shore man that was no matter either; Sappho earned more than enough for both of them.

'About time too, God,' she said aloud, as she pattered down the stairs to her office in her bare feet, dressed only in a short white slip, to go through the morning's emails before Laura got in.

It is probably wiser not to provoke one's maker, and she was usually very conscious of such danger, but such was her elation that she forgot even to cross her fingers. It may or may not have been coincidence that within the half-hour the doorbell rang and she opened it to Isobel, whom she had last seen seven years or so back, eating a boiled egg, supervised by her grandmother Gwen, in the household of the man now lying upstairs in her bed, on the day when she had been fired as an au pair, or had walked out in dudgeon, depending on whose side you were on. (Backstory is easy in film: you just cut back and show it, but in prose it is difficult to be graceful.)

Perhaps it was the demiurge of the Gnostics, not God, who heard and resented the reproach – the demiurge is considered to be an imperfect deity, and by some even downright evil; be that as it may, thereafter life did not go for Sappho quite as she had hoped. What she had hoped for, naturally, was unadulterated and perfect happiness, but since she had taken on a man with baggage, as they say, she could see she would have to accept some compromise. So far that morning things had been okay.

In the half-hour before the demiurge ordered that the doorbell would ring and the eleven-year-old Isobel appear, she had time to go through her email; six spam, three personal, three requests to speak: one from the BBC asking her to 'nominate the arts landmarks in the expression or representation of sex and sexuality from the past fifty years'. A call had even come through from her agent in L.A. while she was at her desk.

'Hi, Saph darling, this is Jennylee. I'm so thrilled. I've just heard from Luke that *Automated*' – Sappho's latest play, about a girl who faked orgasm and lived to regret it – 'is screening here in September.'

'It can't be screening, Jennylee, it's a stage play.'

'You know what I mean, darling. This is a cinema town, we don't do theatre much. Now I don't even have to go to New York to get to see it – aren't you excited?'

Yesterday morning it would indeed have seemed thrilling news: today she was so full of self-congratulation it seemed no more than her due. She wrote a memo to Laura asking her to email Jennylee and get the details of the new production. She was slightly nervous and wondered why and remembered it was because today was the day she would have to break it to Laura that there was now a man permanently in her bed, and not some passing stranger. Laura did not like disturbances to her routine. At eight forty-five in the morning, seldom ill, never late, Laura would let herself through the new security gates, deactivate the alarm, and clip-clop in smart heels up the garden path, dodging the branches of the apple tree to let herself in, pick up the post, and be at her desk waiting for Sappho's appearance in the office at nine o'clock.

'Now we can get on, can we?' she would ask, as if the hours spent away from the office since the previous evening had been all indulgence, a waste of real time.

This morning at seven-thirty, when Sappho had shaken Gavin awake and said it was time for him to have breakfast and either go back to his flat or get the bus to his office in Holborn before Laura turned up, he had frowned and said, 'Either you're having an affair with me or you're not. She's going to have to get used to it, and better sooner than later, because I'm a fixture.' And he'd buried his head in the pillow, saying, 'It smells so wonderfully of you. Goose down, isn't it? I hate foam,' and gone back to sleep.

A fixture, a fixture, Gavin was a fixture! She'd danced out of her room and down the stairs and instead of prudently thanking God reproached Him for having taken so long to find her a man who would stick to her and she to him. Of course she could face Laura. She could face anyone. Laura could not expect her to stay a spinster all her life, just because Laura disapproved of love. The details of any new power-sharing could be easily sorted out.

Three weeks since she had met Gavin, or rather re-met him, seen him across a crowded room and thought, that man is so familiar he can only be the one, the knight in shining armour come to rescue me, who is that odd red-haired woman he is with, how dare she interfere, and then realised of course it was Gavin Garner. And he, seeing her the other side of the white-clothed table where drinks were being served, thought, similarly, of course, Sappho... And that was it. (She thought her mother would have a more compulsive agenda on hand for both of them, but sod that for a lark.) Mine, mine, Gavin is all mine!

Or perhaps, Sappho thought, she could just go back to bed and Laura would have to put up with no boss already up and functioning when she came through the door. She, Sappho, was the guru round here, not Laura, who was only the secretary. Perhaps there was a new life possible in which you just lounged about and drank coffee and ate croissants at your leisure, and looked after your looks and your sex life and decided you were an artist, not a working hack. And you only wrote when the inspiration struck and not just to meet deadlines. She had just decided to go back to bed and let Gavin pull her between the rumpled sheets when the doorbell rang.

Too early for the post, too early for Laura to have forgotten her key – not that she ever did. What did it matter? It was bound to be more good news! The morning sun struck through her window and apple blossom rubbed up against her window, and Sappho opened the door. A girl child stood on the step, no urchin she, but well-reared and healthy, with already the look of good judgement about her. Pale and slight, mind you, though pretty enough in an unformed way, with a short upper lip, surprisingly full lips, thick blonde hair cut short and sharp against a long neck and big serious greeny eyes. She was not smiling: indeed, she seemed rather cross, even censorious. Sappho did not recognise her at once.

Mother, go away! Get out of my head. I'll swear I didn't recognise her. I am not in denial, I just hadn't wanted to think too much about his children, let alone Isolde; the whole thing had been too traumatic. I wanted to put it off as I was putting off telling Laura. Okay, that is denial. You win. But Isobel and Arthur had been safely packed away with Gwen in my memories: they were outside the picture frame. As soon as I had Gavin firmly established inside it, then perhaps I could afford to think about what came with him, extend the frame to include his children and a dead saint for an ex-wife – and after that even bring myself to consider an age difference of nearly twenty years, my wealth, his comparative poverty, and I absolutely argue with you about women being basically masochistic: it is too un-cheerful a view of the universe. Anyway this is a novel, for Christ's sake. If I did it in real life I can do it on the page.

So no, Sappho did not instantly recognise this tweenie as the egg-eating, daddy-possessive toddler she had spent nearly three years raising. That child had the big head and rounded limbs of long-ago: this girl was very much pre-pubertal, and going through that sulky, gawky stage before the bloom of oestrogen softens the muscles and makes the complexion glow. Sappho supposed her to be eleven or twelve. The summer was not yet advanced: the morning was sunny but brisk: the girl wore cropped jeans, sandals and a sleeveless pink cotton top over a still flat chest. Was she not cold? What could a girl as young as this be doing roaming the streets so early, knocking on strange doors? Well of course. A child searching for its father. The name came into Sappho's head almost before she realised who it must be.

'Isobel!'

The girl looked puzzled.

'How do you know who I am? I don't know you.'

'But you do,' Sappho said. 'I looked after you when you were three.'

'I don't believe this,' the girl said. 'Daddy wouldn't do this to me. Are you the au pair from way back then?'

It was one thing for Sappho to refer to herself as the au pair, but she did not like anyone else doing it. She had been family friend, nurse, interpreter, ghost writer, entertainer, mother's help, and provider of laughs, life and drama for the girl's mother for years. Had she not been there at Isobel's birth, or as good as? 'I saw a lot of your family just before your mother died.'

'Are you the one who walked out on us?'

'I guess so,' said Sappho, wrong-footed already.

'Well I'm here to talk to my father,' the girl said. 'He spent the night here. I need him to sign something for school.'

And she stepped elegantly past Sappho and went on into the hall. Had Isobel said 'want' not 'need' Sappho could see she might have resisted and barred the way, but a child in need of its father must be satisfied.

'At least it's one up from his last girl,' Isobel said, with a faint twitch of the red lips which indicated approval, looking round the big hall, with its elegant, newly painted staircase and the view through glass doors to an extremely fancy new kitchen and conservatory beyond, where once stood what Sappho's mother referred to as 'the old garage'.

I should bloody hope so, Sappho thought but did not say. The new layout of the ground floor had set her back many thousands of pounds, and had been achieved with the help of expensive architects and a great deal of agitation and plaster dust in the hair and under the nails as interior walls were removed and placed elsewhere to advantage. The living room where once Emily had received patients and possibly lovers was now Sappho's office, and Laura's territory. The room where Sappho endured or did not endure the quasi-primal scene, heard from below, was now empty, next to the master bedroom where she had been conceived, and where now Gavin lay asleep.

One up from the last girl. A double-edged compliment. The last girl had no doubt been Elvira, the one Gavin abandoned at a party to take her, Sappho, home. Their eyes had met across a crowded room: each saw their destiny in the other. Since then they had not spent an hour apart that they could help.

'He doesn't hang about, does he?' said Isobel, mournfully.

It seemed an age ago, but Sappho realised it had scarcely been three weeks. She felt slightly bad about the last girl, but not much. Gavin, by his own account, had only a casual relationship with Elvira, a theatrical dress designer with red unkempt hair and stocky, slightly bowed legs, who lived modestly as befitted her station in life.

Elvira, thought Sappho, with a degree of conceit, hadn't stood a chance, not in the face of Sappho's determination that she, the famous young playwright who had everything she wanted and could do no wrong, whose hair was reddish but never unkempt, whose legs were perfectly long and straight, had finally met the man of her dreams. And if she happened to have gone to a party with Gavin, what could she expect, but that having once encountered Sappho, he should not go home with Sappho, should Sappho so desire? This was the way of the world.

Sappho had suggested to Gavin that he called Elvira the next day to apologise – a girl did expect the man who took her to a party to at least take her out of it – and he had done so, from Sappho's bed, but Elvira just slammed the phone down. With this had gone Elvira's chance of being included in a circle of Gavin/Sappho friends.

Apart from Elvira, Sappho had rather gained the impression that since Isolde died Gavin's life had been free of romantic interludes. But he was a sexual being: it would be unlikely for him to have been celibate in the interval. Sappho was enough of a realist to realise that. If she did, so could he. But why go there? Their lives had started anew. The past was irrelevant.

'Upstairs?' asked Isobel. Sappho looked blank.

'Is Daddy in bed upstairs? It's a really big house.'

Sappho nodded, and Isobel, without so much as a by your leave, went up the stairs calling, 'Daddy, Daddy, are you in there?'

And Sappho thought, oh fuck, Laura is going to be in any minute and there goes any chance of a gentle introduction to Gavin's new place in my life as resident lover. Not just a man in her bed to explain away, but his child as well, littering up the place, which by now seemed to be as much Laura's as hers, and another one, Arthur, hiding in the woodwork. Arthur had been six when his mother died, old enough to remember how Sappho had not been there at the funeral. And she wished then she had listened to her mother, who had tried to persuade her to stand at the graveside and weep with everyone else. But she could not bear to have gone. She was the one most hurt, but no one would recognise it. She was, after all, only the au pair, not family.

Well, she would make it up to the children somehow. She loved Gavin. She would love his family and make them love her and all would be well. They would all go and visit the grave together and leave flowers. They would be a family. And she would be victorious, how could she not be, since Isolde was dead and she was alive?

A Minor Interruption From Emily

'Does she really not remember the "incident" in the spare room?' I ask Barnaby.

'It is a novel,' he says. 'She is entitled.'

'It's not a novel, it's an autobiography. She's even used her own name.'

'But she's going to change the names before it's published,' says Barnaby.

'I should bloody hope so,' I say.

'Bad luck,' he says, 'having a writer in the family.'

'I remember every detail of the way I lost my virginity,' I say.

'I don't want to know,' he says.

He doesn't love me. He just wants what I have, which is a washing machine that works, a sandwich toaster for pressed cheese sandwiches, and someone to nurse him when his health goes. We are neither of us getting any younger.

Sappho's Novel Continues...

In the couple of weeks since they had re-met, Gavin again had spoken of his children but talked about the common past as if it were too long ago to be accurately remembered. Neither of them much wanted to bring the subject up. Speaking of Isolde was still painful to him, so Sappho seldom did.

'You worked for us for quite a long time,' he said to her once. 'I know that. But after Isolde got ill – well, you put it behind you or it destroys you as well. So let's not talk about it.'

'Okay,' said Sappho. It was early days. He would talk about it eventually. Her mother, who was a psychoanalyst, said that the force of repressed memories was such that they eventually surfaced.

'A new life starts, don't you feel that?'

'I do. So what shall we talk about? The theatre?'

His body became tense against hers. She could see that might be a subject to be avoided. He didn't like her plays. He had written one of the few bad reviews of *Ms Alien*. He found what she wrote destructive and depressing; he deplored the new wave of youth-worshipping, anti-intellectual, anti-middle-class drama that now flooded the theatre. It had been a fine piece of polemic, and started a hare running which the literary press still pursued, but not flattering to her. Why was she now in bed with him? Her mother would complain that she was masochistic, but wasn't it better to embrace the enemy, become one with them, conquer them, convert them, than to run scared? She had sought him out at the party, gone over to him; he'd apologised.

'I'm just an old dinosaur,' he said. 'Anything written since the age of the computer tends to offend me. Take no notice.'

'Only business,' she'd observed.

'Only business,' he agreed, and the need to be in each other's arms stopped that particular conversation. More, talk of theatre would bring them back to Isolde and the rumour, which Sappho's critics so liked to disseminate, that *Ms Alien* was a direct crib from a TV drama written by Isolde way back. There were indeed similarities, if only because of Sappho's hand in that original, but how could she say that without betraying Isolde?

So they spent a lot of time in bed, at her place by night, his place by day, which suited them both, or eating out, or walking on the heath, which Gavin liked and Sappho did not so much. On one occasion they lay for hours on their fronts on Hampstead Heath waiting for a Red-tailed Hawk (*Buteo jamaicensis*) which someone had sighted, only giving up because Gavin's knees began to ache. There were his academic friends to meet: she got on with them well. Their other-worldliness entranced her. He found her friends rather frivolous and thespian, and to tell the truth so did she. She loved Gavin's conversation, his skill with words, the breadth of his knowledge, and the way he loved her. Compared to him, she was a lightweight, and she knew it.

She had visited Gavin's small book-shelved apartment in Bloomsbury, and they had swept aside the books on the sofa to make love on it, and noticed the portrait of Isolde that hung upon his wall, but she did not comment on it and nor did he. It had been painted in the months before she died by an artist they both knew, but still they kept quiet. Next time she came it had vanished, and he hadn't even moved another painting to take its place: the faded wallpaper announced where it had been. He said nothing about its absence, so Sappho didn't either. It became obvious to Sappho that the rules of the relationship were going to be set around minimum reference to the past. It suited her well enough.

They came together as new lovers. The past was in another country, where Gavin had been in Isolde's bed until Isolde had died in it. Sappho had witnessed the slow decline, and who wanted to journey there?

I can see I have been trying to distance myself from these events by putting them in the third person, but it is me I'm writing about so I'm going to put it into the first person and see what happens. Third person tends to get a bit pompous and ponderous.

So I daresay I approached Gavin rather nervously, even while knowing I was his favourite and he loved to indulge me. I can't tell you how good the sex was. He was more experienced than me, being older, but it was more than technique, it was the psychic electricity between us that made us somehow melt into each other and fuse, as in those special effects you see in Terminator films when metal liquefies and reforms as something else. Sex to date had been pleasurable at best and embarrassing at worst – I have this habit of being the onlooker; noticing my own sensations and emotions in the interests of reportage, which doesn't help. But with Gavin I felt I had permission to be there then, as it were.

Now, with Isobel stamping upstairs to surprise her father in a strange bed, my alarm was more about Laura than anything else. So far I had managed to keep Gavin out of Laura's way, and fielded Laura's occasional 'What's the matter? You look like the cat that's swallowed the cream,' and, 'Do pay attention, Sappho, your mind is wandering,' and, 'Late night again, I observe. Who was it? No one important, I hope,' and so on.

Till now I'd managed to get him out of the house before Laura had arrived, bringing the new day with her heels, orderly, precise, one-two, one-two. No more languidly sloping in and out of bed once Laura was through the door. It felt morally wrong to be not working while she was. She'd have had me clock in if she could. The builders were always asked to sign in and out, and their hours noted, checked and initialled. She would have had a time clock if there was one left in the land that I could live with, and that was another thing, if Gavin were to move in, which seemed inevitable, he would be bringing yet more aesthetic conflict into our lives. Laura liked Ikea, I liked antique and junk shop, and Gavin liked Heal's. Trouble ahead.

During Laura's reign I'd become rich and borderline famous: 50,000 articles on Google and rising. Laura put my hand-written scripts onto the computer, opened the mail, paid the bills, kept the diary, had access to all my money, employed the builders who kept Apple Lee from falling down, and took as well a six-figure salary. As I grew rich she grew rich: it paid off. She answered the phone beautifully: the day's business was seen to within the day; we prospered and flourished. The commissions came in thick and fast. Laura saw to it that I did not waste my time, spend too much, drink too much and frowned so ferociously if I took drugs I did not dare. Deadlines were met, all queries answered, all permissions granted if reasonable.

It was all 'If my friends could see me now!' time. I'd started out the child of a widowed mother in a derelict house, while my mother pursued some arcane knowledge to do with psycho-analytical theory. My father had died in a car accident, but that did not deflect Mama from her obsession. I was a Freud orphan.

'Why don't you live in Ireland?' my accountant suggested. 'As an artist, and you qualify, you won't have to pay tax.'

'This is my country, and I love it,' I replied. I felt part of it, and its struggle to be new and different and diverse, and if the price I had to pay was broken needles and used condoms over the garden wall, so be it. Mind you, things were looking up. The Council was spending millions of EU money on the area, and Laura had organ-ised a landscaping firm to bury the old sour and sooty earth beneath tons of new top-soil, and the garden was back to pastoral bliss. The apple tree had been treated with all the fungicides and insecticides known to man, but I looked out on it from the same front window as had my father, my grandfather, and my great-grandfather.

'How strange,' said Gavin, 'to reckon your descent in patri-lineal not matrilineal lines.'

'I will have to have a son, I daresay,' I said, 'just to keep the house in the family.'

I am half joking; I want to see how he will react. This is a week into the relationship. If only I liked children more. I associate them with the years spent au pairing: Isobel and Arthur were as good as my own, yet how quickly I forgot about them. They are associated with too much grief and trauma. Isobel comes to the door seven years on and I don't even recognise her. All that early drudgery comes to nothing. Anyone else could have done the cleaning, the wiping, the pacifying, the flash cards, the hauling of shopping up and down the hill, and no one would have noticed the difference.

'Then I will have to father it,' said Gavin. 'No way am I going to let another man near you.'

I like it when he's possessive. But perhaps he is half joking, too? I don't think so. He is fully committed to me, I can tell.

I put myself back to my resolve to give Isobel and Gavin five minutes together. She is his daughter after all. I can afford to be generous. Then I shall go and impose my will upon whatever situation has materialised. Poor little Isobel. She lost her mother when she was small. She now lives with her grandmother, whom I remember as a cold, fairly loathsome, if beautiful, woman. Her father doesn't seem to take much notice of her or any that he communicates to me. Not that that doesn't suit me. Of course I will take on stepchildren if I have to – but stepchildren imply marriage. What am I thinking of? Yet thinking of it I am – Good Lord! The things one tells oneself if one lets a stream of consciousness evolve! My mother would be proud of me but would have a fit if it ended with a wedding ceremony – an actual walk-down-the-aisle marriage. For what's the point of that? A legal contract to prove true love? Very last century. Yet here I am contemplating it. It would certainly make a stir amongst our friends – and they'd only known each other a matter of weeks: are they mad? – which would be fun, but hardly grounds for marriage. Yet it all seems so right, so certain, so inevitable.

But aren't people meant to be suited? Can I honestly say we are? He's older and academic: I'm younger and frivolous. He hates what I write: I pretend to be interested in birds but am not in the least. All we have in common is a shared memory of a dead wife we aren't even allowed to talk about. I'll bet it's just that I'm fed up with feeling lonely having no one permanent in the bed, want a baby and need someone to defend me from Laura. I will expunge all thoughts of weddings from my thoughts. What will I wear?

There is a window for a wedding in June. I was going to take Laura on a trip round the Ring of Fire somewhere in the South Seas. I had hoped to take my mother but she is too tied up as per usual with her patients and a new lover called Barnaby. At least he is suitable and not rough trade. This problem of suitable. I'm by nature an early riser: Gavin wakes late. Do these differences matter: or do they contribute to the perfect whole, the ideal mean? If the sex which invigorates me seems to tire him is this to do with the difference in our ages or just our natures? Is his propensity to lie abed after a night of lovemaking due to the weakness of years or to the sensual pleasure he takes in so many things: from Italian food to sex to making bonfires to simply lying in bed late on a good mattress. No workaholic he: I am often accused of it. I am not good at living in the present; Gavin is. It's a male trait, that. Women feel the need to leap up and do something lest worse befall: men focus on the now. Single-taskers.

If I go up and see what Isobel and Gavin are doing, I am going to look silly. Supposing they think I'm jealous? I will lose face. But what is there to talk about that takes so long? Or perhaps she's slipped out the back way and not even been bothered to say goodbye. Well, I can understand that. For her I'm just the next in succession: the one after 'the last girl'. How is she to know that I'm a fixture in her father's life, that I'm going to be a formal step-mother, that she's going to have a baby stepbrother? Oh down, down, errant thoughts! It would be nice to have a baby, a bit of her, a bit of him, to go on to the next generation and take over the world. Isolde didn't manage to let much of Gavin in to her children: Isobel used to be a miniature of Gwen, and Arthur was like no one else in the family inasmuch as he wasn't at all creative or even very bright. I would do better than that. My son will have Gavin's build, presence, brilliance and power and the gift of the written gab from me. But hang on a minute – why am I thinking this? To outdo Isolde? I must be joking. This is not a competition between me and her.

I decided I didn't care about losing face: I must go up and see what was going on.

He would have had more than enough of Isobel by now. I went up to the master bedroom, my bedroom for three years – as a child I'd had what was now the spare room – where I was conceived, which before that had been my grandparents', and before that back and back to God knows what relatives, the original genes being no doubt fairly thin by now. There was Gavin lying under the duvet, asleep. And next to him, on top of the bedclothes, the girl, his daughter, Isobel, just lying there, awake. Their hands are entwined. Seeing me she un-entwines them. That is somehow unsettling me. She knows the effect it will have on me. But she is a child, not an adult. Family, not rival. All the same, I'm trembling.

The trouble with men is that what seems so simple – love and living – can suddenly become so complicated. There are people you don't want to hurt, things in the past you don't want disclosed, a more complicated path into the future than you ever contemplated.

'He says he's going to marry you,' said Isobel. I'm gratified: I am right: his mind works like my mind. 'How long have you known each other? Three months?'

'Three weeks.' I am proud, I can't help it. Gavin Garner, literary man about town, snaffled under Elvira's nose in three short weeks. 'Come down and I'll make you coffee.'

'I don't drink coffee,' said Isobel. 'I don't believe in caffeine. I'd like a drink of water. Tap water not bottled because of the air miles.' She slipped off the bed and followed me down.

I poured her a glass from the tap and she sipped. It smelt of chlorine but I didn't suppose that would do her much harm. It crossed my mind that she was anorexic. Well, Gwen would have to deal with it. Isobel and Arthur would only be with us the occasional weekend. She looked pretty and wan and vulnerable. My heart melted. Any minute now Laura would turn up, but that couldn't be helped: I would deal with it. My house, my work, my stepdaughter-to-be, after all.

'It's a nice house,' said Isobel, appreciatively. 'Bigger than Gwen's and lighter. It would be really handy for my new school. The bus goes past the door. I remember you now. You used to be the au pair, before my mother died.'

'You were very small,' I said, and felt a wave of affection for what she once was.

'Something about the way you moved,' she said, 'and all of a sudden there you were in my mind. You splashed a lot of egg yolk into my hair. You had a funny name.'

'Sappho,' I said.

'I used to play under that apple tree out there,' she said. 'One fell on my head. Actually, Daddy didn't really say he was going to marry you, Sappho. I just said that. It was in my head as the kind of thing that happens if you're me.'

'Oh,' I said.

'I handed him the form to sign for school and he just initialled it and went back to sleep.'

'I see,' I said. I was trying to re-grasp a future in which I and Gavin did not get married.

'He's joint guardian with Gwen so there's all kinds of forms he has to sign,' the child said. 'Mostly I can forge them but they can get funny about it at school, so if I know where he is I find him.'

'Really,' I said.

'Early morning's best, because if he's asleep he doesn't argue, just signs.'

'He likes his sleep,' I said, wondering about all the beds to which this child had pursued her father, and how many of them there were. 'Married to Gavin' was a silly, gauche, fleeting kind of idea. He was a serial philanderer: he fell into bed with women, declared they were the love of his life, and departed, and I had fallen for it.

'Why do you say "likes his sleep" and not "likes to sleep"? It sounds very lower class.'

'I am lower class,' I said. I have a long line of generals and politicians in my background and this child had a long line of Polish immigrants through Isolde, and Yorkshire peasants through Gavin, but what the hell. I know where my loyalties lie.

'You are only the au pair,' said Isobel, generously, 'so I suppose it's to be expected. Do you work here? Are the real people away?'

'This is my house,' I said. 'I am the real people.'

The child looked round the room, taking in stainless steel, ceramic surfaces, and the rest.

'It must be nice to be rich,' she said.

'It is,' I said, and Isobel rewarded me with a slow smile, and for once you could see a glimpse of Gavin in her, and I thought we might get on together after all. Because Gavin hadn't told his daughter he was going to marry me didn't mean it was not his

147

intention. How had she managed to confuse me so? Little children were easy: you looked after their physical needs. It tired you out, but it didn't upset you. Older children played games, like adults do.

I made Isobel toast, which she insisted on eating dry, not buttered. She didn't like grease, she said. I asked how she'd known where to find her father, and Isobel said it was because Elvira had been taking her and Arthur riding and Elvira hadn't turned up.

'So we went round to her place and found her like – gross, buggy-eyed and weeping all over the place.'

Apparently Elvira had been standing outside Apple Lee every night for six days – and she, Isobel, knew the house she was describing because of the apple tree. The bus went by on the way to school.

'That's not too safe for her,' I said. 'It's quite a gritty neighbourhood.'

And I thought how strange it was, how one behaved in front of children – pretending that everything is okay when it isn't. Forget the neighbourhood, the thought of a weeping Elvira standing outside watching lights go on and off and shadows silhouetted against glass and so on, freaked me out. It also excited me, somehow. I tried to decipher my own feelings, but I couldn't get to the bottom of them. My breath was coming faster: I wanted to climb back into bed with Gavin, stake my claim, forget this silly child, forget Laura. I hated feeling like this. God would punish me. And I wasn't going to tell Gavin either. Let Elvira watch, and suffer, and know just how thoroughly she was defeated.

'Elvira would love to be mugged,' said Isobel. 'Then she could blame Daddy, and I expect she could sue you. If Daddy did marry you and moved in would he automatically get half the house? Is this what happens?'

'Only if I put it in his name. Married people often do that.'

'Elvira owns her own flat,' said Isobel. 'But it isn't up to much. Even pokier and smaller than Daddy's place. Daddy's lease is running out, so he has to find somewhere. Gwen says he can come and live with us but he won't.'

And she looked at me sidewise, is the only way I can think of describing a look she sometimes has, an elfish look, eldritch, as if more was known than ought be known, than can possibly ever be known, and I remember that her middle name is Morgana, who was King Arthur's sister, Morgan le Fay, or Fata Morgana, a shape-shifting enchantress, who seduced her brother, and brought down disaster.

I remember thinking at the time it was a fairly strange name to give a baby girl. It was Gwen's idea. She was a romantic.

'I'm a direct descendent of Guinevere and Lancelot, darling. Lance is such an old, old family name. We really are Knights of the Round Table people. Arthurian blood runs in the veins. I'm Gwen, which is Gwendolyn, Isolde is my daughter and her father was Caradoc, and of course Gavin is a corruption of Gawain. Isolde and you give birth to baby Arthur, so Arthur's sister really needs to be Morgana.'

'No child of mine is going to be called Morgana, even to please you, Gwen,' Gavin had said. 'I can't bear abbreviations. She will get called Morgan, or worse Morgue.'

So they settled on Isobel with an O, and Morgana for her second name. And here she was, Morgana the half-grown seductress, with her sharp blonde hair and large, slightly slanting green eyes, so like Gwen's – and I found myself thinking that I had better be nice and watch my step or something awful would happen. She'd cast a spell and one's womb would dry up. I shivered. You believe you live in a rational universe, or at least some halfway rational one of the kind my mother inhabits, even though predicated by symbols and motives and compulsions, and then you get a glimpse of some hidden undercurrent which no amount of theorising will explain away.

I'd been to Gwen's flat in South Kensington once or twice; I'd taken the children round there when they were small, to get them out of the sick-house atmosphere of home. But the doomy feeling seemed to follow us up the stairs of the bus which took us there, and then patter after us like some sinister little black dog all the way to Gwen's place, where it would curl up on the horrid, shiny, pale-green cushions of the chintz sofa, as if to say, 'You can't get away from me. I'm with you for ever.' And perhaps it was the other way round – the little black dog lived at Gwen's house and followed us home.

I'd hated the little objects that Gwen said were so valuable.

'Don't touch; don't touch, careful, it's vulgar to touch! Those are the earrings of a Roman lady, found in her grave: a very famous archeologist gave them to me: no, Isobel, leave them alone. This is a sacrificial altar from Papua New Guinea: a very rare hardwood, worth thousands; please don't clamber over it, Arthur. There may be traces of dried blood. It was a gift from an explorer I once knew.' Honestly, it was bad as that: the children were fascinated, but I would feel spooked and longed to get out of there as soon as I could.

I thought that morning that perhaps Isobel saw too much of Gwen, that Gavin should make a stand against the grandmother's influence, but at the same time I knew I wasn't going to say that to him. Having Isobel to stay with us was one thing: having her to live with us another. I didn't want her lying next to Gavin on my bed whenever it took her fancy.

I can see that it might be wiser not to get legally involved with Gavin. Marriage was probably a silly idea. Reason had to cut in at some point. We could live together. We didn't even have to live in Apple Lee, though God knows it is convenient, tens of thousands having been spent to make it fit for its purpose, a place where I can live, write and earn. And Laura would do her nut if I married. So would my mother.

I took Isobel to the bus stop. I wore my nightie and my silk Chinese wrap and no shoes. As we went up the path to the main road Isobel fell on her knees under the branches of the apple tree and said, 'Let's look at it from a toddler's point of view,' and peered up and around and said with satisfaction, 'Now it's familiar. It feels like home.' And again the smile, and again the flash of not quite affection from me to her, but understanding, and I think from her to me. But after it as a kind of visual echo, like the sound halo you used to get on transatlantic calls, came the sidewise look.

The bus came along. I waved from the gate. When it came to it I did not want to venture out into the real world without shoes. The path from the house to the gate was well swept and clean, but once you were the wrong side of it you did not know what you might tread in.

'Give Daddy my love,' said Isobel, as she got on it, and Laura arrived just in time to see her go. 'And it's okay for him to marry you. Elvira was hopeless on a horse. People can be so embarrassing.'

And I thought how easy it is for a woman to turn into the past tense and be dismissed. And so sudden...

I followed Laura back into the house.

'Who was that girl?' she asked, as she took off her smart cropped black jacket and hung it carefully on the hanger on the back of the door. I tend to throw my discarded garments on the floor or sofa or bed. I daresay this is why she always looks so smart and orderly, and I look ramshackle.

'My boyfriend's daughter,' I said. 'Her father's asleep upstairs.'

Seven words and it was done. What had I been so frightened of?

Emily's Alarm

I read extracts of Sappho's novel aloud to Barnaby.

'You don't come out of it too badly,' he said.

I was making him breakfast in my flat. Or rather he was making me scrambled eggs, with eggs he had brought himself – newly laid, organic and so forth, at twice the price I was prepared to spend. Well, if he wanted to, why not? Though they taste no different as far as I can see. An egg's an egg. A night's sleep had settled my nerves. Sappho had told me she was going to ground, so there was no need to get into such a state. Anxiety levels had sunk to around four.

'I think Sappho expected me to read it,' I said. 'She probably censored it on my account.'

'Then be glad,' he said. 'Many a child goes out of its way to hurt its parents. See most autobiographies as a case in point. Literature gives permission, truth is justification, and revenge is the real motive.'

'What I don't understand is why she went ahead with the marriage. Since she could see perfectly well what was going on in Gavin's head.'

'Why? Well, for example, I want to marry you,' Barnaby said, 'though I can see it's folly. You are a terrible cook.'

I said it would be folly to marry him since he only wanted a nurse for his old age and access to my income. He said it was also because he wanted to have Sappho for a stepdaughter. I screamed aloud with horror. The window was open to the spring sun and a passer-by looked up in alarm. I smiled at him to reassure him. He passed on.

'Only kidding,' Barnaby said, and I believed him.

We ate our eggs. They were very good. I agreed I could taste the difference, while keeping my fingers crossed. He liked his toast under-done, little more than warm bread; I liked mine crisp and brown. For once he had done the slices as I preferred. I said I wouldn't marry him but perhaps we could live together. I didn't bring up the matter of my sexual freedom, which I would insist on, because I am conscious that at my age such conversations are not seemly. But in due course the subject would have to come up. I do not mean to live without sex for the rest of my life.

Barnaby asked if there was a lesser name than stepchild for the children partners brought into the relationship, and I said not that I knew of. Such a word had not yet been coined.

'I see,' he said. 'The archetype has not yet been established.'

'You Jungians are obsessed with archetypes. It's too early in the new world order to know what such an archetype will be. Gone are the days when we could assume that when there was a new marriage the stepmother was the villain, and automatically wicked.'

'When it was all "Mirror, mirror, on the wall, who is fairest of us all?"' observed Barnaby, and I so liked him. He is a clever man, and I do love clever. Clever can be quite erotic when you are someone like me. But it's not enough.

'We will see,' I said. 'The diaries will tell us. The child of divorced or bereaved parents fights furiously against a new relationship, but tends to give up and accept if marriage occurs. We will see how Isobel behaves when Sappho marries. It could go one way or another. The ceremony might moderate or exacerbate envy and jealousy. We can be pretty sure that when partners merely drift apart, when there is no marriage, and no divorce, and no ceremony, the outlook is bleak. The child must grow bitter and indifferent as the familiar adult bed fills, as fill it will, with a changing series of uncles or aunts, and the walls of home ring to primal scene after primal scene. No wonder our estates fill up with young criminals. And who is to say what changes happen in the child when established partners give in to social pressure and marry? That too can go either way.'

'Very persuasive,' said Barnaby. 'You Freudians and your primal scene! But if we are going to move in together you will have to let me get a word in edgeways.'

Why does he automatically assume the role of the one who lays down the rules? Because, the answer is, he is a man. What am I doing with him? I ignore his impertinence.

'Poor Sappho,' I said. 'She lost her father when she was small. As Isobel did her mother. They have that in common. That no doubt is why the two of them have a feeling of mutual understanding. Death is a violent separator, but even so, for the growing child, the Grim Reaper might create less emotional turmoil than the wilful divorce of the parents.'

Barnaby did not offer to clear away – having made the eggs, he apparently felt relieved of any further domestic duty – but he did seem to understand what I was saying, and prepared to engage with it, which is more than can be said for many a man.

'People's pets die,' he remarked, 'and you never know how they will react. I see it in my patients. Sometimes they're out within minutes looking for a replacement, any rescue cat will do: sometimes they wall up the cat-flap and say never again. Yet the degree of loss is the same.'

I grow quite excited.

'Perhaps it's the same with children: the loss of the parent is like the loss of the household pet? After the mother dies Isobel – and Sappho, too, when her father goes – either wants a fresh one, a replacement, a rescue girlfriend for the father, a rescue boyfriend for the mother; or else bars the entrance to the parental bed and lets no one in. It could go one way or another. We shall see.'

We sit in the sun over the dirty dishes and I go back over what I have read. I feel bad – slightly – at using my daughter as a case history, but it's too late now to change my ways.

I am proud of my daughter and fearful for her. For she has not escaped psychosexual damage. The masochist is also the sadist. Her pleasure at the thought of Elvira standing outside the window of her beloved in miserable jealousy excites Sappho: the pleasure is overt; it turns her on. She observes it in herself.

Nor will she let Gavin know: it is the excitement of the forbidden and the excitement of sexual power that afflicts her. She will keep it to herself. The infant's narcissism grows into voyeurism, and the turn-around is exhibitionism: Sappho both stands in the street in Elvira's footsteps as voyeur, and makes the shadows in the blinds as the exhibitionist. She catches her breath: she is aroused. Soon she will actively search for the greater masochistic pleasure of emotional pain. She will punish herself. She will marry Gavin.

I offer my interpretation to Barnaby.

'Good old Freud,' says Barnaby. 'Which comes first, the chicken or the egg? Sadism or masochism? Personally I go for sadism. The emotional sadist is a popular man – he gets asked to dinner while the betrayed wife weeps at home.'

It is too old-fashioned a view. He is a dinosaur. It is all impossible.

'I get asked out enough,' I say. It is true enough. I have many admirers and always have had. Age does not wither nor custom stale my infinite variety. Or perhaps it is just that I am available? Sappho goes the other way and is far too discriminating. I wear low tops and Sappho prefers to go buttoned up.

'You are a sadistic woman,' my quasi-lover says. 'You like me to suffer.'

See? I am talking about Sappho but nothing will do but that he turns the conversation to himself. Well, this is how men are. One puts up with it, or does without them. And I do fear loneliness.

'I notice you have skipped the key scene,' says Barnaby now. 'It is too strong for you. Isobel lying on Sappho's bed, her hand locked with her father's. The significator. The master card, which represents the querent. Are you the querent or is your daughter?'

He is laughing at me, talking about Tarot cards. Like many a Jungian he reads the cards, and consults the *I Ching*. I am made of sterner, less superstitious stuff.

'Like you,' he goes on, 'Sappho is in denial. She fails to respond with outrage, only a mild irritation.'

'Isobel is not in the bed, only on it,' I say. 'Though no doubt she would like to be in it. She has seen out many a rival, including her mother, and is staking her claim. But the taboo, the innate sense of the forbidden, is too great even for her: she stays the healthy side of the sheets. There is hope for her. True, Sappho takes it comparatively calmly. But the emotions inevitably aroused – outrage, jealousy, the envy of the older woman for the younger – are too great to surface. They remain buried.'

'And no doubt,' says Barnaby, 'you have decided this is why your daughter wanders the streets, emotionally homeless? This novel was written three or four years ago. Why should it surface now?'

'The unconscious has a different clock than the conscious,' I say, complacently. 'The conscious counts in minutes, the unconscious knows no time. It can take for ever to process its findings.'

'How convenient,' says Barnaby. 'And how about you? The inevitable envy of the older woman for the younger? Why do you wander through my life, emotionally homeless, causing pain?'

'I think it's time you went,' I snap. I hate the way he twists things. In any decent relationship we would have been in bed as soon as the scrambled eggs were finished, having sex.

'Do you think I should find out about Viagra?' he asks. He reads my mind. I wish he wouldn't. But it's true, without sex the relationship between man and woman is hard to sustain. It's hard enough even with it.

'Viagra's out of date,' I say. 'There are new improved drugs on the market.'

'Trust you to know,' he says, bitterly.

Now he is sulking: his development, on current form, stopped when he was about eight years old. His chin sticks out, mutinously.

He grows red in the face; a vein pulses in his forehead. He will have a stroke if he doesn't calm down.

'Can we get back to Sappho?' I ask. 'I am on to something here. Don't you think it's revealing that on encountering Isobel she begins to think about marriage for the first time, and then moves on to babies? The unconscious has the self's psyche at heart, just not its practical concerns. What does the unconscious care about iPods, private health insurance, six weeks' holiday per annum? Not a jot. It simply comes up with archetypes, white weddings, cradles and yummy mummies – there's a new one – and throws them at her.'

'You are ingenious,' admits Barnaby, 'and probably right.'

He has calmed down, given in. As for me, I can see I was tactless. He had just come round to admitting that he suffered from sexual dysfunction, and I had pre-empted him by suggesting Cialis. I really will start grinding the stuff and putting it in his goodnight hot chocolate. Cialis is one up on Viagra. It can work within the half-hour and lasts for days.

Sappho's Novel Continues...

'Isn't it rather late to have a man in your bed?' enquires Laura. 'It's almost nine and a week day. You have deadlines to meet and any halfway decent man would be on his way to work by now.' She's half joking but only half.

'It's my bed,' Sappho says, 'and my life.' And she is not joking. Laura raises her shaggy eyebrows in surprise. The faster she plucks them the faster they grow. 'Don't tell me we're talking something permanent,' she says.

'May well be,' says Sappho.

I don't want to speak from out of my own mouth any more, my own sensibility. I am going to be an impartial observer of myself. My first-person encounter with Isobel exhausted me emotionally. Back to the third person.

'I knew something was going on,' says Laura. 'You're behind in your work. You told me you could finish the first act of *I Liked It Here* by today, and I don't see it on my desk. You have to deliver by the end of September.'

'I need to spend more time on it.'

'Don't tell me he spent the whole weekend.'

'He did.'

'Tell me the worst. Who is it?'

'It's Gavin Garner,' Sappho said. There was a short silence.

'But he's Methuselah,' said Laura. 'You could have anyone. Was that his daughter?'

'Yes. I've known her since she was a baby.'

'Her mother died,' said Laura. 'I remember all that. I read his column. My God, Sappho, what are you getting into? And you've been going through the emails again. I wish you wouldn't. I can't tell what's been opened and what hasn't. And you look shagged out.'

That is not true, thought Sappho. I look really good. Everyone tells me so. Glowing.

'Do you want coffee?' asked Laura.

'No coffee. There's some Oolong tea, though.'

'Oh dear, so habits are already changing. I can see this is serious.'

'It is,' said Sappho, in such a tone of voice that Laura changed tack. She set the computer to defragment while she went to the kitchen. Time management was her finest skill.

'So what's going wrong with *I Liked It Here?*' Laura asked. 'It seemed to be flowing along very nicely.'

'That's the trouble,' said Sappho. 'It's too easy. It's surface stuff. It's not serious.'

'Gavin Garner gave you a bad review in one of the Sundays,' observed Laura. 'He said beneath the gritty realism lay a profound ignorance. Something like that. What's going on?'

'He may have been right,' said Sappho. 'Bear that in mind. Gritty realism may not be my forte. You have to agree it is not exactly in my life experience.'

'Your profound ignorance earned you a lot of money,' said Laura. 'And that's all I'm going to say on the matter.'

She clip-clopped into the kitchen, and Sappho heard her utter a faint scream. Sappho ran to see what the matter was. It was Gavin, naked, making himself tea. He stared at Laura enquiringly, making no attempt to cover himself up. He looked good naked: late forties he may have been, but he was lean, hairy and broad-shouldered. Well-hung, too.

'And you are?' he enquired. And then: 'I know. You must be Laura the secretary—'

'P.A.,' corrected Laura, and fled back into the office and thence to her typist's stool.

'Gavin "Flasher" Garner,' was all she said. 'Sappho, what is the matter with you?'

'Gavin,' said Sappho, 'you have to make an attempt to get on with Laura.'

'Why?' he asked.

'Because this business enterprise of mine requires her.'

'But you're not a business enterprise,' he said. 'It suits Laura to persuade you that you are. You are a writer. Come back to bed.'

'I ought to be going through the emails with Laura,' she said, but she went.

I am falling into the bad habits of the playwright not the novelist: it is all dialogue. I must work harder at cultivating the prose passage.

'Sappho,' said Gavin, 'will you marry me?'

Sappho appeared to think about it a little, though she had been rehearsing her answer for some time. Which was: 'Perhaps not marriage, not yet, but we could move in together.'

They were at Gavin's place when he asked, and she was in the bath. She found it hard lying in bed at Apple Lee waiting for Laura to arrive. Gavin did not get up until nine-thirty and Laura came in at eight forty-five. She liked to lie in bed with Gavin; even though there was not always sex there was the pleasure of the warm, lean body next to hers. She felt she was making up for lost time; she had wasted so many years man-less. So if they had been to the theatre or to dinner it made sense to stop off at Gavin's place, and lie in late, though then she would still have to face Laura's cool, impassive face later in the morning. Laura no longer raised her eyebrows: she had grown prudent. She was formal, and distantly polite, but worked as efficiently as ever.

Nor could Sappho afford to talk to Gavin about it, for fear he would simply say, at best, 'Sappho, she is an employee. And you are an artist, not an office worker.' Or, at worst, 'It is absurd to have someone working for you that you are frightened of. Fire her.'

Instead she told Gavin she liked it round at his place; it was all male and Apple Lee was all female, and she liked the mattress and she liked the bath, because there was somewhere sensible to keep the soap and a glass of champagne, even though the plaster on the ceiling was cracking where the tenant upstairs had once left a tap running. And the comparative narrowness of his bed pleased her; and the books which were everywhere, books on theatre history and the fall of empires, and the usages and development of languages, compared to which her place was hopelessly bourgeois and un-intellectual. It had ruched green silk curtains everywhere and was carpeted, which she could see now was a mistake; even her mother had raised her eyebrows. But Laura said carpets damped noise and saved heating bills, and had been so excited about the curtains Sappho had quelled her own misgivings. It looked pretty and expensive but it wasn't *her*. 'She liked the house,' Sappho had said, of Isobel's visit, and Gavin had said, 'Well she would, wouldn't she. She's eleven.' Which pretty much summed it up.

When Gavin asked Sappho to marry him her heart soared. She felt it physically. A lightness in her chest, a weight removed. It was as if all the elements of her life and nature came together and made sense. Her own answer sounded petty and boring. She stepped out of the bath and he watched her dry herself, enchanted.

'I am so lucky,' he said, 'to have found someone like you. You are the most beautiful woman in the world.' She thought he had accepted her verdict, that she was in charge of the relationship.

'Elvira had longer legs,' she observed. She hadn't mentioned Elvira before. He looked astonished.

'Elvira?' he enquired. 'What has Elvira to do with anything? I didn't love her.' Which somehow settled that.

But a little later he said, 'I would rather we were married. I would feel more secure. You're younger than me; I don't want you running off.'

'Why would I run off? Why would I want to? It's taken me long enough to find you. And I daresay you would keep an eye on me.'

'Then why did you mention Elvira? You wouldn't have if the possibility of other partners had not come to mind.'

'My God,' Sappho said, 'I am not shacking up with my father, I am shacking up with my mother!'

But he did not laugh. He seemed pained.

'I only mean because my mother is always looking for hidden meanings,' she said, but he wasn't listening, he was too angry, and her voice faltered and she fell quiet.

'Shacking up!' he said, eventually. 'So that's how you see it? It means so little to you? I am real, you know, not some kind of fantasy. I can't bring indignity on my children, on me, on you. Shacking up! We are serious people, Sappho, you and me. You love me or you don't. You marry me or you don't.'

He called a taxi for her and said he would go straight to the office. He left before the taxi came, and the firm called to say there would be a twenty-minute delay. Sappho looked for Isolde's portrait. She found it in the broom cupboard, but hung on the wall, so that when you opened the door Isolde looked straight at you. Isolde was to Sappho mentor, oracle, mother, wise woman. She had taught Sappho everything she knew, including how to be married to Gavin. She had died painfully and publicly and over a long time, and Sappho had betrayed her, abandoned her on her deathbed to die alone. Isolde had made Sappho rich through the play *Ms Alien*, the roots of which had been in Isolde's brain, not Sappho's. It had been Sappho's inheritance but Sappho could not tell anyone.

Sappho knew that whatever happened she could not leave

Isolde in the broom cupboard. Gavin had left the hooks for the painting on the wall, from whence he had removed it after Sappho's first night at his place. Sappho took Isolde from the cupboard and hung her once again above Gavin's bed, standing on the bed to do so. A rocky ride. She dusted the frame and settled the painting in. She did not care when specks and even flakes of grime just fell and lay on Gavin's bed. 'That's where you belong, Isolde,' she said, and Isolde seemed satisfied.

The doorbell buzzed and Sappho went home to Apple Lee.

Emily Is Outraged

'Can't she see he's manipulating her? What's the matter with her? He means to marry her, probably for her money. His lease is running out. He needs somewhere to go. He wants to get his children away from his mother-in-law. The way he thinks he'll get my rich, successful, lovely daughter as a bride, and thus solve all his problems, is to trump up some phoney indignation. He's made her feel bad, cheap and insecure because she uses the wrong word. Then he knows she'll come running after him. It's emotional blackmail; he's nothing but a mind-fucker and a con man.'

'Calm down, Emily,' says Barnaby. 'You're paranoiac. He's a romantic. I'd be upset if I loved a girl and she talked about shacking up when I'd proposed marriage. She needs someone steady. He's eminently suitable and she likes him sexually. You just don't want your daughter slipping out of your control. You might even be jealous.'

'Um,' I say, and calm down as Barnaby suggests. I can see he may be right. The well-hung bit did rather get to me. And I found myself sympathising with Laura, who, like me, feared losing her influence over my daughter. Sappho, in my head, had turned suddenly into 'my daughter'. I would have to watch myself.

'She should have dusted the painting before hanging it,' I said. 'Never was there such a domestically incompetent girl.'

'I wonder where she gets that from,' said Barnaby. He had a measuring tape out and was measuring the floor, to work out where the spiral staircase would go, the staircase which in his mind would join our pads and our lives. Let him speculate: I would never allow it.

'It makes painful reading,' I said. 'I brought her up badly.'

'Then stop reading,' he says. He is so sensible, and so male. He has made an appointment to see the doctor, though I say he should just buy potency from the Internet.

'Children grow up into what they were born to be,' he says. 'You have to work very hard at it to distort them. Beat them, seduce them, or bully them and you can hamper their chances and turn them neurotic, but by and large they grow up in spite of their parents' best endeavours.'

'A very comforting and, if I may say so very Jungian vision,' I say. 'Recipe for a guilt-free life.'

'So what is your source of guilt today?' he asks.

'It was around that time Sappho came to visit and asked how partnership as opposed to marriage affected the children, and I said badly.'

'All that primal scene stuff?'

'Yes,' I said. 'I didn't know at the time that she was seeing Gavin. That was before Laura told me.'

'And if you had known your advice would be different?'

'Yes,' I said.

'Women have no scruples,' he said.

I went on reading, while he went on scuffling about the floor with his tape measure. I didn't react even when he said,

'By the way, I'm thinking of taking the girl upstairs as a patient. She has nightmares. She was screaming in the middle of the night and I had to go upstairs and knock on her door.'

All I said was uh-huh. I didn't believe him.

Sappho's Novel Continues...

When Sappho got back Laura was at her computer. She did not remark upon Sappho's lateness – she was playing it cool – other than to say that the BBC had rung and someone in the Drama Department wanted a proposal for a series set in the inner city. She had arranged for Sappho to go in and see them and written it in the diary.

'Hang on a moment,' Sappho said. 'I think the answer to that one is no. I've done too much TV lately. I don't want to get known as a TV writer.'

'It's good money,' said Laura. 'Until you deliver *I Liked It Here* we're living on residuals. How is that going? They called up this morning to enquire.'

'They can't hurry it. It comes in its own time,' Sappho said.

Laura raised her eyebrows.

'I've never heard you say that before,' she said.

'Simply, I am not a hack,' said Sappho. 'I am not a work-horse.'

'Good Lord,' said Laura. 'Next time you'll be claiming to be a great literary figure.'

'Actually, Laura, I am,' said Sappho and went to her bedroom and sat on the four-poster bed, where Maria the Philippina help had just changed the linen. The bed looked fresh, wide and inviting. She could see the advantage of living here rather than with Isolde's portrait. She would need to get the children away from Gwen's influence.

She watched a robin settle on the apple tree branch that now rubbed against the glass of the master bedroom. So a branch had rubbed against her window when she was a child. The tree had been lopped a couple of years back and now spread outwards as much as upwards, reaching this room as well as what was now the spare room. There was change, progress, improvement. The bird put its head on one side enquiringly. Sappho thought it was some kind of sign. She had to answer a question. She thought she would ring her mother and tell her she had re-met Gavin Garner and was thinking of getting married and see what the reaction was. And then she thought perhaps she wouldn't.

Sappho rang her agent Luke. Luke was young, theatrical and gay.

'Luke,' asked Sappho, 'what are your views on my getting married?'

'Bury yourself in the hetero ghetto, darling?' said Luke. 'If you don't mind I'm sure I don't. But am I going to get asked to the wedding?'

'Of course,' said Sappho. She could see the advantage of a wedding. She could ask all the people she owed hospitality to and do them all in one day. Laura would arrange it. Laura so loved doing things well she would surely overlook the arrival of Gavin as a long-term addition to Sappho' s life and just get on with the job in hand. Meanwhile she, Sappho, spurred on by the thought of the occasion, would concentrate on her work and finally get *I Liked It Here* finished. Her failure to do so was beginning to weigh heavily on her mind. She was wasting too much time daydreaming, or taking a taxi down to Selfridges to buy sexy underwear – they had a good department, much frequented by Russian tarts – or going in to town to have a coffee and grappa with Gavin, who was always most intrigued by her desire to 'get back and get on'.

'You've got to be here now just a little,' he would say. 'You have to have a life as well,' and she was only too eager to believe him. He took life at a more leisurely pace than Sappho, which was all very well but somehow the pages did have to be covered with words.

'By the way, Sappho,' said Luke, which was what he always said when he got to the crux of a conversation, 'the Vanbrugh Theatre people rang to see how *I Liked It Here* was getting along. They expect delivery in June.'

'But June is when I'm getting married,' said Sappho. 'They may have to wait a little.'

'We don't want to interfere with their production schedule, do we?' said Luke. 'And I hear the BBC have called about a TV series, lucky old you.'

'I don't write TV plays,' said Sappho. 'I'm a stage writer.'

'Darling,' said Luke, kindly, 'we are whatever people pay us to be. How long since *Ms Alien* swept the boards? Seven years? A girl has to prove herself again and again, if she wants to get on. And the more I think about it perhaps I do prefer my clients unmarried.'

'Why is that?' enquired Sappho.

'Because husbands get all kinds of ideas in their heads, that they are married to geniuses, that kind of thing, so it doesn't matter about delivery dates and money flows in an unending stream, and then they begin to think who needs an agent anyway? Hubby can take the job on and save fifteen per cent and then no one ever hears of the writer again.'

'I hear you, Luke,' said Sappho. 'See you at the wedding.'

Sappho rang round a few friends. Belinda whom she'd known at school, who'd married an older man with a stepson, and was now thinking of running off with the stepson, and Polly, from drama school, who had a young son by a sperm bank donor. Belinda advised against marrying an older man for sexual reasons – experience and finesse were no match for energy – and Polly said she was insane to want to marry anyone at all. If she ended up doing it, Belinda said, she should sleep separately: too much physical proximity sapped individual will and thought. Belinda's married friends tiptoed round their husbands, working out ways of not upsetting them: it was demeaning and pointless. Since all women had to work anyway, there was no point in it. Once it had been a contract: legalised slavery. The woman provided sexual, childcare and domestic services in exchange for her keep. Keep was no longer provided or indeed expected; on the contrary these days many a wife earned more than her husband. So what was marriage all about?

'I just don't want him to get away,' said Sappho.

'Women are mad,' said Polly. 'Thank God my child is a boy.'

Sappho decided not to phone her mother for advice but to send her an invitation through the post, as if casually. She went downstairs, consulted her diary, found a window towards the end of June, and told Laura to book the register office and organise a party and be sure to remember all the people to whom she owed hospitality. Laura sat at her desk with her eyes closed for some minutes, but then decided, doing a quick profit and loss calculation in her mind no doubt, that her best interests lay in remaining at her post, opened her eyes, gave a pained smile which involved pulling back her rather thin lips and said, 'Very well. The register office won't open until ten o'clock but I'll be on to them as soon as possible. I will need full details about the person you are marrying: the sight of a passport would be useful. Do remember the legal implications.'

Emily Agitates

Sappho had been like this as a child. If anyone advised her not to do something she would do it just to see what happened. At least she'd changed her mind and had the courtesy to let me know about the wedding before the invitation arrived by post. As mother of the bride I should have no doubt paid for it, but what with? We had quickly all got used to a situation in which Sappho paid for everything out of the proceeds of *Ms Alien*. I was still offering formal three- or four-times-a-week psychoanalytic therapy when others had long gone over to better-paid short-term Jungian fixes, and patients were no longer so thick on the ground. In its time Apple Lee had swallowed up any surplus funds I had acquired in the days when Freud was God and fashionable amongst the moneyed classes. Fortunately Sappho said, 'Just send all invoices to Laura and she will organise money.' So that's what I did.

I was musing on these things when the telephone rang and I leapt to answer it. I knew before I picked it up it would be my lost and pregnant Sappho.

'Where are you?' I asked. 'I've been so worried!'

'I'm sorry,' she said. 'I just couldn't cope with anything more for a bit.'

I asked if she was back at home, and she said no. I asked her if the baby was okay and she said yes, she had been for a check-up the day before. I asked her if it was true Laura had been fired and she said she didn't know but she wouldn't be surprised. I asked her why and she said because of certain things that had happened and she wasn't going to tell me now, but later. Matters had to be allowed to settle. She just needed to be alone for a little longer but she was okay. I told her Gavin had been round to try and find out where she was and she said she hoped I had not told him and I said no, how could I, since I didn't know where she was.

'But if you'd known would you have told?' she asked.

'Of course not,' I said.

She laughed and I was happy to hear it. She sounded quite in control and cheerful. She said she was glad I was still on her side, and I said I was sorry it had come to sides, and she said,

'Oh well, at least we can all stop playing happy marriages now. You can be as critical a mother-in-law as you like.'

I said I had never had anything against Gavin but his age. My experience of ailing marriages is that they suddenly leap back together again and everyone is forgiven except you, for having said in effect, and too early, good riddance to bad rubbish. In truth, I had lots of things against Gavin. Aside from my paranoia about his motives he had presided over the loss of my daughter's literary reputation, interrupted the flow of her financial success, cut her off from her friends, made her feel second-best to his children and so on and so on, but I had kept my mouth shut and would continue to do so until I had sight of her divorce certificate, and the absolute not the nisi. You can't be blamed for age, so my mentioning it could be the more easily excused.

'I'll be in touch in a day or two,' she said. 'In the meanwhile look after the diaries. And on no account read them.'

'Of course not,' I said. 'Are you trying to keep them from getting into the hands of anyone in particular?'

'Isobel, for one,' she said. 'Not to mention Gavin.' She rang off.

I went upstairs to Barnaby to tell him Sappho had been in touch, let myself in without knocking and found him sitting in the sun in the window just as he had with me earlier in the day, in conversation with Ursula the aromatherapist. I was so disconcerted I went downstairs again without telling him my news. I can't tax him with it: I know he is only trying to make me jealous. The trouble is, he is succeeding.

I go back to the novel and try to concentrate. It's hard. A few paragraphs in and Gavin ensures himself a good wife and a mother to his children by means which suddenly feel alarmingly familiar. No Freud or Jung is required to work it out.

Sappho's Novel Continues...

Sappho called Gavin at his work and asked to be put through to him. She had not visited him there but the receptionist recognised her voice.

'Is that really *the* Sappho Stubb-Palmer?' she asked. Sappho replied 'probably', as was her habit when a member of the public she did not know, but who apparently knew her, offered such a greeting. She felt it was unsafe to claim too much certainty in her own identity, and besides, there might be others. It was flattering to be known to strangers, but made her uneasy, as if she were being found out.

'I went to listen to you at the ICA a few weeks back,' the other woman told her. 'You were the best thing on that panel. I've been following your career ever since *Ms Alien*. How do you know so much about being a woman?'

'I daresay because I am one,' said Sappho civilly.

'Well, yes that's true, I suppose,' said the other, but sounded disappointed, as if that were not the required answer, and put her through.

'Gavin,' said Sappho, 'I'm sorry about this morning. I should not have said shacking up. It was insulting. You are quite right: it is marriage or nothing.'

There was silence the other end.

'Shall we have lunch,' said Sappho, 'or I could come by for an espresso and grappa? I haven't ever been to your office and the receptionist will give me a friendly welcome. She's heard of me.'

'All kinds of people have heard of you,' said Gavin. 'I am well aware of that. Very few have heard of me.'

'Anyone who knows anything about the theatre knows of you,' said Sappho. There was a kind of chilly feeling running up from her toes to her heart. She was not sure what to attribute it to. She realised she was barefoot and was standing on a cold marble floor. But it was a different kind of cold: her body was reacting before her mind did, that was all. He did not want her to come to his office: he probably did not want to marry her. It had been an affair; it was over; she had played it all wrong: she did not know how to behave with men: she never would. She had told Laura and now she would have to un-tell Laura and Laura would hide her smirk. Thank heavens she had said nothing to her mother. The cold had turned into a sort of lukewarm numbness. You should not make forays into irrationality. You should not say things like 'shacking up' because life was too serious.

'Lunch would be great,' he said, 'only you told me you were working so I've arranged to meet someone else.'

'Anyone interesting?' Sappho asked, as casually as she could. All might not yet be lost.

'Elvira,' he said, 'as it happens. She's upset and I thought I could calm her down. Don't read anything into it. She's written a piece for the magazine.'

'I didn't realise she was a writer,' Sappho said. 'I thought she was a theatrical dress-designer.'

'Leave out the dress,' said Gavin. 'And you've got it. I'm surprised you haven't met up with her, but I suppose you're the other end of the market.'

'What does that mean?' Sappho asked, bridling, and he laughed and had lost the coldness.

She felt her heart beating and knew she was at least alive.

'She mostly does Restoration,' said Gavin, 'and you do contemporary grit. Put it another way. She earns peanuts and you earn Brazils, theatre today being what it is. Alas, there tends to be a negative correlation between success and finesse.'

'So what's the article?' I pretended an interest.

'Kierkegaard and popular theatre,' he said. Well, I have better legs than hers and know better than to stand outside rivals' homes all night, weeping. I wouldn't dream of getting on a horse if I didn't look good on one. I have Isobel as an ally. Isobel preferred Sappho to Elvira. Like daughter, like father.

'I'll come round tonight at seven and let you know how it went,' he said. 'And we'll discuss the pros and cons of marriage. After all, there's no hurry.'

But there was, suddenly. If I had been playing with love before, now it was real.

This is beginning to sound like a romance novel. I've gone back into the first person present. Look at love from the outside and it's absurd.

Seven o'clock comes. I am wearing a white dress I bought in a charity shop. It's not something Laura would like. Laura thinks I look good in firm, solid fabrics so I look as if I know what I'm doing. As if. This dress is pale and thin and my nipples show through, and if I watch myself wearing it in the long mirror in the bedroom I quite fall in love with myself. The gesture of my own arm as it rises to push my hair back behind my ear enchants me. Is this me? This object of desire and pleasure? Yes, it is. The fine muslin is gathered in at the waist by a very expensive thin gold belt I bought at Bergdorf's on 5th Avenue. My name was up in lights on the famous Times Square hoarding for *Ms Alien*. I thought I could do anything – except perhaps find true love. I might be up again in lights if only I could finish *I Liked It Here*. I fall back on the bed and my breath comes in short gasps. I am sexually aroused by myself. I put up with it. Other women keep vibrators but I am too proud. I love my feet. They're thin, the skin very white, not a sign of a chilblain or corn, the toenails recently pedicured, shiny scarlet full stops at the tip of each of them, marking where I end and the white bedspread begins. It is a marvel, I think, how we are so neatly encased in our perfect skins, so much beating and throbbing and pulsing inside, such a web of bloody interconnections and electrical excitations, the whole at our worst so hideous and at our best so beautiful, I am quite in awe of myself. And I will join in carnal intercourse with Gavin, and a bit of him and a bit of me will produce another being entirely – how do we come to be here? What is going on? Why did Isolde have to die, in ugliness and pain, in front of us? That this should happen?

If it were not for the painting of Isolde that I rescued from the broom cupboard, if it were not for the physical actuality of Arthur and Isobel, I could believe she had never existed; that she had less reality than any of the characters I had ever written. I put her out of my mind. That was the time before this: it didn't count. The past was another country.

It was ten past seven and where was Gavin? He was usually as punctual as I was always late. Suppose the lunch had gone on and on, supposing she had lured him back into her flat to discuss Kierkegaard? Supposing he valued her mind more than my body? I had a mind too but it failed at Kierkegaard. Was this a great loss in me? I open the bottle of wine. I am not a great drinker. I have seen what it did to my mother. She succumbed to self-pity after the first glass of wine. But I could see that it numbed pain and limited oppression.

Seven-twenty. No Gavin. No phone call. I test the line to see if it's working. It is. I close the curtains. The phone rings. It is not Gavin, but Belinda. I get her off the line as soon as I can.

I think this is pathetic. I call Polly who lives in Soho five minutes by taxi from Gavin's flat. I ask her to go round and see if the lights are on.

'This is terrible, Sappho,' she says, but she goes to look, and reports back: they are off. The windows are dark. I say I am going to ring the hospitals.

'Sappho,' she says, as people speak to madwomen. 'Gavin Garner is three-quarters of an hour late. How long have you known him?'

'All my life,' I say, and I feel it is true.

I call Luke on his out-of-hours line and ask if he knows the name of a theatrical designer called Elvira, who is a whiz at Restoration theatre and writes essays on Kierkegaard, and he says, 'You mean Elvira Woolsey. Not my scene, darling, but she's on my contacts screen. She's on everyone's. She delivers on time and doesn't mess up other people's production schedules.'

'She's not a writer,' I say. 'She interprets, she doesn't create. It's easy for her.'

He snorts but he gives me her number.

An hour late. I call the number. A voice which fitted someone who was in theatre and in academia, somehow strangled, says hello. It is she. I adopt a child's voice.

'Elvira?' I say. 'This is Isobel. Do you have Daddy with you?'

A moment's silence.

'Isobel? You sound peculiar.'

'I've got a cold and I've been crying.' The latter is true enough.

'Darling, you know I haven't,' she says. 'Your daddy isn't with me any more.'

I put down the phone. I hope my deceit will not catch up with me. I am also immensely proud of myself.

At eight-twenty the phone rings. It is Gavin.

'Where are you?' I say. I am without my usual cool. It is Gavin the stern censor who replies, not the lover with the longest and most attentive dick in the world.

'It's nice that you're so possessive, but a little surprising.'

'You're one hour and a half late.'

'Darling, I said I'd be there at eight. It's twenty-past and I'm ringing you.'

'You said seven,' I say, but perhaps I'm wrong? I do not pursue the matter. The agony is over; it is wonderful. He says he will have to call dinner off. Isobel was poorly and asking for him, and now he is at his mother-in-law's.

'Ex-mother-in-law,' I say.

'I don't think so, technically,' he says, rather shortly. 'I am widowed, not divorced. Don't you want to know how Isobel is?'

I say of course I do, crossing my fingers. I am ashamed of myself but I care for nothing at that moment but myself and him. Later on I will have space for his children.

'I went by home,' he says, 'and I saw you'd put Isolde's portrait back. That was very nice of you.'

'She is part of your past,' I say. 'I don't want to deny it.'

'Our past,' he says, and it seems to me some hurdle had been passed, and I am reassured, just missing him. He says Isobel has a migraine, she is very nervy and prone to them – not like Arthur who hasn't a nerve in his body and is off at boarding school being captain of rugby, and I suggest Gavin comes over to me when Isobel is settled. He says no, he'd better spend the night over there with her; she is prone to nightmares and might wake and need him.

'She has her grandmother,' I almost say. 'Surely she can cope?' But I know better by now than to say it aloud. I hear Isobel's little voice calling him and he says he must go.

He puts down the phone saying he will see me tomorrow. There is nothing I can do. I take off the dress and decide I hate it. I try to tear it to bits but the fabric is amazingly resilient so I roll it into a ball and put it in the kitchen waste. I cut the belt to bits with poultry scissors. That's satisfactory. The gold is only veneer. I paid too much for it anyway. It's early. I could go round and have supper with my mother but I'll have to shut up about Gavin and I can't do that. I try writing some *I Liked It Here* but it doesn't seem to be about very much. I take three Temazepams and go to bed and cry myself to sleep in a languorous not wholly unpleasant way. I wonder if my mother is right and I am a masochist. It is such a sensuous pleasure.

At five in the morning someone creeps into my bed. It is Gavin. He has climbed in through the bedroom window without setting off the alarms. I have naturally forgotten to set the system for the night, or the police would have been here by now. He says I need someone to look after me, that Laura alone is not enough. I believe him. He says we will be married, and he will set the alarms every night and never forget.

I say we will sell the house and go and live in the country because it is better to start afresh in a new house, and him not to move into one already established by me, carpeted and painted not to his taste at all.

'Carpets are easily taken up,' he says, 'and walls re-painted. I can do it myself. We don't want workmen cluttering up the place.'

He says he is a city person and so am I, and how would I live without Laura? How could I function work-wise? I say she would follow me to the ends of the earth and he says don't be too sure, you can never be sure of anyone. He says his flat is obviously too small for us both and the children, and Apple Lee is on a direct bus route to Isobel's school and is my family home anyway and it would upset my mother if I left it. I can see it would. I am drowsy with sleeping pills and post-coital pleasure. He says he is an old-fashioned man and the fact that I earn more than him, much more, will upset the natural balance of things, and I laugh and say I am indeed marrying my mother because she is the only other person I know who believes there is such a thing as a natural order. When we get married I will give him half the house and that will make him feel more in charge and he says no, he doesn't want that, it would make him feel like a kept man.

Then we have to worry about Gwen.

'Won't she be upset and lonely if the children come to us?' I ask. 'Perhaps it should be done gradually? They could come to us for weekends and holidays, and later on full-time?'

It is true I would like time with Gavin on my own. I will be mother to his children and a good one but isn't there a space in most marriages before the children come along? Isn't this the natural order of things? But Gavin says Isobel's school is on the bus route and the stop is just outside the door and if Gavin and I are married and he is in Apple Lee it would be hurtful to her not to be with him. Which I can see makes sense.

Besides, he says, he reckons Gwen is pretty much fed up with the kids, and her back isn't good, and if they go she can at last bring out all the breakables, and there will be general rejoicing. A win–win situation.

'I am not sure of this,' I say. 'I wasn't exactly a cause for rejoicing last time round.' And he frowns and blinks and I know it is still a subject we don't go near. He knows rationally I was once the au pair, and Gwen threw me out, or I left, even I can't be sure which way round it was. Sometimes when Isolde's name comes up in theatre talk, as it still does, I remember the feeling tone and my mind says 'just don't go there', so I don't. And I still feel bad about not having gone to her funeral, and marvel at how your bad deeds come back to haunt you, but also somehow that none of it ever happened. If you do not go to a funeral you can't be really sure the person is dead; it becomes a kind of theory not a fact that they're dead, brown bread. It must be the trauma of Isolde's death that makes Gavin – and me too, for that matter – somehow blot all that past stuff out. He wants our life together to have begun when we re-met at the party and I want that too.

He agrees that the transition for the children should be done gradually. There is a bargaining quality about our conversations: 'If you don't bring up this I will concede that.' It intrigues me. It is the only way in which he seems to belong to another generation. It's as if good manners are more likely to save us in the end, rather than truths faced and bluntly told. I like it.

Gavin observes that the real problem is if he stops paying Gwen to look after them she's going to be in dire straits because from next year she has to pay market rent for her flat. I say we can look after that; we can afford it easily enough. If Arthur stops being a boarder and lives at home, we'll be saving school fees anyway. I say all this money talk is boring and unromantic and we stop and concentrate on each other.

I don't get up until ten and Laura is already well at her desk.

'Wedding still on?' she asks.

'Of course,' I say.

'That's good,' she says, 'you're booked in at Judd Street, Camden register office, on the twenty-sixth of June at four p.m. Party afterwards at Groucho's. Are you going to still want me to work for you?'

'Of course,' I say.

'Okay,' she says. 'We'll have to get these invitations out fast.'
She looks quite friendly. There will be peace.
'*Do you, Sappho, take this man Gavin Garner to be your lawful, wedded husband?*'
'*I do.*'
Done!

Emily's Epiphany

Men are such manipulators. When Barnaby drops by I know he expects to find me dolled up and sweet, and in competition with Ursula the aromatherapist. But I will not be. He can go to hell.

As I put the sheaf of papers which represent part one of Sappho's novel back into the Waitrose bag a few loose sheets fall out. I read them.

'What stepdaughters require from their stepmothers is that they will simply vanish, deliquesce. Melt into a pool of brackish water, which the wind of time will pretty soon evaporate. Soon stepmother will be altogether forgotten, her nightdress removed from the peg on the back of the bedroom door. Some girls can be like this about their natural mothers, first wife though they be, so what chance does the second wife have?'

'Daddy is mine, mine, all mine!' the girl child cries: she is primitive, all-devouring. She will gobble up Father's latest squeeze if she has to, just to get rid of her.

These pages are undated. Her writing is getting fancier. The sheets are comparatively crisp and new. It is recent stuff: oh dear. Trouble is certainly brewing. It's always gratifying to be right but that does not compensate for the concern one feels for the participants. Especially if they're family, and I am not like Gwen, I do count Isobel. If I go now I can meet her out of school and buy her a coffee or an alcopop or whatever fifteen-year-olds have these days and see what's going on.

Isobel went to the same school I had gone to myself. Indeed, my name was engraved in gold on the honour boards in the assembly hall inside: Oxford Exhibitioner, 1959, way back in the past.

I don't know how I have come to be so old. One day, her father hoped, and her exam results predicted, Isobel too would be upon the board. I stood at the gate. It was four o'clock.

A bell rang inside the school and a few girls came drifting out. The uniform was the same as I had worn but more loosely interpreted. Navy and scarlet – a kind of mediaeval pleated cardinal's cap, navy skirts, red blouse and whatever leg and footwear came into your head, other than high heels were not allowed. But it is amazing the effect, then as now, you can achieve by simply sawing off heels. A girl can look as if a simple push would land her on her back on a bed.

Another clutch of girls came out, amongst them Isobel. She looked crisp, smart and clean, unusual amongst her companions, who favoured greasy hair, holes in thick stockings and the druggy look. Isobel, it occurred to me, had her grandmother's gift for exuding the kind of batty propriety which I had observed in other high-class call-girls. I quelled the thought. It was unkind.

I hadn't seen her for a month or so. She was looking really good. The menarche had come late because of her low body weight – but now it finally had, and her system was alive with oestrogen. She had raced into a glowing sexual maturity, and was as translucently pretty as only a fifteen-year-old can be, not so long out of latency that the innocence of youth has been lost, not so old that paedophiles have lost interest. She made the most of it: her Alice in Wonderland hair was now long, smooth and shiny. She was, I suppose, borderline anorexic. Certainly Sappho spent a lot of time trying to feed her up. She was long-legged, with a waist little more than a hand's-span, large green eyes beneath a perfect thin arch of eyebrow, and now, most strikingly, a plump, full-lipped, sensuous red mouth, which seemed all too adult. She had a sweet, but slightly mirthful look as if she found the world amusing. That came from Isolde. Like her mother, she too was queen of all around. The others crowded round, admiring and flattering. Heaven alone knew how she managed it. She was early Britney Spears in an Amy Winehouse world. Most girls who tried it would be excoriated, but Isobel was worshipped.

They had gathered on the pavement outside the school. They were waiting for the bus. 'Isobel!' I called. She turned slowly. Her face didn't exactly light up, but she looked quite excited, as people do when they have news to impart.

'It's my other gran,' she told her friends. 'The one who's on the board in the school hall, the exhibitionist. Not the real one who modelled for Parkinson.'

She knew perfectly well what an Exhibitioner was, but never mind. She had had a hard time. It is not nice to lose your mother, think you finally have your father to yourself, and then have him marry what amounted to the au pair. Not surprising if she acted out a bit.

'I'm looking for your mother,' I said.

'My mother's dead,' she said, and gave a sigh. Those around looked at one another, at Isobel, at me, and then as if at a signal all embraced one another and sobbed. I thought they were play acting but could not be sure. This new generation of girls are great ones for physical contact. Always hugging each other, and laughing and weeping on each other's shoulders. One never knows whether they are being sincere or satirical or posing for the media. Sometimes they are doing all at once. Their new language marks them out as different from their predecessors, who saw themselves from the inside out. This lot see themselves from the outside in; they are observers of their own lives, with their 'and I was like: gross!' turn of phrase.

'I mean your new mother, Sappho,' I said.

'She not a new mother,' said Isobel, 'she's a step. It all gets so complicated. Briony here has three stepmothers,' she went on, 'four stepfathers, two siblings and nine half-siblings. Last Christmas she had seven Christmas dinners in two days. Didn't you, Briony? Now she's bulimic.'

'These days they call us gift-children,' said the girl called Briony. She had hollow cheeks and eyebrow rings. I was sure the school didn't allow them. She was drinking lager from the can, which I was more than sure the school did not allow.

'That a nice way of putting it,' I said. 'Gift-children!'

'Not really,' said Briony, gloomily. 'Not if you're a duty present, and unwanted.'

'Like a scented candle,' said another.

'Or lavender soap,' another offered.

'Or a garlic sausage if you're a vegetarian.'

They were a bright lot, these girls. Goths and devil-worshippers perhaps, but bright.

'Isobel,' I said. 'You have one father, one stepmother, and one sibling, and in four months time you will have a half-sibling. And only one Christmas dinner to go round the five of you. That is not bad by today's standards.'

'You're always so sensible and brisk, Gran,' said Isobel, appreciatively. 'You know all this stuff about motivation and so on. But the new baby isn't a stepsibling. It's not even a relative.'

'How do you work that out?' I asked.

'It's not Gavin's baby. My father's not its father.'

What can she mean? I tried to keep shock at bay, or at least not let it show in my face.

'Then let's call the new baby an honorary non-sibling,' I said.

Isobel studied me for a little, impassively, unblinking. I stared back at her, keeping eye-contact a little longer than necessary, during which time it became clear that a state of war had been declared. It evinced itself in a slight scornful flick of the golden hair so it fell over her face. I bent forward to clear the hair from her eyes, and she pushed away my hand. The girls around had fallen silent. I had mishandled this.

Then suddenly I was relieved. I had been trying to believe that Sappho was happy, that the Garner marriage was good, or at least salvageable, and now I didn't have to any more. The Garners could disappear from our lives as if they had never been. There would be a divorce: Laura would come back and organise it. We would be back to where we were. I rejoiced.

'Only kidding,' said Isobel, but it made no difference, other than I was disappointed. But at least I knew where I stood.

'You shouldn't say things like that,' I observed. I tried to draw her away from the others but they followed and clustered, like a Greek chorus. 'What was that for?' She thought a little and then said she was her mother's daughter and would say anything for a good line. She offered that Sappho was probably holed up somewhere trying to finish her novel.

'I don't know why Sap bothers,' she said. 'Even if she finished it they'll never take it. She's history, the tide's swept on.'

What can it have been like, living with this girl?

'And Laura has walked out on us too so no one knows anything, and Dad has just gone to the Faroe Islands for one of his bird conferences. I'm flying out to be with him, and Gwen and I hate Apple Lee when he's away because of the ghost in the attic. Gwen says it's harmless, it's only Sap's dead dad, but all the same. So we're back at Gwen's. Is that okay? So now you're in the loop and can relax?'

'The Faroes!' said someone. 'I hope your dad's not eating whale.'

The new generation is not laggardly when it comes to accusing others of ecological crime. The coach arrived. It was to take them all off to see *Macbeth* at the National. I waved her goodbye, like an affectionate, ordinary grandmother. Her perfect little face dimpled at me through the darkened glass of the window as she waved back, like an adorable grandchild. Her friends seemed to be bent over with merriment. I cannot see these coaches without also seeing the vision of one of them tumbling down a ravine somewhere in the Alps: but that's just me, I suppose, Mrs Worried Mother, or is it Mrs Wishful Thinking? I wish one knew oneself better.

And come to that, why had I assumed the baby had to be Gavin's? Perhaps Isobel had got it right without knowing and the 'only kidding' part was the lie? Perhaps Sappho had wanted a baby badly and finally found a father for it with sperm less worn-out and tired and more effective than her husband's, and told no one. And what was so unusual or surprising about a scion of the Stubb-Palmer family having a baby out of wedlock? Rob and I had never been formally married: he already had a wife. This was something that I daresay I had failed to mention to Sappho, along with the fact that Rob had taken his own life. 'Telling no one' seemed to run in the genes.

The insurance policy would not have paid out if there had been a suicide verdict, or indeed had they realised Rob and I were not formally married. Quite apart from not exposing one's child to unnecessary and painful truths, it is never prudent to stir up trouble, especially if the death-watch beetle is clicking and the dry rot creeping. God, I hate property.

I was so morally and emotionally exhausted by the time I got home that I failed to remonstrate with Barnaby over the Ursula incident. He sat at my computer and checked out spiral staircases, and I felt glad and secure in just the fact that he was there.

Sappho's Novel Continues...

Part 2
Scenes From Married Life: 2004–8

Prequel 1: Isobel Puts In A Claim

One of the few scenes from the blurry days of life before marriage, before Gavin, before fame and fortune, before almost everything, is the one set in the mansion flats where Isolde died. It is when and where, behind those barred windows, Sappho lets down the normal Garner stoicism by weeping and wailing. These are the days when Sappho is the apprentice, devotee and au pair. Isolde lives behind the closed door of her sick room, every day with more trouble breathing and a worse heaviness on her chest, slowly squeezing the life out of her. Isolde struggles not to use the morphine drip; she cannot bear the muzziness of existence with it, but hour by hour uses it more and more. The only end in sight is the peace of death, and wishing it for her is to Sappho the worst torment.

Gavin is standing in the kitchen. Arthur and Isobel are sitting, too obedient and quiet for their own good, dipping wholemeal toast soldiers into the boiled eggs which have become practically their staple food, along with orange juice which Sappho squeezes every day. When she goes shopping these days she cannot think of what else to buy. Initiative is at an end. Oranges and eggs, oranges and eggs.

Sappho comes through from Isolde's room, sees Gavin and buries her head in his tweedie jacket and sobs. Politely and kindly he moves away from her. Physical contact is inappropriate, even before the word came into fashion. She stands on her own and howls. Her mother would point out that she is pre-menstrual: the pointing out itself a kind of homeopathic dose of negative emotion so that at least she can stop howling and start snarling. But her mother isn't here to help.

What happens is that little Isobel stares at Sappho with a look of amazed contempt that anyone should be so out of control as this servant, who shops and cleans and feeds, clearly is. Then she gets up, walks over to her father's tree-like legs and clasps them with her tiny arms. Her father tries to get free, but can't. The arms are stiff and brittle and determined, and he cannot unhitch them without breaking them. So he stands patiently. And Sappho grabs her bags and runs down the corridor past the sick room and out into the street and gets on the bus to Apple Lee. And her mother says, 'You have to go back. You can't just run out on them.' So she goes back.

Her mother has a new lover. At least, Sappho thinks, he is not a patient and seems quite normal, neither twitching nor retching nor howling. He is an architect and is helping Emily with a planning application. Sappho decides there is no room for her in her mother's life. Any spare emotion there is taken up by the house.

Fast forward to:

Prequel 2: Breaking The News To Gwen

Gwen does not like the idea of the children coming to live at Apple Lee. She does not say so directly but it's easy enough to work it out from the things she says, such as:

'But the pair of you are so busy. Children need proper care and attention. This is an office not a home. And for heaven's sake, Gavin, they have to be allowed to watch TV like other children. You have simply no idea how to bring them up.'

'Is that peculiar agent of yours gay, Sappho? "Grim" more like. I know one shouldn't say so, but don't let him go near Arthur. He's a young boy and vulnerable.'

'They're perfectly well settled as they are. They have no mother of their own, but I'm their grandmother by blood and the next best thing. I don't see why Gavin getting married should alter anything. It's a preposterous idea; anyone who knows the history knows he's just trying to relive his youth. Pathetic.'

'As we used to say in Wales, getting married and not pregnant! There's posh for you!'

'Sappho you have to realise my daughter was the love of his life. A great romance, in the old tradition. With you it's practical. His flat is dreary, he's got no money, you look like the answer to his prayers. Dinner on the table, money in the bank, someone to help with the children as I get older. But he's misjudged it: you're no good at domesticity; never were. All you ever gave those poor children was soft boiled eggs. They're so constipating it broke my heart. Mothering is simply not your forte. Leave it to people who know how.'

'Sappho, I don't know how you can live where you do. Nobody, but nobody, lives in N19. The children will get mugged. Bad enough having to go past on the bus, let alone actually having to get off there.'

'It was a mistake spending all that money on the place. You will never get it back.'

'If I lose the children what will I do with myself? Sell up and go and live in some old people's home? Is that what you want? Not that there's much left to sell. One gets nothing for simply priceless pieces. Or of course I could always come and live with the children. I may end up only an ex-mother-in-law but I am at least a blood relative.'

As I am not, of course, thinks Sappho, by now determined that the children will end up with her. Gavin says Sappho should forgive Gwen's impossible rudeness. Gwen is a pre-Freudian. She simply doesn't understand the implications of what she says. It's a kind of blind spot. Sappho, Gavin assures her, is the most post-

Freudian woman he, Gavin, has ever met, so it sounds even worse to her than it does to most people. But he agrees: the sooner they get the children away from her the better. Only they would have to go carefully.

'We don't want her ending up living with us, do we?'

'Anything,' says Sappho, 'anything rather than that.'

Emily Interjects

Oh, Sappho! If only you had listened to me. I could see it happening. The first wife is determined to undo the harm the mother has done, the second wife to undo the unhappiness caused by the first, the third wife of mother, first and second wives, and the stepmother – that's you, Sappho – sets out to be a better mother than the birth mother ever was. It is a great mistake for all of them. 'Making good' should be left to builders. Poor Gwen. She is a silly old woman but she is not as terrible as you think she is. Ruthlessly, you want to steal the children. Gwen is another woman in your husband's life.

It is the maternal element in uxorious love which so binds a woman to a man: she wants to heal him, comfort him, prove to him the world's a fine and welcoming place and he was just unlucky in all the women he happened to encounter along the way. And now, with you, the man has reached his perfect home. And that goes for his children too. Madness, Sappho. Masochism.

Sappho's Novel Continues...

Scenes From Married Life: 2004–8

The Honeymoon

(*First person: hard to stay impersonal.*)

There was a misunderstanding when it came to the honeymoon. We were going to Iceland. The birds are good there and I've always liked the thought of thermal energy and lava bubbling up from the ground. In June it would be light twenty-four hours a day.

Laura got the tickets and booked us into the Holt Hotel. We were going the day after the wedding, which dawned, I must say, a little hangovery. We were to leave the house at midday. Taxis were booked. New smart lightweight suitcases had been bought and packed – Gavin had had no idea such things existed, being accustomed to heavy leather cases with straps and buckles which his father gave him on his twenty-first birthday. For once he was delighted by the lightness, the paleness, the sheer wipe-cleanability provided by the technology of the new world. We breakfasted in the morning sun before we set off. I wanted to gossip about the guests but men are not so good as women at that kind of thing and Gavin got stuck on the ethics of Polly bringing up a child on her own without a father.

'She's only thinking about herself, not about the child,' he said.

I said but if she hadn't had the child he wouldn't exist. Wasn't existence of any kind better than no existence at all? 'If you asked the child he's not likely to say he didn't want to be born, is he? If he really feels that he can always take his own life, and become unborn of his own volition.'

I thought that was rather clever but Gavin told me not to be smart and silly. Polly could simply postpone birth and wait until a proper father came along. And I said, 'Supposing one doesn't?'

We almost had a quarrel which is no way to start married life but is probably pretty normal. People are tired and stressed and faced with the implications of what they have done. But we didn't row. We both drew back – Gavin said he was a very nice little boy anyway even if he did have a Petrie dish for a father, and I agreed that Polly failed to understand what was important to a child. Then we wondered if Luke was the best agent for me; he was certainly trendy, but over-flashy perhaps. The trouble was he made no distinction between what was good and what was popular, profitable and meretricious. I said at least he kept my nose to the grindstone and Gavin said I needed to think more and work less. Which I knew to be true.

We talked about Laura, and Gavin said I overpaid her and I said yes but it worked, and he said in future he could probably take over a lot of the stuff she did. And in return she could type up his handwritten novel. Laura had trained as a secretary and had some training in management, but he was on the board of various literary and theatre magazines and knew up from down.

And then the doorbell rang and I heard the key in the lock before I could get to it, and there stood Arthur and Isobel, with suitcases in their hands, rather like evacuees in the Second World War, and Gwen hopping off down the path into a waiting taxi saying to me, 'Sorry darlings, must rush – fabulous wedding!', and to them, 'See you in two weeks, chickens, have a lovely time; give my regards to the geysers. Arthur, remember your homework, or you'll be in terrible trouble at school.'

I came back into the kitchen and sat down again. Gavin looked surprised at my surprise. Of course the children were coming. I'd been there in the room while Laura made the arrangements with the travel agency. One double and two singles.

Had I heard, and then gone into denial? It was possible. Or more likely there was just so much going on at the time I might very well not have focused. And I couldn't fault Laura, who had given up her ceaseless commentary on my life and times, thank God, and now questioned nothing, which I could see would work to my disadvantage as well as my advantage.

All I said feebly was, 'Couldn't the kids share a room? Iceland is terribly expensive.'

'Please not, Sappho,' piped up Isobel. 'Arthur smells of boy. It isn't his fault. He can't help it.'

And Arthur shuffled his big feet as if he wished they didn't belong to him, and went red.

'You'll have separate rooms of course,' said Gavin. 'Laura booked them for us. And please, please, Sappho, my darling, never call them kids. They're not baby goats, they're my children.'

'Sorry,' I said, and got up to make them toast and marmalade.

'Isolde and I made a promise to each other never to call them kids,' explained Gavin. I couldn't remember the word Isolde passing his lips throughout the whole of our courtship. Mind you, I could see it had been rather a short courtship. 'And we have to get into the habit of using wholemeal bread not white.'

Ever since I left the mansion flats I had avoided brown bread and bought white. Brown reminded me of death and healthy living. White tasted nice and comforting and the children thought so, too. But this was the new life and we would all have to get used to it.

'Of course,' I say.

During our honeymoon – let's just call it a holiday because the children have rooms on either side of ours and the walls aren't all that thick and besides, we have fairly worn ourselves out shagging during the past few weeks – the children are sweet and good and affectionate. It's all going to be okay. I had worried that Arthur didn't come to our wedding because he was so loyal to his dead mother, but apparently he really did have a biology exam. He is not nearly as boisterous now as he was when small: he's a big boy – at fourteen he's nearly six foot already and broadly built like a rugby player, which it is his ambition to be, but manages to move quietly and elegantly about rooms. This comes, I suppose, from having had to live in Gwen's flat, which though large, God knows, is so cramped with ugly furniture and possessions it seems small. Isobel is right about his feet, though. I expect the pong is a kind of unconscious attack against Gwen. He will move silently into a room and the only way you know he is there is because the foot smell comes before him. You get used to it. I almost appreciate it. He is so young, so alive.

Arthur is very like Gavin only broader: the same thatch of brown hair, the same eagle face, but, I fear, without the intellect that both animates Gavin and gives him gravitas. On the other hand he is enthusiastic and well natured and never judgemental. I have only ever heard him criticise one person and that was a rugby referee for giving a wrong decision.

'Bloody idiot,' Arthur said. 'Sad tosser!'

'Arthur's so different from Isobel,' I observed to Gavin. 'Isobel deals in words. Sometimes they can be painful.'

'She doesn't mean to hurt,' he said. 'She's a child: her verbal dexterity outstrips her wisdom. And remember, she's spent years with Gwen, who is not famous for her tact.'

'Here's hoping,' I said, 'that it's learned behaviour and not inherited.' Isolde could be quite caustic, I remembered, and Gavin could stop me in my tracks sometimes; but at any rate the gene of tactlessness had by-passed Arthur. And I changed the subject because I did not particularly want to talk about Isolde. Gavin had shown no signs of comparing me unfavourably with his first wife but I remembered something my mother had said:

'Dead spouses are the devil. Memory renders them perfect. We remember the good times and screen out the bad. That's why I haven't remarried. Who will ever come up to your father? The hated and despised mother becomes an angel once she is dead. The feared and violent father becomes the daddy who is firm but just. The merits of the dead wife, who lives in the past, will always outstrip those of the present wife, who is obliged to love in the present.'

I surprised Arthur in the bath by mistake when I went into our bathroom at the Holt Hotel, just a couple of days into the holiday, and there he was, stretched out naked in the hot sulphurous water – which in Iceland smells of rotten eggs; turn on the taps and it beats even Arthur's feet for pervasiveness. Arthur grabbed for the flannel but I could see that he was remarkably well hung – even more so than his father. I looked away hastily and backed out, wondering slightly why he saw fit to use our bathroom; but apparently Isobel was using his to wash her hair and didn't want him in hers. And one could hardly discourage him from bathing, because of the feet. It is a surfeit of testosterone in the growing lad that does it, I believe.

I think of Belinda and her warning that my stepson would try to seduce me. I can see the danger would more likely be the other way round. But the taboos are very strong. Where they come from in the human psyche I have no idea. I will have to ask my mother. But the mind veers away from any visualisation of the primal scene between me and Arthur, as I'm sure it does from him to me. Forbidden! He reaches for the flannel. I back away hastily. Yet it seems a fairly new development in human nature – until parents have wealth and time enough to start putting children in separate beds the family seems to have been omnisexual: sex with the powerless a source of excitement rather than disapproval, incest a normal part of life, not at all the universal taboo our Victorian forebears insisted it was. They could not conceive of how vile and brutish our ancestors were; or how cold the nights. I would quite like to have a conversation with Gavin on the subject but you don't have it with the father of a daughter just growing into puberty. It's too personal.

On the third night of the holiday I was woken by the sound of our door opening and I started up at once. Gavin stayed sleeping. It was Isobel.

'Daddy, I had such a dream.'

I remembered the one a few days back, when we didn't get our wedding sleep because Isobel was on the phone.

'Daddy, I'm frightened.'

This dream was about the earth gaping and swallowing her up, and at least not about me as a threatening shape-shifter, and perfectly reasonable, since this did tend to happen in Iceland. She got into bed next to Gavin and he woke and said, 'Poor puss, you're cold.'

'Isobel, you're a big girl now,' I said, perhaps a little sharply. 'Too big to be in bed with your daddy. Gavin, take her back to her own room and settle her in.'

And Gavin did. I was half-asleep when he came back into bed and put his arms around me.

'That was a bit harsh and a bit sudden,' he said. 'But I suppose she is growing up. One goes on thinking of them as little when they're not.'

'After we've all been together for a bit,' I said, 'she'll stop getting nightmares.'

In the morning we hire a 4x4 and drive east from Reykjavik into the hinterland of plains and spikes; we stand on the cold black lava sand and stare up at Mount Hekla, which erupts every now and then with no warning. The wind is quite strong. A little bird, a goldcrest, finds a forlorn haven on a rock. It's looking for familiar trees and is not likely to find anything so ordinary round here. Isobel is quick enough to take a photo on her mobile phone before it trusts itself to the skies again and is swept up and on. The bleak, unfriendly scree is dotted with little clumps of bright green, where nature seeds itself and starts again. Isobel finds a little scarlet flower in amongst the green, picks it, and brings it to me.

'For you,' she says, and I am inordinately touched.

Emily's View

If Sappho didn't need the money she could train as a psycho-analyst; with a little more insight into her own compulsive behaviour – using poor Gwen as the whipping boy, for instance – she'd make a good one. I wonder if that is because of her upbringing or because of her genes? Who is to say? What she says about primitive society is interesting. In simple societies, just as animals are seen as sources of survival and wealth, so are the children you yourself give birth to. The boys are for working and the girls for selling, and both are for sexual release and profit if they are halfway desirable. See its remnants in the dowry system. Surplus male animals get killed at birth: in poverty-stricken humans it's surplus females: you have to feed girls for years before they get to procreative age. In the early sexualisation of our girl children today we can see a reversion to a natural state: we dress up the little girls as for the sexual market. We remove the stigma from the prostitute and call her or him a sex worker. Parent as pimp is nothing new. We project our own guilts into the paedophile, and focus on them as the source of all evil.

At least Sappho has been in touch. At least she's okay. I was shocked by my encounter at the school gate with Isobel, and left thoroughly disturbed. The girl is capable of real villainy, and Sappho's pregnancy will have made matters worse. As for Laura – her collapse into compliance was too easy. She too may harbour unconscious or indeed conscious desires for revenge. And Gwen? There may be something suspect in my own defence of Gwen, the mother figure who is bad for the children, who is to be discarded. We will see.

More than thirty years since Rob's death, since the insurance company paid out. I told no lies. All I did was keep quiet when I could have spoken. Why should sleeping dogs suddenly wake and start snapping at my heels? I could have said, hang on a minute, yes, I saw a length of hose, yes, a body fell out of the car when the door was opened, no, it was not suicide. What would that have gained? More misery for friends and relatives and above all Sappho. I could have said, hang on a moment, where it describes us as a married couple, we were not; we said we were married but there was no ceremony. Result? A house sold over our heads, victory to the death-watch beetle and the developers, and some ugly block of offices where now Apple Lee stands. No. There were no lies, just silence where silence was appropriate.

Sappho's Novel Continues...

Scenes From Married Life: 2004–8

A Late Delivery

One afternoon Sappho was getting on with *I Liked It Here*. Or trying to. She had thought when the wedding was over – six months ago – her routine would re-establish itself but somehow it had not. She liked to show Gavin what she was doing. Where once Laura had been her critic and even typed up what she, Laura, wanted to read rather than exactly what Sappho had written – Sappho never noticing, or only some time in rehearsal, by which time it was usually too late anyway – Laura no longer commented but simply got along with the business in hand. Luke was getting fed up with trying to string along the Vanbrugh Theatre, and their production schedule had already had to be rescheduled and programmes reprinted. Now Luke called her on her landline, disturbing her mid-sentence – and she picked up even as she recognised the number. Too late. She should have let it ring, and ring.

'Darling,' was the essence of what Luke said to Sappho, 'you are no longer the most promising young thing on the block. It is not a good idea to be both over thirty and unpopular, which you most certainly are. You have also pissed off the BBC drama department. It is one thing to turn down work, on the grounds of time and money, another thing to explain you are doing it on moral grounds. They will despise you, not admire you, and it will affect both our incomes.'

When Sappho put the phone down she was crying. The door flung open. It was Gavin.

'Luke had better watch his step,' said Gavin, who had been listening on the extension. 'He has no business pressurising a creative artist like that. How much does he charge?'

'How do you mean?' asked Sappho.

'What percentage?'

'I really don't know,' said Sappho. 'You had better ask Laura that kind of thing.'

'Oh my God,' said Gavin. 'No wonder you are in such a mess. You just throw money away.'

Sappho looked round her beautifully organised office, where telephones were answered on time, files were kept, archive boxes sorted, and fan letters and emails never left unanswered, and wondered quite what he meant but she supposed he must be right.

'I'll tell you,' said Gavin. 'Fifteen per cent. Some agents charge only ten.'

'It's true Luke's not very nice to me,' admitted Sappho, 'but I'm kind of used to that.'

'I can't bear to see you crying,' said Gavin. 'You don't have to put up with it. You're worth more than this.'

And he called Luke back and gave Luke hell, and after that Luke seldom called, and Sappho was grateful.

Isolde's Portrait

Isobel and Arthur were over at Gavin's old place helping him pack up his belongings. Most of these were already at Apple Lee, so there was no point in keeping the flat on. Gavin had renewed his lease and sublet to a colleague, Waldo, who'd had a two-hour commute in from the country and now could stay the week in the town. His wife Ellie, Sappho understood, was not pleased about it, but the rent Gavin was asking was not high, and less than the weekly train fare. It was pleasant to take on a new set of friends which someone else had acquired. Waldo was a journalist and film critic with whom she found she could exchange jokes and general intelligence. He was worldlier than Gavin – that is to say he would write enthusiastically about big special-effect family films, as well as the more obscure offerings of the European cinema, which Gavin favoured and Sappho tried to.

At a little past four that Saturday afternoon Sappho clicked out of the programme she was in – she was playing Isobel's *Sims* – when she saw Gavin, Waldo, Isobel and Arthur coming up the path. They were carrying the portrait of Isolde.

Isolde has arrived, thought Sappho, she is following me. The past has come back to haunt me. Then she wondered why she felt so guilty. I should have gone to her funeral, she thought, everyone knows I didn't. Because they don't talk about it doesn't mean they have forgotten it. Waldo had probably been there at the grave, a friend of Gavin's from the old days. She seemed to remember him vaguely as one of the visitors who had come to visit Isolde on her deathbed, to drink champagne and make jokes and be smart and defy death.

She went to open the door to them. The children made off upstairs with the portrait.

'It will need proper picture hooks,' called Gavin after them.

'What are they doing?' asked Sappho.

'We were wondering what to do with the portrait,' said Waldo. 'I have one of Ellie she wants me to have over my bed. Sympathetic magic, I suppose.'

'Women!' said Gavin.

'Mad,' agreed Waldo. 'But it didn't seem right to supplant dear Isolde. Then Isobel said it belonged with them by rights, but there wasn't room on Gwen's walls so it had better come to Apple Lee.'

'So here it is,' Sappho said, perhaps a little flatly.

'I thought that would be okay with you,' said Gavin. 'I moved it but you brought it back in.'

So I did, Sappho thought. Was I mad? Or did I just think that I was invincible?

'It is her dead mother,' said Waldo, reproachfully. 'I mean, poor child!'

'It's fine by me,' said Sappho. What else could she say?

Waldo had brought his washing round for Sappho to do. Her truly fancy machine had a cold wash programme which the one at Bloomsbury didn't, and Waldo needed it for his favoured cashmere sweaters. At home, he explained, Ellie did them by hand. When Sappho had sorted Waldo out she went upstairs and found Arthur stepping down from the marital bed where he had left boot marks on the white coverlet, and Isobel clapping her hands in satisfaction.

'I told you it would fit,' she was saying to Arthur.

'But surely it should go in your room,' Sappho said.

'It's not right for the colour scheme,' said Isobel. 'I like pinks and greens, and this is all bluey. Mummy left it to me in her will but I'm giving it to Dad as a present.'

'Okay,' said Sappho weakly.

Later she said to Gavin that she'd be happier if the portrait was somewhere else in the house than over their bed, and Gavin said, 'But why didn't you say so at the time? It's too late now. Isobel will be hurt, and think I'm rejecting her. But of course, if it really upsets you—'

'Of course not,' said Sappho.

'Anyway,' said Gavin, 'I don't like to think of you being superstitious. Poor Waldo, being stuck with Ellie. I think he's quite relieved to be free of her some of the time.'

More Bedroom Dramas

Sappho notices Isobel's nightmares come in waves, peaking once a month. Isobel's periods haven't started yet, so it can't be described as pre-menstrual. The peak is when she herself is pre-menstrual which is odd. Sappho gets the feeling sometimes that the bad dreams are calculated, because they involve Isobel pit-pattering into the bedroom and disturbing their sleep. Perhaps they are even made up?

'Daddy, Daddy, I've had a dream. I'm trembling. Can I put on the light? I was being chased down the road by one of those coffee machines...'

How can anyone be chased by a coffee machine? Sappho queries it with Gavin, and Gavin puts it to her that she's being paranoiac and is she pre-menstrual? And she has to admit that she is.

'Daddy, Daddy, I've had a dream, there was great crane which came down and clutched me and swung me high above the roof tops and was going to drop me... Daddy I am so cold and lonely...'

'Daddy, Daddy, I was at school and I was going into the library and all my teeth began to crumble and fell out on my science book...'

'Daddy, Daddy, I dreamt I was being tied down and a doctor with a monkey's face had a needle and he was trying to put it in me...'

The girl is thirteen now. Surely it should stop. They are still going two nights a week to Gwen and Gwen lets them watch TV which Gavin won't, or only very selected programmes on the history channel. If Gavin lightened up on TV, as Sappho explains to him, then they wouldn't be so anxious to get to Gwen's. If they didn't have fresh organic food at Apple Lee but were allowed the occasional pizza or McDonald's that might help, too. Gavin will have none of it. Arthur sets up a campaign to go to a top boarding school for the sixth form where he can play rugger not football, though Sappho thinks this is as much to do with escaping to a world of white bread, sausages and pizzas as anything else. He gets his way, and Sappho goes on scrubbing good earth off root vegetables and peeling the flaws out of parsnips for Isobel, who would probably be happy to go round the corner with Sappho and eat an almond croissant at the new Costa's. Gavin's early life out on the Yorkshire moors – where his perfect mother, who died when he was ten, home-cooked and baked, and loved him properly – had been without junk food. If he wants the same for his children, it is surely admirable. And he is right, and junk food is an abomination.

If there's any trouble at home, such as Sappho trying to make her eat more (Isobel is borderline anorexic) the dreams hot up.

'Daddy, Daddy, I'm so cold and frightened. A ghost came into my room. I think it was Mummy but she had a face which worms had eaten – and there was no one to look after me. And there was a hole in the ground and I fell into it and all the earth came over my face and I couldn't breathe...'

Is that aimed at me? wonders Sappho. Because I let her down when her mother was dying? Because I didn't go to the funeral? But that is really paranoiac and not one of the things that can be discussed with Gavin. And what makes her think Isobel's dreams are 'aimed' anyway? Why should they be?

'Daddy, Daddy, are you awake? I dreamed Sap was having a baby and this thing came out and crawled along the bed and came towards me...'

'She doesn't want you to get pregnant, Sap, that's for sure,' says Gavin, and laughs, but Sappho feels she's been ill-wished and doesn't think it's at all funny until Gavin asks her what the time of the month is, and Sappho has to admit it's five days before her period, and tries to reformulate her thinking. It also makes her feel she had better stop having periods and actually get pregnant, which now she wants to do, and the more she wants to and it doesn't happen, the more obsessive the desire gets.

Isobel is always sweet and affectionate and never swears or shouts at Sappho, as other girls sometimes do. She goes to school and gets good reports and comes top in everything.

'She has her mother's brains,' says Gavin, in one of his few references to Isolde.

Sappho is left with the feeling that perhaps she is not as bright as Isolde, not a patch on Isolde. Gavin is so careful never to make comparisons she thinks it might be true.

Everyone, even her own mother, congratulates Sappho on how well she's doing with the stepchildren.

The Haunting Of Isobel's Room

Gwen says how odd it is that Isobel never has bad dreams when she is with her – now Friday and Saturday nights only – and perhaps it is something to do with her room at Apple Lee being haunted? Isobel's room is up in the attic: a large room with high ceiling and rafter beams. She begins to hear noises and feel sudden chills as if the temperature in her room had dropped.

'Daddy, I was up in my room doing my homework and I suddenly felt all shivery, like a ghost was walking over my grave. And I heard footsteps and a man sighing. Has anything horrible happened in that house, Daddy?'

Gwen would drive up on Fridays after tea to pick up the children and take them back to South Kensington, stay and have a cup of tea and chat to Laura and wait for the children to pick up their things. Sappho would usually be out at a rehearsal or at a meeting.

'Do try to be in and be nice to her, Sappho,' said Gavin. 'I know she's difficult, but it's important for the children to feel everyone's at ease with each other.'

So Sappho stayed if she could, and was charm itself.

'Your house just doesn't have a good atmosphere, Sappho, if you'll forgive me saying so,' says Gwen. 'And keeping poor

Isobel tucked away in that attic room. It's like walling up a nun.'

'But it's a lovely room,' says Sappho. 'One of the best in the house. She's decorated it herself, chosen the curtains. She's done it so well!'

'She can't ask her friends back because their parents won't allow them to come down to N19. It's too rough.'

'But that's not the case,' says Sappho. 'They do come and all they have to do is just hop off the bus.'

'That's not what she tells me,' says Gwen. 'And they don't much fancy oatmeal cookies! Tell me, Sappho, didn't your father die in this house?'

'Yes,' says Sappho.

'Which room?'

'The garage, I believe. I was three.'

'Because poor Isobel has got it into her head that he hanged himself in the attic room.'

'That's absurd.'

'Why can't she have the spare room, the one next to your room?'

Because that would spoil my and Gavin's sex life, thinks Sappho, remembering what happened on their honeymoon. The thought of Isobel lying awake next door listening for noises five nights a week is intolerable.

'It has that lovely apple tree outside the window,' goes on Gwen, 'and she won't have to come all the way down through a dark house if she has bad dreams. They're abandonment dreams, of course. She says she remembers you didn't go to my daughter's funeral. I don't remember missing you but apparently she does.'

'She hasn't said anything about it to me,' says Sappho. 'And good Lord, she was only three. Why would I have been there? It was a quiet funeral, family only.'

'Please Daddy, can I change bedrooms? I woke in the night and there was a shadow on the wall. It was a hanging man turning and turning, and flashing his face. He had skeleton eyes and there was a tube in his mouth—'

'You'll have to ask Sap,' said Gavin.

'No, you can't,' said Sappho. 'But you can have the little spare office room on the ground floor.'

'I don't want her having a room with an Internet connection,' said Gavin, so she stayed where she was, while they waited for the computer engineer to come and remove it, and Laura forgot to call him, which was unheard of. Laura and Isobel were getting on really well.

While they were waiting one Friday afternoon Gwen turned up with a man dressed like a Catholic priest, and carrying a bell, book and candle. He had come to exorcise the house, and Gavin had forgotten to tell Sappho it was happening. That is, when dashing out, he had asked Laura to tell Sappho and Laura had forgotten. Somehow Laura's increase in wages had not compensated for her share of the gross. The filing system was not what it had been. Car insurance was left unpaid: she had not been told to pay it. She was not exactly working to rule but sometimes it felt like it. The transition from 'taking responsibility for Sappho' to 'waiting to be told by Gavin' was not as smooth as smiles all round suggested. Gavin would open the mail as it came in; put what he thought applied to Sappho and Laura on Laura's desk and all the rest would disappear into his room. It was a haphazard system and involved discussions which nobody wanted to have, least of all Sappho.

Sappho ran after Gwen, the priest, Gavin and Isobel as they sailed upstairs. Arthur was at school fortunately.

'I don't want you to do this,' said Sappho. 'There's nothing wrong with this house at all.'

'It's haunted,' said Isobel.

'I doubt it,' said Gavin to Isobel. 'But if it reassures Isobel, let's do it.'

'Surely you want the spirit of your poor dead father put to rest,' said Gwen.

The priest says since it's an unquiet spirit which probably died by its own hand he has brought bell, book and candle in case serious manifestations become apparent but with any luck they won't be needed because few major sinners are brought into the world.

'What sort of priest is he?' asked Sappho of Gwen.

'Starhawkian Wikka,' said Gwen.

Sappho threw up her hands and left them to it. The priest performed his incantations and left. The strange noises, the sudden chills, the ghostly shadows continued.

'It's okay,' said Isobel, after reporting the latest manifestation. 'I can just put my head under the pillows at night and do my homework at school. I don't want to cause a fuss.'

But she ate less than ever, and became thinner than ever. Her arms were like sticks and her eyes grew larger in her head, and even her full red lips seemed pale. The school nurse called them in and warned them that she was borderline anorexic and they were not to comment on her eating habits. 'The anorexic is a non-problematic child with problem parents,' they were told.

'Daddy, Daddy, I had this terrible dream. I was being held down and force-fed because people wanted to eat my liver, and there was no one round to help me. There's something wrong with me. I should have grown out of nightmares by now…'

She allowed herself to be taken to the school psychologist. Sappho had to wait outside the room while the two of them talked. Then Isobel sat outside and Sappho went in.

'You are a stepmother, aren't you?' said the psychologist, who reminded Sappho a little of her mother. 'The abandonment dreams are typical of the bereaved child.'

'They seem a little more aggressive than just abandonment,' said Sappho.

'Oh, do you think so?' asked the psychologist. 'A pity she has to be away by herself at the top of the house. I understand there's a room just next to the one you share with her father. She is very attached to her father.'

'I know,' said Sappho.

'And then there's the eating disorder,' the other went on. 'Anorexia is particularly prevalent in broken families.'

'Mine is not a broken family,' Sappho said. 'It is a mended, mending family.'

'All the same,' said the psychologist, and Sappho gave in and let Isobel move into the room next door where the walls were thin, so love-making between her and Gavin only happened on Friday and Saturday nights, because Gavin was so self-conscious about making a noise.

And because Isolde stared down on the marriage bed, if anyone was haunting the place, thought Sappho, it was Isolde, murmuring, 'He married you because he needed you for the children. He fancies your money, not you. He still thinks of you as the au pair and always will.'

But Isobel cheered up as soon as she was ensconced in the spare room, and even ate a few of the date oatmeal cookies Sappho made especially for her.

'She's bulimic with me,' said Gwen. 'She'll eat a six-pack of Mars Bars and a twelve-pack of mixed fruit yoghurts and then sick it all up in the bathroom.'

'That's horrible, awful,' said Sappho.

'Oh, I don't know,' said Gwen. 'Never did me any harm. She'll grow out of it. And the dreams have stopped, haven't they?'

'Yes, they have,' said Sappho and bit back, '*If they were ever there in the first place.*'

Isobel And The Contraceptive Pills

Sappho wanted to get pregnant. She told the family so over breakfast. Isobel said she was not to, she would be embarrassed at school, and her father was too old to have babies.

'But a baby would sort of close us up as a family, surely,' said Sappho. 'Wouldn't that feel right, Isobel?'

'No,' said Isobel. 'It would feel all wrong.'

'What do you think, Arthur?' asked Sappho.

'It's okay by me,' said Arthur. 'I'm not bothered.'

Arthur was home from school and had taken over what Isobel referred to as the haunted room. Arthur had noticed nothing strange. But then he had his iPod in his ears most of the time, as Gavin pointed out.

Arthur was now taller than Gavin and stronger, and Sappho thought that had something to do with the way Arthur was allowed his iPod and his mobile phone while Isobel was not. The food rules at Apple Lee remained strict but the TV situation was slightly improved. With the arrival of the fashion for DVDs and the closing of so many art cinemas it seemed almost unnatural not to have a DVD player in the home and a real effort not to have a TV as well. As Sappho was writing for TV soap opera it was useful for her job, though Gavin didn't seem to think that professionalism applied in this particular area. It was all just trash, albeit useful as an income flow.

And Waldo was round quite a lot, and it was useful for him to have a DVD for new films he had to review. Ellie was divorcing him. Elvira of all people had taken to standing outside the Bloomsbury flat night after night, still pining for Gavin, even though he'd long since left for Apple Lee, and Waldo had noticed and brought her in, and one thing led to another. It had been a short-lived thing but Ellie had found out, and now Waldo was as free as could be and rejoicing – only he seemed to spend a lot of time at Apple Lee complaining of loneliness, rather than out on the town. Sappho thought he quite liked Laura, too.

'What *do* you think, Gavin?' Sappho asked. 'It needs to be a family decision.'

'Might have been a good idea to ask me first,' said Gavin. He could be touchy. 'Let's talk about it in private.'

'That means no,' said Isobel. 'I know my daddy.'

She was wrong, just. Gavin thought he might be too old to embark on fatherhood, it would certainly not please Isobel, who had had a disturbed enough beginning anyway, but he couldn't deprive Sappho of motherhood if that's what she wanted. But she needed to think of the financial implications – children were expensive.

'We have lots of money,' said Sappho.

And Gavin said running Apple Lee was expensive, not to

mention time-consuming, tax was at 40 per cent, agents were at 15 per cent, her annual income was down 50 per cent from last year and she must use taxis less, buy fewer clothes and think about what she spent.

'Are we paying for Gwen's flat?' asked Sappho. 'How much does that put us back?

'Not all that much,' said Gavin. 'Around two thousand a month.'

'But that's just money down the drain,' said Sappho.

'Better than having her live with us, which is the alternative,' said Gavin, and they both laughed. The house was half in Gavin's name. A couple needs equal dignity.

She had finally finished *I Liked It Here* and Luke had been trying to sell it with no success. The deal with the Vanbrugh had long ago fallen through.

'Times move on, darling,' he said, 'and today's favourite is tomorrow's "*who's she?*" It was okay when you were a young lesbian banging on about women's rights, but you are bourgeois now and white, which is worse, and married with children, which is awful, so you are the wrong side of the tracks. So settle down into TV hackwork and think yourself lucky and hope the powers that be don't start remembering you're female and over thirty or there'll be nothing left but novel writing.'

'I was never a real lesbian,' said Sappho.

'Just don't let on,' said Luke. 'Lie through your teeth.'

When Sappho got off the phone from talking to Luke she was again crying, seeing her career, her future and her aspirations in ruins, and Gavin again flew to her defence. He called Luke straight back and fired him, and said he was saving 15 per cent of his wife's income and taking over himself. Words were exchanged. Sappho pointed out that Luke would still be taking 15 per cent of all the deals he had agented since her writing career began and she couldn't see there was much left of it, and Gavin looked slightly taken aback but replied that since motherhood was her aim she had better get on with that.

So she tried. But it did not work. She waited a year, during which she took a one-day-a-week job in the drama department at a London university. Her name still meant something in some quarters, and it was nice to have a pay packet and be useful. At the end of a year she saw the doctor, privately, and he agreed to set things in motion. He did blood tests and said there was rather a lot of extraneous oestrogen around, and he supposed she had stopped taking the contraceptive pills he had prescribed her some time back and she said yes, she was not an idiot. He replied that as soon as it came to wanting babies women seemed to lose all sense and nothing surprised him. She reported this to Gavin and he persuaded her to change to a woman obstetrician. He did not like men diving round in her insides anyway, and she felt protected and grateful. No hassle. On Fridays and Saturdays when Isobel was with Gwen they had lots of sex but still no baby arrived.

'There can't be anything wrong with me,' said Gavin. 'I do have two already. You may not be all that fertile. Come to think of it you have no siblings, and aunts, uncles and cousins are thin on the ground.'

'It is true,' said Sappho, 'as a family we have dwindled, and I don't like that. All the more reason to build a family round me. But remember my father died when I was three: there wasn't much time for my mother to have any more.'

'Not by the same man, certainly,' said Gavin.

'If my father hadn't tried to clean the headlights with the garage door closed I might be one of six.'

'Gwen said something to me about your father around the ghost-in-the-attic time,' said Gavin, 'when she came round with the ridiculous exorcist. Gwen said it wasn't surprising Isobel was picking up vibes. She said your father's death wasn't an accident and he died by his own hand.'

Sappho said that was absurd, Gwen was a mischief-maker and trying to upset her, Sappho, and what could Gwen possibly know? It was over thirty years ago.

'Gwen claims your mother's late cleaner Mary told her,' said Gavin, 'that she saw your father fall out of the car when the policeman came round and broke down the garage door. But Gwen says anything that comes into her head. Take no notice. Your mother won't have been lying to you all these years about something like that. Forget I said anything. The past is another country and they do things differently there. Our lives began the day we met at the party and saw each other across a crowded room.'

'That's true,' said Sappho, and Gavin kissed her and became very romantic and stared quite soulfully into her eyes, and she pretended to gaze back but actually she was gazing inwards.

She had what she referred to in her head as a spare-room moment, in the same way as her mother had senior moments. It was when you remembered things which might not have happened, memories which could just as easily have been constructed out of past conversations. Do you remember the holiday outing or do you remember the photo someone took? You need witnesses. She remembered her father's body falling out of a car as the door was opened and she remembered Gavin falling upon her in the spare room, and she knew she could never ask her mother about the one or Gavin about the other. It was probably better if your life began at some time convenient to you, rather than when it did in reality.

Emily Stresses

'I can't read this any more,' I said to Barnaby. 'I am having a panic attack.'

'Breathe deeply,' he said, 'but go on reading.'

I was handing the pages over to him one by one as I read them. I was not sure whether he had my interests in mind or he simply wanted to know what happened next. How can men be trusted?

'Gwen must be making it up,' he said. 'Sappho's right. How could Gwen possibly know?'

'Because when Isolde was ill and Sappho was the childminder and Gavin was the hero, Sappho would sometimes leave the children up at Apple Lee for me to mind and Gwen would turn up in her taxi to pick them up, and if I wasn't there she would sit and have a cup of tea with Mary, who had been cleaning the house since year zero, and no doubt find out everything there was to know. Yes, it is possible. Why did Sappho not tell me any of this?'

'Because it may not have happened,' said Barnaby. 'It may be a variation of the truth, like so much fiction. Make me a toasted cheese sandwich while you calm down and get your breathing back.'

I did. I made him one of those sealed, pressed wodges of over-toasted bread and under-melted cheese, made in the sandwich toaster, glistening with butter, and half hoped it would kill him and half hoped it would save him and he would be there for me for ever. 'Aloneness', with all its single-woman dignity, was feeling remarkably like loneliness to me. Children went to therapists and were told to cut the ties that bind, and that their mothers were responsible for all the ills that afflicted the children and their own children must never be allowed contact with the grandmother. I had known it happen to friends, though usually after a year or so the daughters shook themselves, realised they'd been had, and normal family relations continued. I wished indeed I had had six children and not one daughter. I was altogether too vulnerable.

Sappho's Novel Continues...

Scenes From Married Life: 2004–8

Isobel And The Contraceptive Pills Continues...

Belinda came round and watched Sappho take her daily multi-vitamin pill and said,

'But I take those and they're huge and yellow, and yours are small and white.'

Sappho spat out the pill and went to her bathroom cupboard and checked though her old unthrown-out medications – Laura no longer sorted out things like that – and yes, her discarded contraceptive pills were small and white and had a little cross on the back like the ones posing as vitamins. She took the blister pack to the table where Belinda was sitting with her new man, Dwight Gordon, who wrote detective stories and had connections with the SAS, so they mostly involved wounded heroes who were ex action men trapped in a civilian world.

'These are the same pills, aren't they,' she said and Dwight looked at them and laughed and said,

'It'll be the stepdaughter. They don't like cuckoos in the nest.'

'Does that mean me or a new baby?' Sappho asked.

'Both,' he said. 'Just be glad it's not a daily dose of arsenic.'

'A fucking year of my life,' said Sappho. 'Wasted!'

'Take on an older man,' said Belinda smugly, 'and you take on his past as well.'

Later she said to Isobel, 'Darling, you haven't been tampering with my vitamin pills, have you?'

Isobel burst into tears and said she didn't want Sappho to have another baby because then Sappho would stop loving her.

Sappho wrapped her arms around her and said she had enough love to go round for everyone, and how had Isobel got hold of them? Isobel said on the Internet at school and Sappho said how had she known what ones to use? Had she gone though her bathroom cabinet?

'I asked Laura,' said Isobel, but Sappho didn't quite believe her.

'Don't tell Daddy,' begged Isobel.

'I won't,' said Sappho.

'Why didn't you come to my mummy's funeral?' wept Isobel.

'Who said I didn't?' asked Sappho.

'Gwen,' said Isobel.

'You know how Granny Gwen likes to make things up,' said Sappho. 'I was there.'

Together they emptied the bottle of little white pills down the loo and flushed them away. Gavin had agreed to have a sperm test done, but from the grim set of his jaw was not looking forward to it. Isobel and Sappho were united in deceit. They did not tell him there was no need now: nature could probably be trusted to take its course.

Nevertheless, Sappho resolved to give up hot drinks thereafter, and so eschew the tea and coffee Isobel sometimes prepared. She would drink water straight from the unopened glass bottle, and explain it was bad to drink caffeine when hoping to get pregnant. How easily and sensibly one lie slipped into another.

Sappho Is Seized By Guilt

'Is something the matter?' Laura asked Sappho. Sappho was crying into her computer. It was the first month of the new pill-free regime.

'No,' said Sappho. 'Never been happier.'

'But really?' asked Laura. 'Because Channel 4 want their changes by the end of the week and it's already Thursday. Your reputation for quick delivery is not what it was.'

'That no longer worries me,' said Sappho.

'Then what? Because the curse has come upon you?' asked Laura.

'Yes,' said Sappho, lying, because it was an easier thing to agree that her period had started – Laura was clearly against babies for Sappho – than to state her real pre-occupation. That is, to say,

'My mother lied to me all her life and my father killed himself. Why? Because he was "depressed"? Because my mother drove him to it by having affairs? Because my mother's whole life has been driven by self-deception, which is why she devotes so much of her time to unravelling it in others? Because once my mother read my diaries and that was an end to my ever really trusting her or confiding in her, so I was deprived of most girls' birthright?'

But she did not say it. She realised, forget her mother, that these days she no longer quite trusted anyone at all with the truth. Others would use it against her, whatever it was. Laura was on an emotional work-to-rule: she had become Sappho's employee and not her friend and twin. Luke was no longer there to chide her and make her laugh as well as cry. Isobel was like a weather vane which some foe had tampered with; you looked, you shivered, but you could never be sure quite where the wind was coming from. Arthur, since she was not a rugger ball, would not care where she was coming from. Gavin? Surely she could unburden herself to Gavin. But Gavin had a male morality: it would not bend to let her off the hook just because she was his wife. He would be right: her own life was her own fault, not her mother's. Everyone's was. No way she could ever bring the conversation back to the beginning: she had lied to Isobel about the funeral for her own convenience: Gavin would despise her if he knew.

In other words Sappho that morning was full of self-pity; the more so because she feared the feelings of foreboding and resentment were pre-menstrual. For the twelfth time in a year, she was about to be not pregnant. It was not unlike wondering whether or not *I Liked It Here* was ever going to find a proper home, and in the end having to accept it was never going to happen. God was against her.

Why was God against her? Because if she faced it, she had neglected to tell the world that *Ms Alien* had been based on a script of Isolde's; that the one she had 'found in a drawer' had actually been sketched out in pencil by Isolde in the first place, and though she, Sappho, had worked on it for months and turned it from Isolde's comedy into her own sociologically significant drama, and re-written it many times so it seemed a different work from the original, none the less it was at heart Isolde's. And she, Sappho, had grown rich and famous on it, and Isolde had died poor and everything she, Sappho, had was morally Gavin's and the children's. Which was why she had put half the property in his name when she married him. And why God was angry with her and why the public had seen through her and wanted nothing she wrote.

In fact, she was very low. So low, indeed, she swung the other way and thought she could trust Laura with a question or two, and did.

'Laura,' she asked a little later, 'what do you know about my father's death?' She was at her computer, no longer weeping, but sensibly trying to pacify Channel 4's whims. Sappho no longer wrote by hand, but straight onto the keyboard. Gavin had sensibly re-negotiated Laura's contract so that her hours were shortened, her holidays lengthened, and her salary reduced.

'Only what Gwen told me,' said Laura. 'Why? It all happened a long time ago. Does it matter?'

'It does to me,' Sappho said.

'Okay,' said Laura. 'There was an "accidental" verdict but actually it was suicide. Your mother covered up the facts of your father's death to claim the insurance.'

'That's absurd,' said Sappho.

'I checked it out,' said Laura, 'and found the records. The policy was taken out only a month before the death so as things were at the time if anyone found out your mother could be done for fraud.'

'Even all this time on?' asked Sappho.

'It happens,' said Laura, 'but so long as no one talks it should be okay. And I'm not going to talk so who is?'

'Laura,' asked Sappho, 'why did you check it out?'

'Because it's in my fucking nature,' said Laura. 'And I didn't think Gwen should go round talking about it. I told her not to and she accepted that. It wasn't done out of malice. You know what she's like. No worries. If you've finished that can we go through the emails now?'

'Try not to swear in front of Isobel,' said Sappho. 'It gives her ideas.'

'Bloody children,' said Laura. 'Why do people want them?'

Sappho saw a life based on lies and theft and dark clouds with brilliant silver linings. She saw that if Gwen had not lied, her mother had, and more, that if her father had not killed himself Apple Lee would have been sold long ago. And her father had done it for her, his daughter, Sappho. It was not vulgar depression, or mad sexual jealousy, but a noble sacrifice; one complete, sufficient, perfect sacrifice, for his child. No wonder her mother had been so eager to put the house in her, Sappho's, name. Her mother was the villain of the piece. She had not been wrong. And silver linings lighted her way.

Sappho Takes Steps

Isobel was showing signs of teenage defiance. Her skirts had become amazingly short and her bare midriff amazingly long.

'You can't go to school like that,' Gavin said.

'I can,' said Isobel and did. But she was sent straight home again, and now her skirt just touched her knees and her midriff was clothed – perhaps because whenever it wasn't Sappho complained about the girl's sticky-out ribs and pressured her to eat more. Now she just swore occasionally which was not too bad. Sappho did sometimes, too, but now she made an effort to stop.

'Isobel's feeling insecure,' said Gavin. 'She really doesn't want you to have a baby. That doesn't mean you shouldn't, of course. There are more of us in the family than just her.'

'If I put my half of the house in her and Arthur's name,' said Sappho, 'do you think that would make her wear her skirts longer?'

She was half joking.

'I had thought of that,' said Gavin, 'but it seems a bit extreme. And then of course I could make a will – I need to, anyway, you're so much younger than me you're bound to outlive me – leaving my half to you. It might not be such a bad idea.'

'My mother wouldn't like it,' said Sappho.

'I don't see why she should object,' said Gavin. 'She is perfectly well settled as she is and Apple Lee will come back into your family on my death.'

'Don't even think about it,' said Sappho. She could not envisage life without Gavin.

So they made an appointment with the lawyer. He advised Sappho quite strenuously against what she was doing, but then he did not know what she knew. The papers were drawn up, sealed and signed. Gwen would look after the children's share until they were of age.

'Now I live by courtesy of you,' said Sappho to Gavin. 'It is a very old-fashioned feeling and very erotic. I have no power and you have all. I am your slave and your servant.'

Gavin seemed a little shocked.

'That's very masochistic,' he said. 'Hardly from the pen of the writer of *Ms Alien*.'

Sometimes she wished she was married to someone less prudent and thoughtful than Gavin, or perhaps only a younger version of Gavin, who had once gone out and shot a crow as a gesture against death.

But the sex that Friday night was particularly good and was the night she became pregnant. God had rewarded her.

Sappho At The Breakfast Table

Sappho sits sipping a caffeine-free latte while the sun shines in through the branches of the apple tree. She is convinced of the existence of God. The baby, nine weeks into its being, sits happily and contentedly in her belly. The doctor says all is well. She is content not to be a famous writer any more. She does not mind having no money to spend. She thinks back to the morning Isobel first came tapping at her door and her concerns about challenging the demiurge and realises she need not have worried. The demiurge did not overhear or at least pretended not to. She has told the children that she is pregnant and Arthur has grunted amiably and Isobel says courteously and formally, 'I am happy for you.' A soft warm wind blows from the south and Sappho relaxes.

Gwen has offered grudging congratulations and said she had a letter from her landlord complaining that the rent had been late and the cost of living had gone up and she was going to have to ask for more money for the children's weekend keep, and perhaps it was time she gave up living alone and moved into Apple Lee and gave a hand with the new baby. Gavin has apologised for the lateness of the rent and said it was a mistake at the bank and of course the weekly allowance would go up. He agrees with Sappho that the thought of another generation being trained in the proper use of milk jugs is intolerable. He says Gwen has no real desire to move in to Apple Lee – she just knows how to keep the threat hanging over their heads.

Sappho is now writing for *EastEnders* and enough money is coming in to make headway against the debts. Gwen tells Sappho to provide her with an extra store card so when she takes Isobel shopping she can use that instead of writing cheques, and Sappho signs the necessary forms. Sappho explains to Gwen that she'd rather Gwen didn't bring up the matter of her father's death because it upsets everyone and Gwen looks surprised and says she hasn't done that for years and she hadn't realised it upset people anyway, but she'll keep mum. Her skin is beginning to look papery and thin, but she is still grand and beautiful. She wears her hair like Isobel's, only hers is white and Isobel's is fair and longer. Both have the same somehow out-of-time elegance.

Even Laura seems settled and pleased at the thought of a baby.

Sappho's mother Emily is delighted. Sappho has forgiven her, without telling her she had offended in the first place. Emily should have told Sappho the truth but Sappho can see why she didn't. Sappho won't tell this new child, either; who wants a suicide included in family history if it need not be? She has not told her mother that Apple Lee is now owned by her son-in-law and her step-grandchildren. She has not told the children either.

The espresso machine finally gives up, perhaps in protest at being fed caffeine-free coffee. Sappho bought it at the height of her money-making potential. Now it hisses and spurts and collapses into a silence which makes Sappho uneasy. It is the end of an era and Sappho is not quite sure she wants it to go, even though she herself drinks no real coffee. Gavin had someone in to look at the machine recently and the man said it was hopelessly scaled up and wouldn't last long. They had neglected it, and it would cost £800 to strip it down and rebuild. Which was absurd. They would take it round to the charity shop and hope someone could make use of it and Gavin and the others could make do with the cafetière.

In the days of Laura's power she would never have let an espresso machine go unserviced. Sometimes Sappho thinks it would not be beyond Laura to mention a few things – 'Hey, do remember to have the espresso machine looked at' or, 'The hem of your jacket needs fixing at the back' or, 'Your road tax runs out next week', but she rather studiously doesn't. This is work, not family, her attitude implies. Sappho feels powerless to change anything. And anyway it's been going on like this for years. Marriage, Sappho decides, is a strange business. It saps your sense not just of identity but of purpose. Sleeping in the same bed with a man ends up with you sitting at a table in the sun, accepting your destiny instead of raging. Or perhaps sex is just a form of medication: the weekly injection renders you helpless.

Isobel is off playing netball for the school. Arthur is back for his half-term, and is peacefully eating cereal, and has a maths book propped up against the milk jug. Left to her own devices

Sappho would have had the milk carton on the table and not bothered with a jug, but Gwen had in her time inculcated in Isolde the notion that pouring milk from the carton was vulgar and Isobel in her turn had adopted a similar attitude. A dead woman, Sappho has long since realised, is harder to placate than a live one. In the modern world a glass jug is outdated; it clouds or breaks in the dishwasher and takes up extra space and energy, but Isolde is trapped in her own time. Sappho must in some respects live in the past alongside Isolde. It is one of the taxes she must pay for the privileges of marrying Isolde's husband. The other one is having a portrait of Isolde over her marriage bed. Sometimes she resents that. But on the whole she is happy.

Isobel And The Flurry Of Trouble

(I am writing 'Isobel and the Flurry of Trouble' in the first person. It started life as a short diary entry, but it is what made me start writing the novel in the first place, in an attempt to work out what had been going on in my life. Isolde's idea that one should observe one's experiences from afar and record them as for the stage may have therapeutic advantages, but is limited, and besides, needs an actor to bring it to life. It is also fundamentally evasive. Not me, not me, blame the actor, blame the director, leave me out of it, cries the writer. This may be why so many men end up stage writers and so few women, even today, and if they are women they are often lesbian. This may be the inhibitory nature of motherhood. You don't want to invoke the furies. I remember Isolde saying at one of the brink-of-death literary parties that Angela Carter felt she had to stop writing

the icy cruelty of the fairy stories as soon as she had her baby:
it felt too dangerous. After that she wrote harmless if long
novels about things which could not possibly summon disaster.
I am braving the furies, however, and am writing this in first
person novel form, undistanced and unsafe though it may be.
Courage, courage!)

A storm blows up on a normally still lake and everything turns
choppy and then all is still and calm again and it is as if it has never
happened. Or the sun is shining and suddenly there is a flurry of
snow whirling around the head and then it stops and lies for a
minute on the ground and then melts and disappears. And someone
says, 'But it was snowing,' and someone else says, 'I didn't see it. I
was map-reading in the car, you must have imagined it, whatever it
was, it's gone.' Yet snow fell: a butterfly shivered and shook its
wings free of the transitory white weight, and there was an earthquake in China. You can see how reluctant I am to write what
follows; I would rather talk about earthquakes in China.

It happened shortly after I had been sitting in the kitchen at
Apple Lee thinking life was good and untroubled, and that I had
won through to a comfortable place and could now leave bother-
some memories behind. Arthur sat, as he had that other morning,
a book about sharks propped up on the milk jug. Gavin was shut
away in his office, which was now in the attic where once Isobel
had suffered in the night from the swinging ghosts of dead men.
He worked surrounded by unfiled letters and documents which he
could never find. He didn't like me going in there when he was
working; I respected that. We had our own separate areas for
working. I had the conservatory, which had once been the garage,
at the back of the house.

Gavin had decided the time had come to write a novel. It was about a bird-watcher: he did not show it to me. He read bits of it to Isobel, though. She would go up to the attic after school bearing him a cup of tea and biscuits, and he would let her in, and I would hear them laughing and talking, though I tried not to go upstairs to the bedroom if they were there, because I would hear and it felt as if I was spying. And sometimes after about twenty minutes she would come back down and collect her homework and sprint all the way up the stairs with it, so he could help her.

'Isobel,' I said once, 'are you meant to ask Daddy so much? Is he actually doing your homework? Because if so I'm sure the school wouldn't approve.'

'It's better than Google,' she said. 'Which is what most of us use. But they can catch you out on that, these days, so Daddy's best. He knows everything.' And then she added, 'Why, are you jealous?', with a look from the green eyes, which usually slid side-wise and shyly to look up at you, but which this time was head on, and amused, and somehow victorious. I realised she was now as tall as me, and would soon be taller. And she was slim and young and full of promise, and my pregnancy, which I had been so proud of, suddenly made me feel awkward and clumsy and taken advantage of. I had realised the promise and was now of no real interest to any man.

'Of course I'm not jealous,' I said, flustered, because I realised I was, and so did she. I shut up about the homework, as she had intended.

'Darling,' I said to Gavin, 'it might not be wise to read your novel aloud to Isobel when you won't to me. It gives her power over me and it isn't healthy.'

'Oh my God,' he said, 'don't tell me you're jealous. Isobel said you were and I laughed at her. Don't tell me it's true? She's Snow White and you're the stepmother? "Mirror, mirror on the wall, who is fairest of us all?" All that?'

'No,' I said. 'Nothing like that. Just don't read your novel aloud to either of us.'

'But I fear your judgement,' he said, 'and I don't fear hers. You'll make suggestions and she'll just accept. You know what men are: they like acceptance.'

'She is certainly very fond of you,' I said. 'And always has been.'

'Sometimes you are so like your mother,' he complained. 'Why can't you say she loves me. I love her. It's allowed. She's my daughter. It's very simple.'

I remembered something my mother had said: 'The face on the pillow is liable to change but a daughter is for ever.' It stopped worrying me, as things that happen a lot, and which you survive, do. And as soon as she had made her point Isobel stopped doing it. The cup-of-tea-and-biscuit-homework-safari dwindled away. I think the bird-watching novel was not all that lively for a fifteen-year-old. And at least she was not dating, or on drugs, or running round with the wrong crowd, and as Gavin said, I should think myself lucky.

At any rate, the ground beneath my feet, slightly shaken after the 'Why, are you jealous?' remark, had steadied again. I had made the breakfast coffee for me and Arthur and squeezed the oranges for Isobel and put the juice in the fridge to chill. I was waiting for her to come down and wondering if I should call and hurry her up, in case she was late for school, when Isobel came into the kitchen and I had the terrifying sense of earthquake.

Back track. Rewind. Let me do this as a scene. I keep thinking of other things to do rather than write it.

Scene: The Kitchen At Apple Lee On A Bright Morning

Enter Isobel in full school uniform from the waist up, tie, cropped blazer and all, very tidy and neat and virginal. From the waist down it's different. She wears a scarlet ra-ra skirt of the kind Gavin, whose sixties' youth sometimes shows, refers to as a pussy pelmet though everyone wishes he wouldn't. She has on pale-grey fishnet stockings which do not come up to the level of the skirt, a suspender belt and a pair of elaborate and very beautiful and also probably very expensive pink high heeled-shoes. I could not begin to wear them even when I was not pregnant. They are too fragile and cantilevered to stand up in. Isobel manages. She looks like a very expensive tart posing for the paedophile market.

ARTHUR (*looking up*): Wow! Jail bait.

ISOBEL: Like it? I went shopping with Gwen.

SAPPHO: Isobel, you'll be late for school. Stop messing around and get your uniform on.

ISOBEL: What would happen if I went like this?

SAPPHO: You would look silly and you would be expelled.

ISOBEL: Supposing I didn't care.

SAPPHO: Isobel, take it off before your father sees.

ISOBEL: Why? I think he'd like it.

SAPPHO: Because you're his daughter and old enough not to provoke him.

ISOBEL: You mean sexually?

SAPPHO: Yes, I do.

IISOBEL: Well, you should know.

SAPPHO: What is that supposed to mean?

ISOBEL: Gwen told me. When you were the au pair and my mother was coughing and dying in the bedroom you had sex with my father in the spare room and I saw it. I can't remember it but it must have had a very bad effect on me. You are meant to face the abuser with their crimes.

ARTHUR: It's some stupid TV programme she watched. Do shut up, Izzy. You are embarrassing everyone.

SAPPHO: I don't understand this. What do you mean, 'Gwen told me'?

ISOBEL: It just came out. It wasn't her fault. I asked her why you hadn't been to my mother's funeral, because Arthur told me that, and she said it was because she had fired you.

I asked her why and she said because of what happened in the spare room. She found me sucking my thumb and watching you and Daddy having it off on the spare room bed.

SAPPHO: That is not the case.

ISOBEL: I bet it is. Gwen always tells the truth. That's why everyone hates her except me.

ARTHUR (*Standing up*): I can't stand any more of this. God, I wish I was back at school.

Arthur goes.

SAPPHO: And all this is total fantasy.

ISOBEL: Yes. I know. But Freud said fantasy was as real as fact, or was it the other way round? I've been doing Freud with Daddy. Famous World Thinkers. It was the primal scene with knobs on, because it wasn't even Mummy and Daddy. I've got it confused, he says, so it comes out you and him.

SAPPHO: You've talked about this with your father?

ISOBEL: Yup. Freud said the child interprets the primal scene as the father attacking the mother, but in my fantasy it seemed to me you were enjoying it.

SAPPHO: Isobel, please go and take those clothes off. It isn't fair on your father.

ISOBEL: Why not? I don't understand all this. Why shouldn't I fuck Daddy if I want? Why shouldn't he fuck me? What's the matter with it? Don't go all pink, I really want to know.

SAPPHO: Incest is a universal taboo because the babies come out wrong. Stop this and go and change.

ISOBEL: Daddy says that isn't true. You have to have about three generations of incest before the babies are affected. And there isn't a universal taboo. It's normal in lots of cultures. It's all about power relations. You're half Daddy's age so I don't see it's any more taboo than me and him. Your baby will probably come out wrong because of the age difference between you and Daddy. I, totally, think it's disgusting of you to have a baby. Have you any idea how my friends are going to laugh? How old were you when you seduced him? How much older than me? Why should you have him and not me? Well?

She is half laughing, half crying. She is hysterical. Sappho slaps her and Isobel shuts up and then begins to cry. Sappho hears the slip-slop of Gavin coming down the stairs. It's his favourite worn-down slippers. She hates them. It makes her remember that he's an old man.

GAVIN: What's the matter with Isobel?

SAPPHO: I told her to go and change and now she's hysterical.

ISOBEL: Sap's being mean to me again.

GAVIN: Isobel, you can't go to school like that. I like it but your teachers won't. Come on now, you're not six.

ISOBEL: No I'm not. I'm a big girl now. I'll take off the stockings but the skirt covers my bum. That's all they care about.

(*I come up against the real problem when writing for the stage: people have to talk their thoughts aloud. You can do a lot with expressions on faces but not everything. In the circumstances Sappho can't let on to Gavin or Isobel what is going on in her head, so the writer has to do it. Back to novel form. Sorry.*)

Isobel turns so her back is to her father and bends over, so her bum sticks out and she's right, her skirt just covers it. She does it apparently unselfconsciously, as if she were a child, but she is not a child and knows it. It is a sexual display. She is offering herself to her father and taunting her stepmother. Gavin looks away quickly. Sappho notices that the backs of Isobel's knees, stretched by the high heels, are wonderfully slim and taut. If I were her real mother, thinks Sappho, I'd give her such a healthy heartfelt slap, but I am not her real mother, I am her rival and she is bound to win.

Now Isobel's face appears between her knees, her blonde hair falling like a curtain to her lean ankles and she smiles at her stepmother but it is not a friendly smile. Mind you, her face is upside-down. Sappho may just be imagining it. What expression did Isobel have on her face when she pushed open the door of the spare room when she was small? Wouldn't she, Sappho, recall that at least, if it had happened? But she doesn't. And wasn't the door locked? Surely it was. They knew the children were in the house. Besides, there was nothing to see anyway. Was there? No sharp pain, no spots of blood which went with the loss of a classic virginity. Just a comforting fumble, before they were on their feet in response to a plaintive child's voice, 'Where have you two gone?' But then the washing of the quilt? What was that about? What Gwen remembers is neither here nor there. Gwen would remember what she wanted to have seen, not what happened, using it as an excuse to get Sappho out of the house – though it seemed a mischievous enough thing to report to a child. But Gwen can hardly be expected to be rational. Isolde was Gwen's daughter, and Gwen would love to think badly of Gavin, but can hardly afford to if she wants to keep her grandchildren, so Sappho must get the blame.

Sappho shuts her eyes and tries to sort out the memories. Why does Isobel's upside-down face so disturb her? Because everything is now upside-down, devilish. Because girls are not meant to use incestuous desires for their father as a weapon in a domestic war.

Sappho opens her eyes. Isobel has straightened up. She seems a child again. Gavin is laughing. He sees nothing wrong. Sappho knows it would be wise to refute, here and now, and loudly, and jointly with Gavin, the ideas Gwen has put in the girl's head. Emily as fraudster, herself as a young seductress, Gavin betraying his dying wife. They could all have a sensible conversation about incest taboos. But it is too dreadful and embarrassing. She says nothing. And so all are guilty, as charged.

Gavin tells Isobel to just go and get changed. Isobel lingers.

'Gavin,' Sappho rashly takes the opportunity of complaining, 'Isobel and Gwen went shopping. This is the result. Gwen encourages her. The shoes must have cost a bomb.'

'A hundred and seventy in Harrods' sale,' says Isobel, 'reduced from three hundred and ten.'

Sappho splutters indignation and tells everyone it's absurd and that she's stopping Gwen's card.

Isobel says, 'You'd better not, you cow.'

Gavin raises his eyebrows and Sappho tells Isobel she's being grounded. Isobel jeers.

'Grounded!' she says. 'You've been watching US imports again. Daddy's right. You have no cultural taste or judgement. You're just the au pair.'

Sappho gasps. Gavin looks superior. Isobel stalks out, bum wriggling, with a complicit smirk over her shoulder back at her father. And Sappho knows the moment for revelation has gone. Now she is in Isobel's power.

'She's got too much brain for too small a frame,' says Gavin. 'You handle her all wrong, Sappho.'

Sappho takes a little time to recover from this. Then she says,

'I suppose Isolde would do it better.' And she is so careful never to say things like this: to set up a competition between herself and Isolde. Usually she succeeds. Not now. She watches Gavin's expression change from benign to hurt and remote.

'We'll never know, will we?' says Gavin, and follows Isobel out of the room. They go to separate rooms.

Emily's Outburst

'I blame the house,' I say. 'I blame Apple Lee.'

Barnaby watches me as I stalk up and down the room.

'Hecate is here,' he rejoices. I ignore him.

'Hecate the vengeful mother,' he goes on. 'Hecate the inspired, the primordial, rendered beautiful by rage – look at you!'

I go on ignoring him. It is all very well, but being told you are beautiful by a sexually dysfunctional man is not the same as when compliments are made by a man moved and powered by sexual energy. Barnaby's links with the throbbing heart of Gaia – phallus and womb, phallus and womb, in and out, in and out, charging the universe – are just too inadequate for me. I am a Freudian, he is a Jungian, and it shows. My dark hair is all over the place. I am wrapped in an old dressing gown, it is far into the small hours, I have thrown the manuscript on the ground, I am a yowling crea-ture of the night, crawled out of the forest coven: the devil was there with his bright attentive yellow eyes, his hairy cloven hooves, waiting for me. I saw him, I glimpsed him. I did. I wanted him but I was too afraid.

'I blame Apple Lee,' I say again, and shake my fists and Barnaby for once falls silent. Let him prostrate himself at my bare feet; he is a pitiful wretch. 'If it were not for that house, that wretched, crumbling pile of wood, dry rot and death-watch beetle, Rob would not have died. I would not have been widowed; I would have had six children, not this single wretch of a girl child, Sappho, set on this wilful course of self-destruction. She deserves no sympathy from me. Suicide is in the genes, I see it clear. What else is this marriage of hers to Gavin, this old, spiteful, manipulative and greedy man, but the death of her spirit, her talent, her selfhood? Rob died that Apple Lee should live. That was madness and I blame him, and I curse him, and may he rot in hell.'

'Emily,' says Barnaby, 'this is not good for your karma, and heaven knows how it is dulling your chakras. It is not poor Rob you are angry with; it is yourself, and Sappho.'

'And you,' I say, 'and you.'

'It is projection.'

'Fuck that for a laugh,' I say, and I go to the desk I brought with me from Apple Lee, that once was owned by Rob's great-grandfather and dates back to 1814 and has a secret drawer. It is where I keep the note Rob left and I found in the garage and showed no one. I would have put the piece of rubber hosing that might have linked the exhaust to the car window there too but it was too thick, so I tucked it beneath rubble in a neighbour's skip and no one noticed. I fiddle about with various wooden inserts and the drawer eventually opens. I show the note to Barnaby. He has to find his glasses before he can read it. I want a young man with tight jeans and perfect eyesight.

The note reads, 'My darling, look after little Sappho. I am doing this for you. You must spend the money on getting rid of the dry rot. Make sure the window frames are painted before the winter or the whole lot will need replacing. The glass in the bedroom window is the original Georgian. Do try to keep it safe and the apple tree well pruned. I love you, Rob.'

'Do you see what I mean?' I ask. 'Do you? How appalling this is? What a shit he was? Leaving me with the mess and the agony and the child and simply slipping out of it?'

'Emily,' he says, 'this note is rather compromising. Did the insurance cover include suicide? Otherwise, Isobel is right, you can be accused of rather serious fraud.'

'No,' I say, 'the policy specifically excluded it. But it was not suicide. It was not *felo de se*, it was *felo de DIY*. Crime against the self by reason of mortgage-induced madness.' And I laugh heartily.

'At least Sappho is saved from it now,' I say. 'Legally the stupid girl has no responsibility for Apple Lee, any more than she has any claim to live in it, other than the goodwill of her husband and stepchildren. She will have to mind her manners if she wants to stay.'

I invoke a curse upon all who love their houses more than themselves, who put possessions above happiness, who would sacrifice an extra child for a bathroom extension, who put their children out to childminders so they can build a new deck for the garden, who own houses and do not rent them (for were we not all born to live in caves?), who identify their status with their 'homes' at the cost of their humanity. I curse and condemn the mad usurious system which invented mortgages the better to control us, to render us passive and powerless, dangling on the rope of interest – the shadowy form swinging in Isobel's attic – so we live our lives in anxiety and fret. And as I rant and rave, lying upon the floor, possessed, kicking my feet into the carpet, I see Barnaby approaching me engorged, inspired by my rage, willing servant of Hecate, so much anger can do, and perhaps a visit to the doctor, and he falls upon me.

Later, a lot less angry, and me actually seeing a future for us together after all, we decide to go together in person to Apple Lee in the morning, to see what we can see. In the meanwhile I get on with Sappho's novel, which pray God she never sees fit to publish. I cannot sleep.

Sappho's Novel Continues...

Scenes from Married Life: 2004–8

Isobel And The Credit Cards

When it had been clear for a few weeks that Sappho was pregnant Gavin and she hosted a modest celebration at the Groucho club. It was held between 5.30 and 8.30 on a Friday night, just to let people know they were still alive and fruitful. They had been four years married. All kinds of people didn't come because it was a long time since Gavin's column, Isolde's funeral and Sappho's newsworthy wedding eight years after the death; certainly no one much cared any more whether Sappho or Isolde was responsible for *Ms Alien.* The *debate* had moved on, and the play was long forgotten and Sappho was no longer snapped falling out of night-clubs with her bosom showing. But there were friends there and it was good.

Gwen wasn't there because she didn't like 'all those trivial media people', Emily wasn't there because she was too busy with her new admirer Barnaby the Jungian, Isobel because she would be embarrassed by a pregnant stepmother. Arthur was newly at college – he had got into Keele to study Marine Biology – and Sappho had driven him up there, complete with microwave, comfy pillows and a computer with WiFi and Skype newly installed. They had clasped each other affectionately as they parted. Arthur, as it turned out, lusted after nothing other than to hurl himself upon a rugger ball and not let it get away. Girls passed him by. He was not interested in conflict with his father. They were too different. Some are ruled by their intellects and some by their bodies: Isobel and Arthur were born out of the one womb but represent different species. The one views the other as an alien.

Laura no longer came to such events: though once she had not just organised but as good as hosted them, asked her own friends along, too, and quite often run off with Sappho's. She said it was not appropriate for her to come along. She was an employee.

It was around 5.45. Guests were still arriving. Champagne was being poured – grape juice for Sappho, of course. And then the phone rang and it was Laura.

'Sorry to interrupt the fun,' she said, 'but I just had an email. It's from the League for the Protection of Birds of Prey. You know that thing of Gavin's? It's for you. It said thank you for the donation received yesterday: twenty-five thousand pounds. I thought you might like to know.'

Laura had taken it upon herself to open the American Express statement, addressed to me, which had been lying unopened on the hall table for a couple of weeks, and £75,000 had been paid into various animal and bird charities. The Platinum card was now up to its limit. Sappho was relaying this information through to Gavin as it came from Laura.

'She had no business opening our mail,' said Gavin, loud enough for Laura to overhear while Sappho listened, 'the interfering bitch!' But then he was so upset he hardly knew what he was saying. More, he had been drinking champagne, which did not agree with him.

Sappho was already feeling some of the first effects of pregnancy, namely that everything is strangely muted, censored, filtered out before it reaches the ears. There is a time lag between cause and effect.

'You'd better tell Gavin to call the card people and tell them,' Laura was saying. 'I hope you're insured!'

'But you'll have insured them surely,' said Sappho. 'You do that kind of thing.'

'It's on Gavin's list. I drew up a list of the things which were his concern and which were mine, and got him to sign it in case of argument. I hope he put it up on his wall and didn't just lose it. I don't go into his office: he doesn't like that.'

But of course they weren't insured. 'How can you do this to me?' demanded Gavin of Sappho, on the way home in the taxi to sort things out. 'Any idiot knows credit cards must be insured.'

'It was on your list to do,' said Sappho. They left their guests to themselves and went back home to sort things out.

'A list! Laura and her mad preoccupation with lists. I am not your nursemaid,' said Gavin. 'You are not a child. The cards are in your name. Obviously it's up to you to insure them.' He seemed half mad. Sappho tried to pacify him. It would all be okay in the end.

When she explained to everyone a child had done it, the charities would cancel the gift and American Express would be understanding. This incensed him still further.

'What do you mean, a child did it? I am a victim of identity fraud. Yet your sick mind goes straight to my poor daughter.'

She remembered the way he had killed the crow. If he had a gun she felt he might kill her now. His eyes glittered: he was edgy. What was the matter with him?

'It's a possibility, that's all,' she said.

'Why on earth would Isobel try and destroy me?'

'Me', these days. 'Us', so seldom. It was the feeling she had known a long time ago, when Gavin and Isolde were together: that she was not even a bit part player, merely an extra, in a drama others were playing out. She was still on the edge of the same stage. One of the protagonists had died but she was obliged to remain. It was drama, it was not real life. It was Isolde's life not hers: she was just the body Isolde now used. She drove Arthur up to Keele and paid his bills so he didn't have to be burdened by a student loan. But Isolde was driving her. When she fell asleep she moved into the painting on the wall and Isolde moved down to sleep beside Gavin.

She too was tired, worried and, upset, and as she remembered, pregnant. Perhaps this sudden shift of perception, this awareness of dark horrors, was to do with having a baby? Gavin was drunk, that was all it was.

'It'll all be okay,' she said, soothingly.

'I asked you a question,' he said. 'Pay me the courtesy of replying. Why in your trashy *EastEnders* imagination would Isobel do a thing like this?'

'Because she's pissed off about me being pregnant,' said Sappho, finally furious. 'She fed me contraceptive pills for a full year before I found out.'

He fell silent. It was news to him.

'The poor, lonely, insecure child,' he said eventually. 'So much your mothering has done for her.'

He wasn't half mad, he was mad. Or else infatuated by Isobel. She kept silent. She could not trust herself to speak.

'And you, you put me through all that, you bitch.'

All that, she wondered? Oh, the sperm test. Yes, she could have spared him that, she supposed. But she couldn't get beyond the 'you bitch'. He had opened a door behind which a furnace of distrust and resentment raged. How well he had hidden it from her. The smooth words, the kindly smiles, and all the time the well-sealed door. Not even a flicker of hellish light from round its edges. They were nearly home. The streets were full of nightmare people. Starbucks and the tapas bars were lighted, and bright, and glittery, but they were props, insubstantial things. Apple Lee was no longer under siege, outside and inside was all of a piece. The pressure of the evil milling around outside was such that it had finally lapped the defences and got in, and had taken root, and was secretly growing, like the dry rot her mother spoke about. A history, an ancestry, a Grade II listing, a front drive, somewhere to park and security lights were no defence.

'I told you to shred all paperwork you threw away,' Gavin said, 'but you couldn't be bothered. What have you done?' She thought perhaps she was so used to blame she no longer noticed if she deserved it or not. But why didn't he shred it?

When they got back Laura had gone home, but she had left the credit card statements out, and the store cards, and a pile of receipts waiting to go to the accountant.

Sappho looked at them briefly, and the store cards with more attention. Most were up to the limit. Gwen had been using her cards to buy antiques for herself. There was an eighteenth-century antique clock for £625 from Liberty's, and wine from Waitrose, and fashion labels from designer houses, the size 6's and 4's for Isobel, the 12's for Gwen. She told Gavin what she had found.

'But all the credit cards were meant to be paid off at the end of every month,' she said, helplessly.

'Then why didn't you do it?' he asked. 'You were the one who gave Gwen one card after another. I told you not to do it. She has no sense. She's not even my mother; she's my dead wife's mother.

I owe her nothing. You're the one who needs her around to take the children so you can concentrate on making me a father. You know what you are? An insatiable whore? The tales I hear from others; rough trade, builder's mates, anyone.'

She had wandered into some extreme soap opera of her own designing. Her ears were dull; the sound was coming from a distance, as if from a stage with very poor acoustics. She thought he might hit her. If you hit people with words there is not such a difference between hitting people with your fists.

'I probably gave her the cards,' she said, nevertheless. This could still be salvaged. A life, a marriage, could not collapse so simply and suddenly around one's ears. 'I don't want Gwen going round telling everyone my father killed himself and I don't want Isobel trying to damage the baby, which she is quite capable of. She doesn't mind destroying herself in order to destroy me. So see the cards as simple bribes. I had not realised they would be quite so large. The odd sandwich toaster for Gwen, the odd Topshop jewel for Isobel, but no – no skirmishes in this sick war. Just violent attack.'

'You're the one who's sick, and vicious, too. You don't care what harm you do.'

'And you're a bit drunk,' she said. 'Wait until tomorrow when you're feeling calmer. We can sort it out then, I'm sure. I shouldn't be upset. I'm pregnant.'

'Yes, you would be, wouldn't you,' he said. 'You choose your time.'

He looked at her as if he hoped the baby died, and the sooner the better. She had not seen him like this before, or if she has, she has forgotten. She seemed to forget so much. She thought it was the way sex washed away memory. Was it that someone else's personality had descended upon him, like an evil cloak, or was it some disguise, there from the beginning, he was finally shrugging off?

'We'll just have to re-mortgage the house,' she said, 'if the worst comes to the worst.'

'I own the house with the children,' he said, 'and rightly so because the profits from *Ms Alien* are morally ours, which is why you did it. You had a bad conscience. So you have no say in what happens next.'

They went to separate bedrooms. He went to his attic and she went where she usually did, but took the Isolde's portrait off the wall. 'You've run my life for too long,' she said adding 'you bitch' to keep in tune with her husband, which made her laugh. It was a heavy painting but she tried to take the weight with her arms and not with her stomach muscles. She did not want to miscarry. She put the painting in the airing cupboard where she hoped the damp and warm would make it peel. She wrote up her novel. When finally she slept, it was good.

Sappho And Gavin Part

In the morning she called all the card companies and cancelled the cards 'while she worked things out'. They seemed quite accustomed to such requests. After Laura came in she called the Birds of Prey people and they said they would of course send the donation back. It would take them a week or so to do the paperwork and she called American Express and they said they would note the cancelled transaction but of course interest would have to be paid. Laura said that was normal.

'Laura,' said Sappho, 'why have you let me get into such a mess?'

'But you wanted to do things your own way,' said Laura.

Gavin came downstairs in his slip-slop slippers and apologised for things he may have said when drunk and upset. Sappho said that was okay. It wasn't, and probably never could be, but Laura was in ear-shot and eager to overhear. She told Gavin that her dealings with authority had met with partial success. The £75,000 was safe, or at least would be eventually. The store cards were another matter. Gavin said that was a relief: they would have to think up a story to cover their sudden absence from their own party. They didn't want rumours going round that Isobel had had anything to do with it. The girl had a hard enough time as it was. Perhaps they could say a break-in back home had been reported by the police? No one would be surprised: Archway was hardly anyone's idea of a sensible place to live. Personally he thought he would like to move out to the country.

'I know you were born here, Sappho, I know you have a sentimental attachment to the place, and you've wasted enough money on it, God knows, since any developer – which is all you will get – is going to pull the whole place down anyway, but facts have to be faced. Gwen is right. This is no place to bring up children. And it isn't really fair on me. I moved in here and adapted myself to your space, but we might be happier starting again, somewhere new to both of us, with the new baby. What do you think?'

She said she'd think about it and he laughed and said 'think' might not be quite the right word, since when it came to Apple Lee and Sappho, 'feeling' was probably more appropriate.

He was going upstairs to prepare his lecture for the Faroes. He was leaving at the weekend.

Sappho thought it might be possible to repair the damage that had been done between them the previous evening – words had been spoken, that was all: no one had *done* anything out of order, or only Isobel and Gwen. As it was she had been struck by semi-deafness: had it been total, she would not be feeling so alienated. Perhaps she should go to the Faroes with him? She went up to the attic and said as much.

Gavin said actually he'd thought it might help Isobel if he spent some time with her on his own, and when she came in later that morning he was going to ask her to take time off school and go with him to the Faroes.

Sappho said she thought perhaps when Isobel came in he might ask her about the sums sent by the various charities, including one for the protection of newts, and a substantial one to Victims of Parental Abuse.

'It was a childish prank,' said Gavin. 'And rather funny when you think of it. She was probably egged on by her friends. You've stopped her access to the store cards – and Gwen's, too, which may mean trouble – so what's the fuss? Pregnancy is turning you into a rather serious person.'

'Well, that makes a change, doesn't it.' She knew she should stop, but she couldn't.

'Bitchiness doesn't suit you, Sappho,' said Gavin. 'It's not why I married you.'

'You married me for my house, and my money, and my contacts,' said Sappho. 'And so Laura could type up your bloody novel. You needed someone to look after your children because you wanted them away from Gwen.'

'You haven't done very well on any of those counts,' said Gavin. 'I should never have married you. You make no money to speak of, you have no contacts any more, no one wants your work, you are a wicked stepmother and you are boring in bed.'

It occurred to Sappho, and she could see it was rather late in the day, that Gavin was manoeuvring her out of the house and out of his life. And that it was calculated. What he said was probably true enough, other than the part of being a wicked stepmother. He had sucked her dry, got the house, and was now happy to spit her out, all in the name of love. Nor would he see that he was in any way at fault. She waited to see what he would say next that she would not forgive.

'I was sorry for you,' he said. 'You'd got to thirty and no one wanted you for more than a night. So I gave you a mercy fuck, and to make Elvira jealous. And you were all over me, the floodgates opened. The good thing about you, Sappho, was that you had space. Apple Lee is a proper space with big rooms. I needed big rooms. Only kidding.'

Except of course he wasn't. She wondered if you could divorce people for what they said without witnesses, or did it have to be something they did.

'Don't worry about the house,' he said. 'I'm sure you are. If we split up I'll put it back in your name.'

'Yes, of course,' she said. 'You'll get round to it one day, the same as you got round to making your will and leaving it back to me.'

'You're no good at repartee,' he said. 'Never were. It falls flat. And how concerned you are about material things. Poor Isobel spent this, Gwen has got that. You don't have an artistic or creative bone in your body. It was only after you came into our lives that my wife got ill and died.'

'I see,' said Sappho, though it took her a little time to recover from her astonishment. 'I sapped her energy in some way and destroyed her immune system?'

'Yes,' said Gavin, bleakly. 'Something like that. You destroyed your own father in the same way. Death walks with you.'

That was fairly bad but it got worse. She should never have followed him up to this room. There was a little fluttering in her stomach. She thought it would be as well if she miscarried. She did not want Gavin's baby. A bit of him, a bit of her, to go on into eternity. No. It needed to stop. She was only in her thirties. She could start again.

'The au pair,' Gavin said. 'That was all you were to either of us. And a whorish one, too. Even when poor Isolde was dying you couldn't stop. Slinking round the room half-dressed, playing poor little me. Embracing me, putting your arms around me in front of the children. They noticed, little as they were.'

Sappho found she was crying though she tried not to. It was shock, she supposed. She was not particularly unhappy, just puzzled.

'I wanted to fire you. Isolde said no, it would upset the children. You walked out on us anyway.'

'Down Memory Lane,' she said, 'all of a sudden.' That made him laugh.

'You and your gift for cliché,' he said. 'Marvellous! Isolde and I really loved that. And those pathetic anagrams. And your mad mother. You were a great source of entertainment.'

Sappho thought it was time for her to go.

'Don't go away,' he said. 'I haven't finished. And the time you crawled into bed with me, and Gwen found us.'

'That is not true,' Sappho said. 'Gwen wasn't in the house.'

'Then why did she fire you?'

'Perhaps you told her,' said Sappho. 'People remember all kinds of thing when it suits them. I think you may remember things the wrong way round. I was very young and upset, I was a virgin.'

That really made him laugh. She supposed when people got divorced it always got like this. People said the most hurtful things they could think of. They knew the buttons to press and pushed them. Nothing had hurt so much as the anagram business which was absurd because it was not important. And he was taking Isobel to the Faroes, not her. By now she hated him but it still hurt. It was extraordinary the very different universes which people constructed to live in and preserve their self-importance.

There seemed little need to say anything else, or any question which she couldn't answer herself, such as, 'Why did you marry me then if you had such a low opinion of me?' since he had answered it way back. For her house, her income, her contacts, and for the sake of his children. He had the house now and she had failed him in all other respects. Isobel's £75,000 worth of inner disturbance had tipped the balance.

If he were then suddenly to say, 'Because I love you,' would it overwhelm the other reasons? The terrible truth was, it probably would. It was only since he had stopped saying it that the other reasons loomed so large, that she came to her senses.

Her carefully constructed universe had ended with a few slaps and bangs but mostly a sort of disagreeable whimper. It had taken only a couple of days. No doubt there had been any number of warning signs which she had overlooked. But then, and she thought it was rather like a piece of music which the composer has trouble ending, and will keep bringing in another final chord, and then another, just when you think surely it must have stopped, there came another noisy event, another reminder that nothing ever quite ends neatly. It was Isobel running into the attic room, throwing herself upon Sappho and biting and scratching.

Sappho held her at arm's length and even Gavin did his best to restrain her.

'You bitch,' shrieked Isobel. 'You nasty cruel woman! My mummy's painting. What have you done with my mummy?'

'What have you done with her mummy?' asked Gavin. She was still flailing but calming down.

'I put her in the airing cupboard,' said Isobel.

'You are completely mad,' said Gavin, and Isobel retreated into Gavin's arms, where she sheltered, gasping and staring wide-eyed and distraught at Sappho as if she were some foul and dangerous fiend.

'It's all right, puss,' said Gavin. 'She's going for good, right out of our lives,' and Sappho, as she turned to go, thought she caught just a glimmer of a smile from Isobel, before she turned and flung her arms round Gavin's neck and wept into his shoulder for comfort as she, Sappho, had done once before. The father becomes the man: she knew the syndrome well.

I turned her into me, thought Sappho. They're probably right that I'm a danger. How long before there was a re-run, for Isobel, of the spare room incident? Isobel would be distressed: Gavin would comfort her. Comfort was what Isobel wanted, and she would find her own way of getting it from her father, and all the old taboos were broken, and the comfort would be sexual because that was what everything had been leading up to. Sappho hesitated at the door. Something was incumbent upon her but she could not be sure what.

'She's writing a novel, Daddy,' said Isobel, a final triumphant attack, and again the smirk, which Sappho could see and Gavin not. 'You are, so she is. She's so jealous! Only you write nice things about me and she writes these horrible, poisonous, lying things about you.'

'I always rather thought that's why you married me,' said Gavin to Sappho. 'Not just for a literary respectability but to have something to write about. God, you're a sour, perverted, disloyal bitch. I want you to give me what you've written.'

'No,' said Sappho.

But Isobel wanted her father's attention back. She was beating her little white fists with their perfect nails against her father's tweedy jacket. 'Why does she hate us so much? Why?'

'It's over, darling, it's over,' said Gavin, and Sappho went downstairs to the bedroom and found the pages of her work in progress all over the floor where Isobel had flung them, and looked for the Waitrose bag which she had used to take clothes to the cleaners, and put all her papers together quickly and shoved them in, and went down to the basement and found Arthur's woolly hat and backpack, the one he used for potholing. It made her feel comforted and understood. Arthur was okay and not her enemy and never had been. Emily had a thing against backpacks but that was because she was old and hated new things the way Gavin did. She went back upstairs and packed a few personal things in the backpack and was ready to leave. She wondered if she could go to the airing cupboard and thrust her foot through Isolde, but decided against it. Enough harm had been done.

Sappho looked in at Laura as she went.

'I'm off, Laura,' she said. 'It's all of us for ourselves. I'm sorry,' and Laura just nodded.

'Did you know what Gwen was doing with the store cards?' she asked, as an afterthought.

'Yes,' said Laura. 'Of course. I went out with them myself, once or twice, on a Saturday morning. They're great shoppers.'

'But why, Laura?' Sappho was stricken.

'You've got to sound just like your husband. "*But why?*" Because people have to live with the consequences of their actions. I'll get what I can back in order,' added Laura, kindly, 'since you're off. In memory of old times. They were good, weren't they?'

'Yes, they were,' said Sappho and left. She heard Gavin stomping and Isobel tripping down stairs. They were probably looking for the novel. She had wiped it off her computer but she had the hard copy.

Gwen was still outside with the taxi, and with the aid of the driver and a passer-by was decanting suitcases and objects of desire from the pavement to the safety of the path inside the gate.

'You moving in, Gwen?' asked Sappho.

'I am,' said Gwen. 'Someone has to look after the family.'

'Quite a re-run, isn't it?' said Sappho.

Gwen tossed her head in dismissal. She was wearing a real fur, not at all ratty and old, and looking elegant, and in her element instructing inferiors.

Sappho realised she was not quite sure where she was going. It was strange how you could know so many people but none of them seemed quite ready to look after you when you needed them, or else they were the kind who would say, 'I told you so.' She took the next bus which came along.

Emily Is Off The Hook

When I had recovered, when my rage had abated, my maternal anxiety quelled by the thought that at least my daughter was away from that hell-hole, wherever she was – and it took me a couple of hours to calm down and I am a trained analyst – I said to Barnaby,

'My main worry is that she might get rid of the baby. Supposing next time I see her she's flat as a board and not swollen in the middle? How will I cope?'

'How will she cope?' asks Barnaby. 'That's the problem. It's much too late for an abortion. It would be murder. It's not in her nature, is it?'

'God knows any more what is in her nature,' I complain. And I think back to Sappho when she was small, standing up in her cot on two sturdy legs, beaming a welcome at me as I came into her room. She was all happy expectation, all faith. The clouds of glory she trailed into the world at her birth, that lay around her in her infancy, had dimmed and it was I who let it happen. I suppose love always fails between mother and child, child and mother: self-interest prevails. Both start as one, but split, and both need to survive. There is no getting it right. Poor Sappho – it can't have been much fun for her, being brought up by a simulacrum, any more than it was for me, being one. No wonder she adopted the Garner household as her own. I have no right to feel resentful. We have finished the diaries: I am still snivelling. It is all too painful. My carapace, like Sappho's, is cracked and broken. At least she unshelled herself within years, not decades.

'I blame myself,' I say, assuming Barnaby will deny it, which he doesn't and I suppose is why I give him house room in the first place. The capacity to confront and disturb, not to mention, I can now see, the possibility, now realised, of sex. Let no one suppose desire fades with age. One needs to see less clearly but age itself looks after that.

'So you should blame yourself,' says Barnaby. 'A great deal of projection goes on between mother and child. The child blames the parents for its own misdeeds. The parent blames the child when their own inadequacies make their appearance in their offspring. Both judge each other over-harshly.'

The doorbell goes. It is, as I knew it would be, Sappho. She is looking better, though dressed in what look to me like new clothes off the rail from Tesco. Thank God she still has her bulge.

'You'll have read it by now?' she asks. 'My full confession?'

'Yes,' I say.

'Are you still speaking to me?'

'Just about,' I say.

'That's good,' she says, and hands me a flimsy Tesco bag with a few sheets of paper inside.

'This will bring you up to date,' she says. 'Me, I'm going over to the coffee bar. I'll come back when, and if, you wave.'

Sappho's Confession Concludes

The place to go of course is the college. I'm on a 1/7 contract which means I am employed one day a week. But I have my own room, and a computer and a few books and a telephone. I need time on my own to work out who and what I am, or was, or will be. It is a good place to be, here in the forest, where Hansel and Gretel once covered themselves with leaves and hid, away from the wicked stepmother. Mother was right: the archetype has changed. The stepmother must hide from the murderous children. This particular forest is a labyrinth of rooms dedicated to learning and the passing of examinations. The pile of leaves under which I creep is made of paper and emails, notices, warnings, instructions, first year pigeon holes here, post-grads there, leave your dissertations here, lateness can cost you grades, compulsory equality and disability training and bullying workshops for all academic staff.

It's okay. It's just life, or 40–50 per cent of it, that being the percentage which goes to college now, and rising. It's okay. Everyone has everyone's best interests at heart. At night I sneak over with sheets and pillow – cheap to buy at the Campus Store – to the closed Senior Common Room, using my swipe card to get in, push two armchairs together, change in the dim emergency lighting into my nightie, and sleep.

When morning comes I am woken by the cooing and nudging of pigeons on the window sills of the SCR. I fold my sheets and my nightgown, smooth out the armchairs and push them apart, plump up cushions, open such windows as are free of birds, wash, brush up, and take the elevator to my office on the first floor. Sappho Garner, Lecturer, Dramatic Studies. If I keep my door closed no one even knows whether I am in or not. They are too polite to disturb me in case I am in the middle of my creative work, for which they have this deep respect. It is very different from being with Gavin. I am in suspended animation. I try not to think about anything that relates to my immediate past life. I call my mother just to let her know I am okay.

'No sleeping in the offices' showed up on my email from External Affairs the other day, but it was circulated to all departments and there was no mention of penalties, so I ignored it. There may be others doing the same thing as me but I have not seen them. All the same the forest is not safe, not really, I must face that. I daresay there are witches living somewhere hereabouts, and a gingerbread house into which I will be lured and cooked alive along with all the other runaways. I wonder if Gwen is a witch? She ill-wished me and it worked. I wonder which room she has moved into? Probably my office. No stairs and a truly good shower room grander and better than most bathrooms. I call Laura but the office is not manned – personned, as she would say. I am getting a little better, beginning to function, emerging from shock. My white knight in shining armour, the one who was meant to rescue me, did turn up, but alas he was already married to Isolde, and soon his armour was discarded and moths got in and rust, and now he is nothing but a heap of gnawed, still stirring bones, animated only by his hatred of me. But that doesn't mean I can't still survive.

I wash my clothes out in the sinks in the art department – they are larger than the ones we have in drama – remove as much water as possible with paper towels and hang them over the back of a chair in my office to dry. I am seldom disturbed. I sneak over to the students' union for a cooked meal when I feel the need of one – canteen food from tin containers: broccoli, curry, fish in sauce, chips – it's okay, as I say. I can read a book when I eat. Gavin hated me reading at meals. Sometimes they're 'good' books – mostly they are thrillers. Paperbacks. You can drop food on them and it doesn't much matter. No one recognises me, why should they? Students are pre-occupied with their own lives. One is safe amongst them. This is a multi-cultural university – two hundred and thirty languages spoken, though probably not written. People are expected to be strange, as I am.

I am hiding, of course I am. But whether from Isobel's murderous rage, or Gavin's displeasure, or my own stupidity, who is to say? All I know is that every day that passes makes it less likely that I will get rid of the baby. I am tempted, of course I am; how nice it would be to start again, without the baggage of the past. But I can't do that. The baby is my penalty and my reward. It is at the fluttering stage. With the first kick I will be okay with it, and it will be safe from me.

I love the university at night, when everyone has gone home but me. The spirit of pure intellect hovers in its corridors. Its presence does not quite make up for the loss of my home but it's a near thing. I was coming back from the loo at about half past twelve one night and there it was, something both dark and light at the same time, twisting and darting down the corridor, like St Elmo's fire. I can't think what else it can have been.

I come to some decisions. I have decided all that is required from the stepmothers of sons is that they provide palatable food, practical support, clean clothes, stay out of their bedrooms, do not interfere with their lives, comment on their activities and do not quarrel with their father in public. All these things I achieved in the years we shared a common roof; and many were the good times and laughs we had, Arthur and I.

All that is required of second wives is that they know their place, which is at the end of a long-line up of memories, duties and rituals to do with the first marriage. I did my best but that hope common to second wives, that he will put the past behind him, soon faded. I should have managed to subdue my protests better, looked more favourably at the portrait of the first wife above my bed. Or not got married at all.

Should, should. I should have married a banker or someone suitable, and not lived the rackety life of a writer. I should not have stolen Isolde's idea and used it as my own. I defied the demiurge as I walked down the stairs barefoot that morning and he heard me. Now I lumber down, pregnant, in comfy, rubber-soled shoes. I would not be getting the blame for so much but I am Eve getting the blame for Adam eating the apple. She should not have handed it to him but eaten it herself. It would have saved no end of trouble.

Sons can be awkward when their mothers re-marry, but they're not a patch on girls when their fathers find a new occupant for an old marital bed. That too I have learned. And I had wanted so much to love Isobel and be loved. Alas, it is simply not in the nature of the stepdaughter to love the stepmother. Females of all species will love and nurture helpless creatures: it is something to do with the proportion of the eyes to the skull. But the loving is a one-way street.

They say the two peak times for first marriages and partnerships to split are one) when the first child is born, and the mother falls in sensuous love with the new baby and forgets the father, and two) if the marriage survives that, why then when the first daughter reaches puberty. The complexities of staying are altogether too much for the male. It is not the pleasures of the new that entice the male away to other, younger arms: it is the terror of being old. In 'reconstituted' families, such as the one I tried to create, a new pregnancy will bring old tensions to a head. Yes, indeed.

People warned me but I took no notice. She was a sweet girl and I knew her mother well. Now I hate Isobel and she hates me, and her hate is stronger than mine because she is younger than me, prettier than me, her legs are longer than mine and because she will stop at nothing.

And Gavin? The body misses the one who keeps it warm at night. That is all I will say.

I am well out of it.

Emily Nods And Waves

I nod and wave at Sappho from my window as she sits in the coffee shop across the way. I hope she is drinking hot chocolate without additives, and no caffeine. But probably, as for so many of her generation, 'hot drinks' are not a priority. Water will do. She is anxious, I can tell. She sees me waving and her face breaks into the same smile she used to have when she looked at me over the rim of her cot. She comes over. She looks both ways: she has learned caution; she does not trust the world as much as once she did. I open the door to her.

'I thought I would come home,' she says. 'I thought you could re-birth me.'

'And the baby?'

'And of course the baby,' she says. 'We could try again, and get it right.'

She comes in and looks at Barnaby.

'Hi, Barnaby,' she says.

'I was about to marry Barnaby,' I say. He's looking rather pale.

'It's a bit small in this place,' she says, 'but I daresay we could manage. If we put in a spiral staircase, put the two homes together. Nothing like a re-run, is there?'

'That's all there is, I sometimes think,' says Barnaby. He sounds a little bitter, but accepting.

'Do you still mean to be a writer when you're re-born?' I ask her.

'Of course,' she says. 'Once the baby is born I've got a novel to redraft.'

I shudder.

I almost feel sorry for Isobel, who from Isolde's first labour pain was grist for Sappho's mill.